THE GHOST

WHO WASN'T

HAUNTING DANIELLE

The Ghost of Marlow House

The Ghost Who Loved Diamonds

The Ghost Who Wasn't

The Ghost Who Wanted Revenge

The Ghost of Halloween Past

The Ghost Who Came for Christmas

The Ghost of Valentine Past

The Ghost from the Sea

The Ghost and the Mystery Writer

The Ghost and the Muse

The Ghost Who Stayed Home

The Ghost and the Leprechaun

The Ghost Who Lied

The Ghost and the Bride

The Ghost and Little Marie

The Ghost and the Doppelganger

The Ghost of Second Chances

The Ghost Who Dream Hopped

The Ghost of Christmas Secrets

The Ghost Who Was Says I Do

HAUNTING DANIELLE - BOOK 3

THE GHOST
WHO WASN'T

BOBBI HOLMES

The Ghost Who Wasn't
(Haunting Danielle, Book 3)
A Novel
By Bobbi Holmes
Cover Design: Elizabeth Mackey

Copyright © 2014 Bobbi Holmes
Robeth Publishing, LLC
All Rights Reserved.
robeth.net

ISBN 978-1-949977-02-8

For my mother-in-law, Doris.
You are missed.

ONE

Isabella sat sideways in the Tahoe's backseat, propping her bare feet up on the middle console. She had never traveled in the backseat before this trip, which wasn't surprising since it was her car. She had to admit it was roomier than what she had expected, yet she would still prefer to be the one behind the wheel. But that was not going to happen—Hunter insisted on doing all the driving.

Judging by the road signs she'd noticed before pulling into the rest stop, they weren't far from Palm Springs, California. Isabella had never been to Palm Springs before, and she certainly never imagined she would get there this way.

Stretching out, she leaned against the inside of the right rear car door and looked out the side window, where Hunter stood in the parking lot with Claire, arguing with Justina. They'd left the windows down, so she could easily hear what they were saying. Hunter claimed it was the alternator, but Justina insisted they just needed a new battery.

As she listened to them argue, she wondered what Hunter saw in Claire. The woman desperately needed a day at the salon to bring some style to her long stringy hair. Only a good cut would eliminate the split ends, which were probably the result of too much peroxide. The white-blond shade was not a good look for Claire's olive complexion. By the amount of dark roots showing, it was obvious she hadn't been to the hairdresser in a long time. Considering her

1

hair's condition, Claire probably got the color from a box purchased at the drugstore and not from a salon.

And then there's the matter of Claire's face. Isabella immediately felt guilty for such an unkind thought. Unkind but true. Claire's hazel eyes were too small for her face and her nose too large. Hunter didn't seem to mind, yet Isabella thought that had to do more with Claire's figure. She was a petite thing, maybe five foot three inches, with a tight little body. While she wasn't voluptuous, she was well toned with ample curves. Hunter seemed to like it, considering how he couldn't keep his hands off her.

Justina was far better looking than Claire. She reminded Isabella of a poor man's Angelina Jolie—one dressed in faded baggy denim overalls and a tie-dyed tank top. Isabella had an idea Justina might prefer girls. She wasn't sure, and she certainly wasn't going to ask.

Isabella had been trying to figure out their ages. At first, she guessed they were in their mid-forties—at least twenty years older than she was. But after a few days traveling with the threesome, she began wondering if they were younger, maybe in their thirties. Considering their lifestyle, she wouldn't be surprised if they weren't as old as she initially suspected. Drugs, booze, and cigarettes tended to age a person, and they embraced all three vices.

"Maybe we should just get another car," Claire suggested.

"You might be right, but exactly where do you expect to get a car out here?" Hunter asked.

Isabella glanced around. Theirs was the only vehicle in the rest stop aside from a motorhome, which looked like it was getting ready to pull out. Hunter walked to the front of the Tahoe and slammed its hood shut.

Glancing to the exit again, she watched as the motorhome pulled out and back onto the highway, without asking if they needed any help. She looked to Hunter, who now paced in front of the car.

Isabella marveled at how a person's appearance could change so drastically after you got to know him better. When she first spied Hunter at the beach, she found him handsome. He wore his hair longer than she preferred, pulled back into a haphazard man-bun. Some of her friends found the look quite sexy, something she never understood until Hunter entered her world.

Days ago, the man-bun had again fallen out of favor with Isabella, and instead of finding Hunter attractive, now he repulsed her. Part of it might be attributed to the fact he hadn't bathed since she had first seen him—nor shaved. The armpit stains of his ragged gray T-shirt grew daily. His stench didn't deter Claire, whose grooming habits weren't much better than his. *They deserve each other,* Isabella thought.

"Maybe a car will come to us," Claire suggested.

"Perhaps Hunter will use his magic." Justina snickered.

"Oh, shut up," Claire snapped.

"It's okay, babe." Hunter wrapped his arm around Claire and gave her shoulder a reassuring pat. "Justina gets a little cynical sometimes. I think she's just hungry."

"I am that," Justina agreed. "Do we have any more of those sandwiches?"

"I ate the last one," Hunter said.

"Why doesn't that surprise me?" Justina grumbled.

"Don't you have any more of those candy bars?" Claire asked. "I'm kind of hungry too."

"You mean the ones she stole at the last place we stopped for gas?" Isabella asked.

Justina shrugged. She walked to the rear car door behind the driver's side of the Tahoe. Opening the door, she snatched her purse off the empty seat next to Isabella. Digging into the handbag, she grabbed a candy bar and then tossed the purse onto the floor before walking to the front of the vehicle, leaving the car door wide open.

Isabella scooted across the seat to the open door and jumped down from the car. Walking toward the front of the Tahoe, she found Hunter sitting on its front hood.

"You're going to scratch the paint!" Isabella snapped.

Hunter seemed oblivious to Isabella's outrage and focused his attention on Justina, who had just unwrapped her candy bar and was preparing to take a bite.

"Did you bring me one?" Hunter asked.

Justina glanced up and glared at Hunter. "Did you offer me part of the last sandwich before you ate it?"

"And since when do I need to ask you anything? Either share the candy bar, or give it all to me."

Reluctantly, Justina snapped the candy bar in two and tossed a half to Hunter. Instead of eating the candy, he handed his share to Claire.

"Thanks, baby," Claire cooed.

"Please get off my car! You're going to scratch the paint,"

Isabella repeated. When Hunter continued to ignore her, she angrily stomped her foot.

Hunter closed his eyes while Justina and Claire silently devoured the candy. After a few seconds, he opened his eyes and asked, "Now did you hear that? Seems Isabella does not like me sitting on her precious car."

"I don't think there's much Isabella can do about it now," Justina said as she popped the last bite of candy into her mouth.

"I don't want to upset her." Hunter sniggered. He slid off the hood and walked to Claire, who now sat on the curb by the front of the car. He sat down next to her.

"I want to sleep in a real bed tonight." Claire leaned her head on Hunter's shoulder. "And I want to take a shower."

"It's about time," Isabella mumbled under her breath.

Hunter wrapped his arm around Claire and pulled her close. "If we play our cards right, we'll be able to do that. I promise."

"I wish you would've listened to me yesterday when I said we needed to dump this car."

"Don't start nagging me." Hunter pulled Claire closer.

"But it was a Mustang, and that stupid woman left it unlocked with the key hanging in the ignition," Claire whined.

"Yeah, and the minute we take off, she'd call the cops and we'd get pulled over. No thanks. We're going to do it smart, like this one."

"Exactly what is that supposed to mean?" Isabella demanded. "We don't need another car. I certainly don't intend to abandon my Tahoe! I bet it'll start if you just try. Put some water in the battery; that's all it needs."

Hunter started to say something but looked up instead. Claire and Justina must have heard whatever he had because they looked in the same direction. Isabella turned around to see what had caught their attention.

A red Mustang had just driven into the rest stop. Silently, the four watched as it pulled into a parking space some twenty feet from the Tahoe.

"It's a Mustang," Hunter said in a low voice. "I believe it's a sign."

"Looks like she's alone," Justina noted.

"How is this Mustang any different from the one Claire wanted to take?" Isabella asked. "I don't think the woman will just let you drive off in her car. She'll have the cops on us before we hit the highway."

Isabella watched as the driver, a young woman in her late twenties or early thirties, got out of the Mustang. The woman, a purse in one hand and keys in the other, slammed the car door shut. Isabella watched as she used the keychain to remotely lock the vehicle before heading toward the restrooms.

"She didn't leave the keys in her car," Claire grumbled.

Isabella watched as the driver of the Mustang walked into the women's bathroom.

"I didn't expect she would." Hunter stood up and offered a hand to Claire.

"So what do we do?" Claire looked up to Hunter and took his hand. He gave her a little tug, and she stood up. Standing beside him, she dusted off the back of her faded jeans.

"We're going to take the keys away from her," Hunter said.

"And her cellphone," Claire said. "I bet she has a cellphone in that purse."

"With or without a cellphone, we can't just leave her here," Justina insisted. "As far as we know, the next car that pulls into this rest stop could be the highway patrol."

"We can't take her with us!" Claire said.

Hunter began to laugh. "I don't think that's what she's suggesting." He looked over to Justina and asked, "Something a little more permanent?"

"Yep," Justina said with a nod, her eyes focused on the restroom building. "Lots of empty desert around here. Shouldn't be too hard to get rid of her. But we'll have to move quick."

Isabella felt a sickening twisting in the pit of her belly. "No, please don't do this!" she begged.

"Justina's right. If we're going to do this, we better hurry before another car pulls in here," Claire agreed.

"While I take care of her, you guys start wiping down the inside of the Tahoe," Hunter instructed.

"Why do we have to do that?" Isabella asked.

"It may not take long for them to find the car, and we don't want to be tied to it," Hunter said.

"They'd expect to find my prints. After all, it is my car!" Isabella snapped.

"And grab the license plate. We'll need to put it on the Mustang," Hunter said.

"Should we put the Tahoe's real license plate back on? It's still in the back," Claire asked.

"I don't care what you do with it. Just make sure it doesn't have our fingerprints on it," Hunter said.

Justina glanced up to the restroom building. "You sure you can handle this by yourself, Hunter? I think you'll need another hand. I'll go with you."

"You're probably right," Hunter agreed.

"Oh, come on, guys, you aren't really going to do this, are you?" When they didn't answer her question, Isabella took off running, racing toward the women's bathroom in her bare feet. Barging into the building, she found the woman inside one of the stalls. Frantic, Isabella began pounding on the stall door.

"If you have a cellphone with you, call 911 now! You're in danger!" Isabella shouted.

TWO

L abor Day weekend officially signified the end of the summer season. It was a short first season for Marlow House Bed and Breakfast. Lily had already returned to California before Danielle accepted her first guests in early August. Yet Danielle had other business she needed to attend to, such as planning her cousin Cheryl's funeral and settling the estate.

Danielle sat next to Ian at Pier Café's lunch counter. It was the first Wednesday in September, and Carla, the waitress, had just taken their breakfast orders and filled their cups with coffee.

Danielle picked up her mug, took a sip, and then said, "I guess there is life for a B and B after Labor Day."

"What do you mean?" Ian asked.

"I got a reservation this morning." Danielle smiled. "They arrive on Friday."

"Congratulations. Anyone I might know? Lily perhaps?"

Danielle laughed. "Sorry, not Lily. Some couple from Portland. They're staying for a week. Of course, they might turn out to be a no-show."

"Why do you say that?"

"The man who made the reservation said he doesn't have a credit card—claims not to believe in them. Promised to pay in cash when he gets here."

"Everyone has plastic, a debit card at least."

Danielle shrugged. "I guess not. No big deal really. It's not like I'm in the middle of tourist season and turning people away."

"Sounds kind of sketchy to me. May not be safe."

"I'll be fine." *After all, I have Walt. He's better than an armed guard. Well, most of the time.*

"Okay, but remember I'm just across the street if you need me."

"Thanks, Ian."

"Have you heard from Lily?"

"Not since last week. She was getting ready for her Labor Day trip."

"Can't believe she drove that far for the weekend. Might as well have driven up here," Ian grumbled.

"She goes every Labor Day. Girls' weekend."

"So why didn't you go?"

"They're people she's known since she was a kid. Not really my friends. Have you talked to her?"

"I spoke to her right before she left. Didn't want to bother her over the weekend when she was with her friends. I was hoping she'd give me a call when she got home. But I haven't heard from her."

"From what I understood, she wasn't planning to get home until sometime Monday evening. Maybe she got home later than she expected and didn't want to call you so late. Labor Day traffic and all."

"I tried calling her last night but no answer."

"Knowing Lily, she probably forgot to charge her phone. So what's with you two?"

"That sounds like a Lily question, not something you'd ask." Ian smiled.

"I guess after living with her for the summer, she rubbed off on me," Danielle joked.

"I'm going down there when I wrap up the Emma Jackson story. I hope to be finished before the end of the month."

"Does this mean I'm losing a neighbor?"

"I think so. I have to admit, if it wasn't for Lily, I'd be tempted to stay. I like working here, although I imagine it'll be getting pretty cold come winter."

"Ah…" Danielle grinned. "So it is serious."

"Yeah, I think so." Ian downed the rest of his coffee and motioned for Carla to bring the pot to the table.

"I'm going to miss you. But I'll miss Sadie most."

"Sadie will miss you too."

No, Sadie will miss Walt, Danielle silently corrected.

"Did you hear they found Isabella Strickland?" Carla asked as she refilled their coffee cups.

"Who's that?" Danielle asked.

In response, Carla grabbed a copy of the morning paper from behind the lunch counter and tossed it between Ian and Danielle. Ian picked up the paper and glanced over the front-page article.

"She's a local girl," Ian explained as he skimmed the paper. "She went missing when you were in California for Cheryl's funeral."

"Missing?" Danielle asked. "I would have thought I'd have heard about something like that. This is a small town."

"Well, no one thought she was missing missing," Carla explained as she set the coffee pot on the counter. "According to her uncle, she took off on a trip, but when he tried to call her cellphone, she wouldn't answer his call. He was pretty annoyed. Said she was ignoring him. I swear, he complained to everyone in town who'd listen."

"I read the article this morning. There's obviously more to the story than an errant niece," Ian said as he glanced over the front page.

"I know!" Carla said excitedly. "They found her body in the desert, a couple hundred yards from a rest stop near Palm Springs!"

"She's dead? That's horrible!" Danielle gasped.

"No, she's alive. But in a coma," the waitress explained. "She's lucky that dog found her, or she'd definitely be dead by now!"

The cook rang a bell, and Carla quickly picked up the pot of coffee. "I have an order up."

"What dog?" Danielle asked after Carla walked away. "I'm totally confused."

Ian set the newspaper on the counter. "A family pulled into a rest stop outside of Palm Springs. When they went to walk their dog, he started pulling on the leash and managed to slip out of his collar and ran off into the desert. They chased after him, and he led them to a body—the unconscious body of Isabella Strickland. She'd been hit over the head and left for dead in the desert."

"That's awful. Do they have any idea who did it?"

"No. According to the article, they found her car in the parking lot at the rest stop. That's how they figured out who she was.

Someone had removed her car's license plate and put it in the back of the car with her purse. There weren't any fingerprints inside or on the vehicle—not even Isabella's, which suggests someone wiped it down."

"Is she going to be all right?" Danielle asked.

"It doesn't sound good. She's in a coma, and according to the article, her uncle had her moved to his house, where she's getting round-the-clock care."

"He moved her from the hospital to his house?" Danielle frowned.

"Her uncle is Stoddard Gusarov."

"The Stoddard Gusarov? The one who lives in that monstrosity on the south side of town?"

"Gusarov considers his house an architectural marvel." Ian snickered.

"It's hideous. Looks like an industrial building. In fact, I thought it was one when I first saw it. Wondered why they built it on such a prime piece of ocean-front property."

"The Gusarovs have money to build whatever they want, even an ugly house like that. I read about it once; it's over six thousand square feet."

"Did the rest of her family just go along with the uncle removing her from the hospital?"

"She really doesn't have any other family. According to the stories, her father married her mother for the money, but when his new in-laws disinherited his wife, he took off not long after he found out his new bride was pregnant."

"Nice guy," Danielle scoffed.

"The mother reportedly had mental issues, and Isabella ended up being raised by her grandparents."

"What happened to her mother?" Danielle asked.

"She died when Isabella was just a kid. From what I understand, she was in and out of rehab."

"Alcoholic?" Danielle asked.

"I think it was more prescription drugs."

"And her father was never in the picture?"

"No. He disappeared. I suspect he's probably dead. I'd expect someone like that to resurface after his wife died and claim his fatherly rights—in an attempt to get to his daughter's eventual inheritance. But apparently, he never did."

"Isabella isn't married?"

"No."

"How did they make their money?"

Ian took a sip of coffee before answering the question. "From what I understand, Gusarov's parents made a fortune in the adult-care industry."

"You mean like retirement homes?" Danielle asked.

"Primarily assisted living. They have facilities all over the country. The family is worth a fortune." With a mischievous grin he added, "Might have as much money as you."

"Ha-ha…" Danielle rolled her eyes.

"After Isabella's grandfather died, his estate was divided between her and the uncle. The grandmother had passed away a few years after Isabella's mother. According to the terms of the will, Isabella became an active member of the business when she turned twenty-one. I assume that's why her uncle got annoyed when she'd just take off on her impromptu trips. Technically speaking, they're business partners."

"How do you know so much about the family?"

"I did a lot of reading up on the area when I was working on the Eva Thorndike story. Although, the Gusarovs are relative newcomers to the area."

"I still don't understand why she isn't in a hospital."

Before Ian could answer Danielle's question, the waitress brought their food.

"Wouldn't she get better care in the hospital?" Danielle asked after Carla left their table.

"From what the article says, it doesn't look good for her. I suppose some will insist she was lucky to have been found by that dog—but was she really found in time? I think her uncle is just trying to make her comfortable, and frankly, if it was someone I loved and I could afford it, I'd do the same thing."

"I suppose…" Danielle speared a piece of scrambled egg with her fork. "It's so sad. I wonder what happened."

"Hopefully, they'll be able to find out something."

"What I don't understand, why didn't they find her earlier?" Danielle asked. "If she was missing, couldn't they track her by her cellphone? Or I'd think someone with that much money would have one of those radio thingies in her car. You know, like when you break down and call for help."

"Like Carla said, she wasn't missing missing."

"What does that mean?"

"I don't think anyone was actively looking for her. Not the police, anyway. After all, she's an adult and doesn't have to check in with anyone. Plus, she has a history of just taking off and being gone for a few weeks at a time without checking in with anyone."

"The way the waitress said, 'Did you hear they found Isabella Strickland?' made it sound like everyone was looking for her."

"That week you were gone, her uncle was going around complaining to everyone who would listen—like Klein over at the bank and people here at the café—that she'd taken off again. Small town, that sort of thing makes its rounds pretty quickly. But by the time you got back, it was old news, and Gusarov seemed to have gotten over his annoyance. At least he'd stopped going around town complaining."

"I wonder if he feels guilty about it now." Danielle spread jam over her toast.

"It could be why he decided to keep her at home and hire private, round-the-clock care."

Glancing up, Ian noticed two uniformed police officers walking into the diner. "Don't look now, your favorite cops are here," Ian whispered under his breath.

"Oh gawd…" Danielle moaned, refusing to look up. "Can't they get donuts somewhere else?"

"They're coming over here," Ian whispered.

"Both of them?" Danielle asked as she shoved a forkful of eggs into her mouth.

Before Ian could respond, Joe Morelli and his partner, Brian Henderson, walked up to their place at the counter.

"Morning, Danielle, Ian," Joe greeted.

Chewing her food, Danielle slowly turned and looked at Joe. She gave him a brief nod in greeting before turning back to her plate.

"Morning, Joe, Brian. I see they found Isabella Strickland," Ian said. "Any leads on who's responsible for putting her in a coma?"

Before they could respond, Danielle wiped her mouth with a napkin and turned back around to face Joe and Brian. "That's prob-ably why they're here," Danielle said sarcastically. "I'm the likely suspect. After all, I was in California the week she went missing. God, you guys are good. Can't ever get anything over on you."

"Did you know Isabella Strickland?" Brian asked.

Joe shuffled uncomfortably. "Right now the investigation's being handled in California. We're not really involved."

"Are you sure about that? Your partner there just asked if I knew her."

"Umm...I'm sure Brian knew you were just kidding," Joe said.

"She didn't sound like she was kidding," Brian said.

"No, Officer Henderson, I wasn't kidding. I was being sarcastic. But then you've never been very intuitive."

"I'm going to grab a booth." Brian turned and walked away.

"Danielle, can't we at least be friends?" Joe asked.

"Fine," Danielle muttered.

Ian sat quietly and listened to the exchange.

"I'm so sorry about everything," Joe insisted.

"Your partner obviously isn't. I tossed that one crumb, and he was ready to pounce."

"That's just Brian. I'm sorry, but considering the circumstances, can't you at least understand why I thought what I did?" Joe asked.

Danielle turned to Ian and asked, "Did you ever think I killed my cousin?"

"No," Ian answered truthfully and took a sip of coffee.

Joe didn't respond. Instead, he let out a deep sigh, gave a nod to Ian, and made his way to the booth where Brian waited.

"To be completely honest, I was somewhat prejudiced," Ian whispered when Joe was out of earshot. "I'm in love with your best friend—and I could hardly imagine Lily's best friend was a cold-hearted killer."

"Oh, shut up, that's not the point..." She then paused for a moment and looked up into Ian's face. Flashing a wide grin, she said, "You're in love with Lily!"

"Oh, shut up yourself..." Ian grumbled. "I didn't mean to say that. Well, at least not until I tell Lily."

Danielle began to laugh.

THREE

When Danielle left the diner alone, thirty minutes later, Joe and Brian were just finishing their breakfast. She didn't stop at their table to say goodbye, nor did she look their way as she left the restaurant. Yet she could feel Joe's eyes on her as she walked by their booth and headed to the door.

Overtly she had expressed anger toward Joe. What she actually felt was more akin to profound sadness—something she carefully concealed. Danielle had genuinely liked Joe Morelli, and it wasn't just his dark good looks and friendly brown eyes. He was the first man since her late husband—not counting Walt of course, yet Walt didn't count since he was dead—to whom she felt an attraction. Her attraction to Walt was obviously that of just a close friend—at least that was what she told herself, considering anything more would be absurd due to the circumstances. Yet, with Joe, she thought their relationship might bloom into something deeper—more personal and physical.

Danielle still believed Joe Morelli was the caring person she first imagined. However, the moment Joe's concern for her shifted from a man interested in a woman to a man concerned for a broken, mentally ill soul, their relationship was forever tainted. Even though Joe now knew she was not responsible for Cheryl's death, Danielle believed he still questioned her sanity. *Perhaps he doesn't think I'm insane exactly*, she told herself—*just fragile and a little unstable.*

Walking back to her house from the diner, Danielle thought about Joe Morelli and their brief relationship. It was so brief he had never gotten around to kissing her. By the time she reached her street, Danielle's thoughts had already turned from Joe to Marlow House and her plans for the bed and breakfast.

When she walked in her front door, she was surprised to find Walt anxiously pacing back and forth in the foyer. He came to an abrupt halt, looked at Danielle, and asked, "Are you alone? Is Ian with you?"

Danielle glanced at the door she was closing then looked back to Walt and shook her head. "No, I'm alone, what's up?" Slipping her purse's strap off her shoulder, she walked to the entry hall table, with Walt close at her heels.

"We need to talk," Walt explained as he stood behind Danielle, who was now setting her purse on the entry table and removing her jacket. His eyes darted to the parlor door.

"Talk? What did I do now?" Danielle turned to face Walt. Startled that he was standing so close, she impulsively jumped backwards, accidentally hitting the entry table with her hip and sending the purse tumbling to the floor.

"Maybe we should go to the library and talk," Walt suggested as Danielle leaned down to pick up her purse.

"What is going on with you?" Danielle asked impatiently as she set her purse back on the table, this time with her jacket. Narrowing her eyes, she studied Walt. He was dressed in his normal attire—a three-piece suit circa the 1920s and perfectly polished leather dress shoes. He was now moving toward the library while encouraging her to follow him, yet his eyes kept flashing in the opposite direction, toward the door leading to the parlor.

"I'll explain everything, but please hurry, we need to talk. In the library."

Just as Danielle was about to take a step in Walt's direction, she heard what sounded like singing coming from the parlor.

"What was that?" Danielle asked, coming to an abrupt stop.

"Ignore that. I'll explain everything," Walt insisted, still edging toward the library door.

"Is someone here?" Danielle turned to face the closed parlor door. Cocking her head to one side, she listened—and again she heard what sounded like a woman singing.

"I said I'll explain everything," Walt insisted.

Ignoring Walt, Danielle walked to the parlor door and threw it open. To her surprise, she found Lily inside the room, sitting at the desk, her bare feet propped up on the desktop as she enthusiastically sang her rendition of Sara Bareilles' "Brave."

"Lily!" Danielle called out in surprise.

Lily stopped singing and smiled at Danielle. Instead of standing up or removing her feet from the desktop, she leaned back in the desk chair and stretched lazily.

"It's about time you showed up," Lily greeted.

"What in the world are you doing here? Why aren't you in school?"

"You aren't happy to see me?" Lily pouted.

"Of course I am!" Danielle laughed. "I'm just surprised to see you."

"I stopped at Ian's first. He wasn't home. Sadie was though, and she was very excited to see me. Much warmer greeting than what you just gave me." Lily grinned mischievously then asked with more seriousness, "Do you know where Ian is, by the way?"

"I just left him at Pier Café. We had breakfast."

"He didn't come back with you?" Lily pulled her feet off the desk and sat up straight.

"He had some errands to run in town. Boy, he's sure going to be happy to see you!"

"I can't wait to see him." Lily grinned.

"So tell me, how were you able to get out of work? School just started; I can't believe you were able to get time off so soon."

"Life is too short, Dani, not to be with the people you love. I had to come back here."

"But what about work?" Danielle asked.

"What about it?"

"How long are you planning on staying?"

"Already trying to get rid of me?" Lily teased.

"Of course not." Danielle sat down in a chair facing the desk.

"So tell me about your new guest!"

"New guest?" Danielle frowned.

"I met him when I got here. Well, I didn't exactly meet him. I think he thought I was a burglar at first." Lily giggled. "But once I told him who I was, he seemed to know my name. You been talking about me, Dani?" Lily flashed Danielle a grin and then continued. "He suggested I wait in here for you. I thought that was kinda sweet.

Made me feel sort of like a guest. But he never did tell me his name."

"I'm not sure what you're talking about. What guest?"

"I seriously doubt you don't know who I'm talking about. The guy with the really sexy blue eyes. He's pretty cute, even though he does dress a little odd. So tell me about him. I want to hear everything!"

"What are you talking about? I don't have any guests right now. It's just me…" Danielle paused a moment and stared at Lily before adding, "Me and Walt."

"Hmmm…that's right…Walt…I almost forgot about him…" Lily frowned and squinted her eyes, as if trying to grab on to a memory.

"What do you mean you forgot about Walt?" Danielle studied Lily, who stared off into the opposite direction.

"That's right…Walt. I never met Walt before. Well, only in my dreams, but that doesn't count. Now that you mention it, your new guest sorta looks like him. At least like the portrait in the library and how I remember him from my dreams."

"We don't have any guests at Marlow House. Honest, Lily."

Lily looked up at Danielle, a concerned frown on her face. "Not even one with really nice blue eyes?"

"Only Walt," Danielle said quietly.

"Don't tell me I'm starting to see ghosts now, because that ain't happening!" Lily shook her head.

"I tried to warn you," Walt said a moment later when he appeared in the room, standing between Lily and Danielle.

Lily looked at Walt. "I didn't see you walk in." She then turned to Danielle and said, "And you were trying to say you didn't have any guests staying with you!"

"Lily, you can see him?" Danielle asked quietly.

"Of course I can see him. What's with you, Dani? Are you going to introduce me to your guest or not?" Lily paused a moment, then glanced inquisitively from Danielle to Walt. "Wait, he isn't a guest at all, is he?"

"No, not exactly," Danielle said weakly.

"Oh my gosh, you met someone! You two are seeing each other, aren't you?" Lily said excitedly.

Danielle glanced from Lily to Walt, who only shrugged and looked back to Lily.

After a moment of silence Danielle asked, "Lily, where is your car?"

"What do you mean?"

"Your car. I just realized I didn't see it when I walked up to the house."

"Boy, Dani, you sure know how to change the subject!"

"How did you get here, Lily?" Danielle asked.

"How did I get here?" Lily contemplated the question for a moment. "I don't know. I suppose I walked. Maybe my car is across the street at Ian's. I did stop there first."

Danielle started to ask Lily another question when her cellphone began to ring. She stood up briefly, pulled it from her back pocket, and glanced at it.

"It's your mother," Danielle told Lily as she sat back down.

"Oh, I wonder if she's mad at me for playing hooky at work," Lily said with a sigh.

"Did your mother know you were coming here?" Danielle asked, not yet answering the phone.

"I don't know," Lily said impatiently. "Why do you keep asking me all these silly questions?"

Danielle took a deep breath and then answered her phone. "Hello, Mrs. Miller."

Lily sat at the desk, watching Danielle, while Walt took the chair next to Danielle and sat down. After her initial hello, Danielle sat quietly—her expression blank—listening to what Lily's mother had to say. Finally, she said, "Oh my god..." and closed her eyes briefly.

"What's wrong? Is Mother okay?" Lily asked, standing up quickly. "Here, let me talk to her."

"I'm sure your mother is fine. Let Danielle talk to her," Walt said, looking from Danielle to Lily.

"How do you know that? Why did Mom call her and not me?"

"Where is your phone, Lily?" Walt asked.

"My phone?" Lily glanced around. "Gee, I'm not really sure." She sat back down, looking confused.

After a few more moments of silently listening to Mrs. Miller on the phone, Danielle said, "No, let me tell him. I had breakfast with him this morning, and he's running errands. I'd rather we be alone when he hears."

"Are you talking about Ian?" Lily asked. "What does my mother need to tell him? I bet she's mad at me for coming back here. She probably thinks I'm chasing him! I bet she didn't believe me when I told her he was moving down to California to be near me. A summer fling. That's what she called it."

Somber, Danielle said goodbye to Mrs. Miller and promised to call her back. Turning her phone off, Danielle dropped it to the floor and looked at Lily.

"Well? What did Mom say? And why didn't you let me talk to her?"

"Lily," Danielle said quietly, "you really need to focus and try to remember how you got here. Why you are here."

"I don't know." Lily sighed. "Like I said, maybe I walked."

"All the way from Sacramento?" Danielle asked.

"Okay, tell me what my mother wanted," Lily insisted.

"First, Lily, I need to introduce you to Walt Marlow," Danielle said wearily.

"Walt Marlow?" Lily frowned and glanced at Walt. "Did you tell him about Walt?"

"He is Walt Marlow," Danielle explained.

Lily narrowed her eyes and glanced from Danielle to Walt and back to Danielle again. "What are you talking about?"

"Take a good look, Lily. You've seen his portrait. You met him in your dreams. And he didn't walk in here a few minutes ago, did he? He just appeared."

"No." Lily looked at Walt and shook her head. "No, you can't be Walt Marlow. Walt Marlow is dead. I can't see ghosts. And Cheryl could only see ghosts after she...after she..." Lily paused; she looked wildly from Walt to Danielle. "No...no...it can't be! I AM NOT DEAD!"

FOUR

W alt and Danielle sat quietly in the parlor, watching Lily pace back and forth, talking to herself as if she were trying to work out a puzzle. Her left hand absently twirled a lock of red hair while her right hand punched and pointed into the air erratically.

"I'm glad to see she hasn't gotten hysterical like your cousin did," Walt whispered.

"I just can't believe this," Danielle said softly, her eyes filling with tears as she watched her best friend arguing with herself. "I don't want to lose Lily."

"You don't have to lose her; she could stay with us."

"No, Walt. This isn't where she belongs, if she is…is…" Danielle closed her eyes and stifled a sob.

"Well, she obviously is," Walt said calmly.

Lily stopped abruptly and turned to Walt and Danielle. "I'm not dead. I don't feel dead. Tell me again, Dani, what my mother told you."

"She said you had a car accident. You were returning from your girls' weekend, and your car ran into a semi and burst into flames. They said you were speeding—going over one hundred miles an hour."

"That's ridiculous. I don't speed!" Lily took the chair behind the desk again and sat down.

"Do you remember driving home?" Danielle asked.

"I guess…" Lily closed her eyes for a moment and tried to remember. "It's funny, until you mentioned it, I had forgotten all about the weekend. I'm not even sure how I got back here. At the time, it just seemed like the most natural thing…but it's all very confusing."

"Yes, it can be like that. At least it was for me," Walt said with a nod. "After I was murdered, things were hazy and out of sync. At the time, I just accepted it all—didn't question it—not really. It was not until I acknowledged my death—accepted it—did things come into focus. I stepped out of the fog."

"I am not dead. I refuse to be dead!"

"Lily, I think it will help if you try to remember. What is your last memory of your trip?" Danielle asked gently.

"Well…I remember putting my suitcase in the car. Dreading the long drive home."

"Okay, then what?"

"Oh, I know!" Lily said excitedly.

"What?" Walt and Danielle chorused.

"We all went to the Indian casino the night before, and I won over five thousand bucks! How could I have forgotten that?" Lily's momentary burst of excitement faded into a frown. "Oh crap, don't tell me it was burned with my car…"

"Focus on your ride home after putting your suitcase in your car," Danielle urged.

"I remember getting on the freeway…then…"

"Then what?" Danielle asked.

Lily shook her head and said, "That's when it gets really fuzzy. I can't remember much after getting on the freeway."

"Your mother did say that's where you were killed," Walt reminded her.

"I know, but I don't speed. I mean seriously, me driving over a hundred miles an hour. I don't think so."

"It was your car, Lily," Danielle said. "According to your mother, there was only one person in the vehicle—a woman. They found your purse not far from the wreckage, with your identification. It must have flown out of the car before the explosion."

"And the woman in the car was definitely me? My mother said that?"

"I'm sorry, Lily. She didn't sound like there was any doubt. I'm sure they've done what they had to, to verify your identity. I didn't

21

ask her about it. I was just trying to wrap my head around things."

"I don't remember speeding or any accident. Although…" Lily paused and rubbed her head.

"What is it?" Danielle asked.

"My head. I remember. Something hit my head. It hurt and then…then everything gets mixed up."

"Maybe you hit your head during the accident?" Danielle suggested.

"The only reason you two think I'm dead is because I can see Walt! Dani can see Walt, and she's not dead. I obviously have some sort of amnesia because I can't remember how I got here exactly. But it doesn't mean I'm dead. Maybe I did get hit over the head somehow, and because of it, it's possible for me to see Walt, like Dani does."

"There are other ways to determine if you…if you have passed over to my side."

"Such as?" Lily asked.

"I suppose you could try giving Danielle a hug, try picking up something—or simply look in the mirror."

"The mirror?" Lily asked.

"Remember, that's when Cheryl truly realized she was no longer alive. She didn't have a reflection," Danielle said.

"I thought that was only vampires?" Lily scoffed.

"Vampires and ghosts," Walt quipped.

"Okay, I'll take the mirror test—and then we can figure out how I got here."

"Should I be offended she didn't want a hug?" Danielle asked Walt after Lily dashed from the parlor into the entry hall. Just as Danielle stood up, she heard Lily let out a loud scream.

"No reflection?" Walt said dryly, arching his brows.

Danielle raced from the room. When she reached Lily's side, she looked into the mirror with her friend. The moment she did, she too let out a scream, one even louder than Lily's.

"Goodness, women, I'm sorry about this, but what did you expect, Danielle?" Walt asked.

"I didn't expect this!" Danielle said, still staring into the mirror with Lily.

"What do you think this means?" Lily asked, her eyes still focused on the mirror.

"I don't have any idea." Danielle shook her head.

"Does she have a reflection or not?" Walt asked, walking toward the pair.

"Sort of…" Danielle murmured.

"Sort of?" Walt frowned.

Danielle stepped back, making room for Walt. Standing next to Lily, Walt looked into the mirror. He had no reflection, yet Lily had one, a faint ghostlike reflection.

Lily reached out to the mirror, yet didn't try to touch it. "I can see myself. Does this mean I'm not dead?"

"I don't know. It's not a regular reflection—looks—well—like you're made up of mist," Walt said.

"I didn't think a ghost could have a reflection," Danielle said.

"Then I'm not dead!" Lily said excitedly, turning to Danielle.

Danielle reached out to take Lily's hand, but her hand moved effortlessly through Lily's. The two women stood motionless for a moment, staring at each other's hands. Danielle tried again, but once again, her hand moved through Lily's.

"Oh crap…" Lily moaned.

"I am so sorry, Lily," Danielle whispered.

"I still don't believe I'm dead. I can't explain it, but I feel…I feel as if I'm here for a reason. Maybe I'm having some out-of-body experience. If a ghost doesn't have a reflection, then it is possible I'm still alive…somewhere."

"I don't know anything about out-of-body experiences. I've never met anyone who had one. Are you saying someone else was driving your car?" Danielle asked.

"Well, if I'm still alive—somewhere—then that would have to mean someone else was driving my car and was killed. I would never race down the freeway that fast; it can't be me. Someone must have stolen my car and was trying to get away."

"But where are you, Lily?" Walt asked.

"I don't know."

"Try to remember. Think back to before you got onto the freeway and then move forward, retrace your steps," Danielle urged.

"Let's see…" Lily stepped away from the mirror and began to pace. "Okay…before I checked out of the motel, I had something to eat. They served breakfast in the lobby. We all got together, said our goodbyes, and I had some cereal and coffee. I checked out and then got on the road."

"You say you remember getting on the freeway?" Danielle asked.

"Yes. I remember now. I was annoyed with myself for not going to the bathroom one more time before I left the motel. I downed a couple cups of coffee pretty quickly."

"Maybe that's why you were speeding—to get to a rest stop," Danielle suggested.

"No…because I remember turning off to the rest stop. I went to the bathroom. I remember now."

"Okay, then what?" Danielle asked.

Lily stopped pacing and turned to face Walt and Danielle. "That's it. I was in the bathroom, and then…my head…I remember my head hurting. Maybe that's where I hit my head. Then it's kind of a jumble. The clearest memory I have after that is being at Ian's, looking for him…oh my god, Ian!"

"I know. I'm going to have to tell him."

"No, Dani! You can't. Not yet. We don't know for sure that I'm dead!"

"I promised your mother I'd be calling her back later. I should probably ask if they've made a positive identification on the body—she didn't mention anything about a funeral, and I didn't ask."

"They can't have a funeral; I'm not dead! And you can't tell Ian; I don't want to worry him."

"Lily, I have to tell him," Danielle insisted.

"Danielle is right; she has to tell Ian. But if your mother tells her they haven't made a positive identification, I suppose she could leave that window of hope open—until you figure this thing out."

"Walt, when did you realize you were dead?" Lily asked.

"When Danielle told me. I think I always knew, deep down, but I suppose I ignored the signs and blissfully moved through a fog."

"That's the thing; I don't have that deep-down feeling. The only deep-down feeling I have is that I am alive! I'll admit I was in a fog, so to speak, when I first got here. But it's gone, and I see things clearly."

"You say you see things clearly, but you don't remember what happened between the time you stopped and may have hit your head and you arrived at Ian's." Walt reminded her.

"There is something there, but I just can't seem to grab on to it."

"That happens—at least it does for someone who has died. Not everything came into focus immediately for me. It took time.

However, you seem to think this is something else, so I don't know what to tell you."

"Why don't I call Lily's mother back?" Danielle suggested. "It was an awful lot to take in when I first spoke to her. She's expecting me to call her later anyway. Might as well do it now."

"Yes! Please do!" Lily said excitedly. "And tell Mom, whatever she does, don't start planning my funeral!"

"Let's go into the library. I'll call her from there."

Once in the library, Walt and Lily quietly listened to Danielle's side of the conversation. She and Mrs. Miller were on the phone for almost thirty minutes before Danielle finally said goodbye.

"Well, what did she say? They haven't positively identified the body, have they?" Lily asked.

"No, they're waiting to get a hold of your dental records."

"That shouldn't take long. Our dentist retired last spring, but he sold his practice, so the guy who bought it should have my records."

"Your mom mentioned that. Unfortunately, there was some sort of mix-up with the records transferred from your dentist to the new one. A few patient records are missing—including yours."

"That's crazy! What does our old dentist say?"

"That's the problem. He's out of town and won't be back until after the weekend."

"My poor mother, I wish we could tell her everything will be okay," Lily moaned.

"I wish that too. But we don't know everything is going to be okay."

"You can remind her the body hasn't been officially identified yet, so there's still hope," Lily suggested.

"Your mom seems to think it's just a formality. Although, they're waiting until after the body has been positively identified to plan the funeral. According to her, the authorities don't suspect foul play, and with the evidence they have, they're convinced you were the one killed in the accident." Danielle's phone buzzed, indicating an incoming text message. She glanced down and read it. "That's Ian. He wants to know if he can come over. He needs to ask me something."

"Ian! I can't wait to see him!"

"Lily, when he comes over, you have to promise not to distract me while I tell him what happened. It's going to be hard enough without you trying to talk to me when he's here."

25

FIVE

Danielle questioned the wisdom of meeting with Ian at Marlow House to discuss Lily's possible demise while Lily and Walt lurked in the background. Even if they both kept quiet—which she doubted was possible—they would be a distraction while she broached such a sensitive subject.

Unfortunately, Ian had caught her off guard by calling and asking if it was okay if he dropped by. Had she considered the question a moment, she might have thought to make up an excuse to meet him elsewhere, such as his house across the street. Of course, that would only have worked had Lily not pieced together her phone conversation with Ian. After all, if Lily had been able to go to Ian's house earlier, Danielle didn't see why she wouldn't be able to do it again.

Danielle made her way from the library to the foyer, with Lily and Walt trailing behind her. Going to the window by the front door, she pulled the curtain to one side and looked out. It was starting to drizzle. When she spied Ian rushing up the front walk, she quickly opened the front door to let him in.

"It started to rain when I got across the street," Ian said when he stepped inside and began wiping his feet on the mat. "I wanted to talk to you about Lily."

"Umm...yes...I need to talk to you about Lily too." Danielle shut the door after Ian walked into the house.

"Oh, Ian, I wish you could hear me!"

"Hush, Lily, we promised Danielle we'd be quiet," Walt reminded her.

"I know, but I wonder why he wants to talk to Dani about me."

Danielle cleared her throat and glared at Lily, who seemed oblivious to her friend's annoyance.

"I imagine if you stop talking, we'll find out," Walt suggested.

"Have you heard from her?" Ian asked, sounding hopeful.

"Why don't we go talk in the parlor," Danielle suggested, leading the way.

"Just tell me you've talked to her," Ian said as he followed Danielle into the parlor. "After we left the café, I tried calling her and got a message that the number is no longer in service. Did she change her cell number for some reason? I don't know why she wouldn't have told me."

"That's impossible," Lily said as she followed them into the parlor. "Mom wouldn't have turned off my phone that quick! What am I thinking, that's exactly what Mom would do. That's what I get for being part of their family plan!"

"Ian, I have some bad news," Danielle began.

"Don't you think you should tell him to sit down first?" Walt suggested.

"That's so cliché, Walt. I hate when they say that in movies. Like really, do you expect Ian to faint?" Lily rolled her eyes.

"He does seem to be stuck on you."

"If you mean he likes me, I hope so! But I don't want him to think I'm dead. I'm certain my body is alive and, well, somewhere. We just need to find it before it's too late."

"I can't focus!" Danielle rubbed the heel of her right hand against her forehead.

"What is it, Danielle? Has something happened to Lily?"

Lily started to reply, but Walt hushed her again. "Quiet, Lily, you're making this more difficult for Danielle."

With a pout, Lily folded her arms over her chest and pursed her lips, locking whatever words she wanted to say inside. Danielle glanced at Lily and Walt before taking a deep breath.

"Maybe you should sit down," Danielle said quietly.

"Something has happened to Lily?" Ian said dully as he sat down on the sofa. "Hasn't it?"

"I'm not sure. But I got a call from Lily's mom a few minutes ago. There was an accident yesterday. Lily's car was speeding on the freeway and it hit a semi. The woman who was driving was killed."

"It wasn't Lily?" Ian sounded hopeful.

"Lily's mother thinks it was her, but they haven't identified the body yet. It was burned beyond recognition. They're waiting for results from the dental records."

"But you don't sound like you think it was Lily?"

"According to Mrs. Miller, the driver was going in excess of a hundred miles an hour."

"Lily? She drives like a little old lady," Ian said. "Unless someone was chasing her, I can't see her speeding."

"Little old lady? That's rude. I'm just a safe driver," Lily grumbled.

Danielle glanced over at Lily and narrowed her eyes briefly, silently hushing her, then looked back to Ian. "That's what I thought. It's just out of character for her."

"Where did the accident happen?" Ian asked.

"Not far from Palm Springs."

"You said this was yesterday?"

"Yes."

"That doesn't make sense. Lily was planning to return home Monday. She had to be back to work on Tuesday."

"That's right! I left on Labor Day!" Lily jumped up from the desk and stood next to Walt, who again hushed her.

"Mrs. Miller didn't say anything about Lily planning to return on Monday."

"And no one has heard from her?" Ian asked.

"I'm afraid not." Danielle shook her head sadly.

"What do the police think?" Ian asked.

"According to Mrs. Miller, they don't believe there was any foul play. Identifying the body is nothing more than a formality from their perspective."

"This doesn't feel right." Ian stood up and began pacing the room. "Has anyone talked to the motel Lily was staying at?"

Lily sat back down on the desktop and watched Ian pace.

"What for?" Danielle asked.

"To find out when she checked out. Like I said, the last time I talked to her, she planned to be home Monday night so she'd make school on Tuesday."

"Mrs. Miller didn't say anything about that. I didn't even think to ask."

"I refuse to believe that was Lily in the car," Ian insisted.

"I love you, Ian," Lily whispered.

"I don't want to believe that either. But if it wasn't her, then where is she?" Danielle asked, glancing back at Lily.

"Even if she wasn't driving the car, this isn't good." Ian stopped pacing. "And if the police believe that was Lily in the car, then they aren't looking for her. When are they getting those dental records back?"

"I don't know. From what I understand, Lily's dentist retired not long ago, and someone bought out his practice."

"The new dentist would have her records. It really shouldn't take long." Ian ran his fingers through his hair and closed his eyes. Taking a deep breath, he stood silent for a moment.

"Ian, are you okay?" Danielle asked in a soft voice.

When Ian finally opened his eyes, they were brimming with tears. He looked at Danielle and shook his head.

"Not really," he mumbled, the realization of Danielle's news finally sinking in.

Without thought, Danielle opened her arms to Ian. He accepted her invitation, silently weeping on her shoulder.

"Oh, stop that!" Lily begged. "You two are going to make me cry!" Lily jumped up and down just a few feet from Ian and Danielle. Helpless, she watched as her best friend comforted the man she loved.

"Please don't." Walt sounded more bored than concerned. "I remember Cheryl's annoying caterwauling. Sobbing ghosts are not pretty."

"I would have to be dead to be a ghost. And like I told you, I am not dead!" Lily stomped her foot.

"Then pray tell, where is your body, missy?"

"You were much nicer when you visited me in my dreams."

"I'm just trying to be realistic, Lily. When someone makes a visit without their flesh-and-blood body in tow, one tends to assume the worst."

"I just don't feel dead. I feel…well, disconnected…what I would expect an out-of-body experience to feel like."

"What exactly is an out-of-body experience?"

"When your conscious self—your soul—disconnects from your body—travels independently of the body."

"Sounds like being dead to me," Walt scoffed.

"Some people claim to be able to have out-of-body experiences through meditation," Lily explained.

"Are you saying your physical self is somewhere meditating while your conscious self is zooming from California to Oregon?"

"No, not exactly. But I believe my body is somewhere—still alive —and we need to figure out where so I can reconnect."

"I'm sorry," Ian mumbled, wiping tears from his eyes as he stepped away from Danielle.

"That's okay, Ian. I love her too."

"I never told her," Ian said sadly.

"You do love me!" Lily beamed.

"We can't give up hope, Ian."

"There is one thing we can do," Ian said with conviction, his eyes now dry.

"What's that?"

"We need to find out what motel she stayed at and see when she checked out."

"What good will that do?"

"We could call the police investigating the accident, and if she left on Monday, like she was supposed to, then they may consider foul play and start looking for Lily, assuming she wasn't the one killed in the accident. My only problem, I don't know where she was staying. Do you have any idea?"

Danielle looked over to Lily. "I think she mentioned it," Danielle lied. "Let me see if I can remember the name of the motel."

After a few moments of silence, Walt spoke up. "Lily, tell Danielle where you stayed in Palm Springs!"

"Oh! Sorry!" Lily felt foolish. She quickly gave Danielle the name of the motel.

After sharing the information with Ian, Danielle went to the desk and turned on her laptop computer. "I'll see if I can find the phone number."

A few minutes later Ian was ringing up the motel and asking to speak to the reservation desk. Silently, Danielle, Walt, and Lily listened to Ian's side of the conversation.

"I need to speak to someone about a guest you had over the weekend, Lily Miller," Ian said.

"Who is this exactly?" a male voice asked.

"My name is Ian Bartley. I'm Lily's boyfriend."

"My boyfriend. I love how that sounds!" Lily gushed.

"Umm…Mr. Bartley…exactly why are you calling?"

"Lily was supposed to leave there on Monday."

"Yes, she checked out on Monday."

"Are you sure?"

"Umm…Mr. Bartley, I think you need to speak to Sergeant King."

"Sergeant King?" Ian frowned.

"Hold on, he left his business card. Let me get it for you."

"Who is Sergeant King?"

"I am really sorry to have to tell you this, Mr. Bartley, but Ms. Miller was in a car accident. You really need to speak to Sergeant King."

Before Ian got off the phone a few moments later, he jotted down the officer's phone number.

"What did they say?" Danielle asked.

"She checked out on Monday."

"I told you!" Lily said.

"Apparently the police investigating the accident already know that."

"They do? Then why don't they suspect foul play? She should have been back home Tuesday, not on a freeway a short distance from a motel she checked out of the day before."

"I don't know. But he gave me the name of the officer who inquired about Lily's checkout time."

"Well, what are you waiting for? Call him!" Danielle urged.

A few minutes later Ian had Sergeant King on the phone. Danielle and Lily waited anxiously for Ian to hang up. His side of the conversation gave them more questions than answers.

"This is really odd," Ian said when he finally ended the call.

"Do they suspect foul play and just haven't told Lily's mother? Are they looking for Lily?" Danielle asked.

"No, they aren't looking for her. He's convinced it was Lily in the car."

"I don't understand? Don't they wonder why she was still in Southern California after checking out the day before?"

"According to him, when she didn't show up to work on Tuesday, the school called her cellphone and Lily answered."

31

"That's not true!" Lily insisted.

"What did she say?" Danielle asked.

"She apologized for not calling sooner but claimed she had been sleeping. Said she got food poisoning on the way home and had to pull over and get another room. Sounded like they woke her up when they called."

"I did no such thing!" Lily shouted.

SIX

The motel was a dive, but they had stayed in worse places. At least their room had running water and two queen-size beds. Justina sat just outside the door on a concrete bench, smoking a cigarette. Hunter and Claire were inside, and Justina could hear them arguing through the open window. Hunter was determined to go to Oregon, but Claire wanted to go to Vegas.

Justina's thoughts were interrupted when a female voice said, "I hear cigarettes can kill you." Justina glanced up and found herself looking into the green eyes of an attractive redhead.

"I'm not too concerned about that." Justina took another drag off the cigarette while staring at the young woman. There was something familiar about her. "You were the one who gave me directions at the gas station, aren't you?"

"Yes. Did you find your friends?" The woman took a seat on the bench.

"I did." Justina nodded to the open window.

Before the woman could respond, they heard Claire shout at Hunter, "I don't want to go back to Oregon! You're going to kill me with boredom if we go there!"

Justina glanced back at the window and shook her head, then took another puff off her cigarette and looked at the stranger.

"Trouble in paradise?" the redhead asked.

"Hunter will get his way, he always does."

"Does this mean you're going to Oregon with them?"

"I don't know." Justina tossed her spent cigarette butt on the ground then looked up at the woman and frowned. "What are you doing here, anyway? You staying at this dump?"

"No." The woman leaned back on the bench. "Just wondered if you found your friends. You were pretty upset back at the gas station."

"I suppose I was. But don't know why I bothered. It's not like they'll miss me if I don't go with them. And frankly, even if I wanted to, not sure I can." Justina leaned back on the bench.

"What do you mean?"

"Things feel different, that's all." Justina sighed.

"Have you considered going home?" the woman asked.

"I burned that bridge long ago," Justina said. "Even if I could, I don't think I'd want to."

They sat quietly for a few minutes, each lost in private thoughts. Finally Justina asked, "So where are you going?"

"I was on my way home when we met at the gas station. Got a little sidetracked. Wanted to check on you; then I'll be on my way."

Before Justina could respond, they heard Hunter shouting at Claire from inside the motel room.

"What's the deal with those two? Are they married or what?" the woman asked.

"No. Hunter has a wife and kid back home," Justina explained.

"So they aren't a couple?" The woman glanced at the motel window and frowned.

"Yeah, sure, they're a thing. Claire is crazy about Hunter. And it's hard for him to resist her adoration."

"So he just left his wife and kid?"

"Pretty much. Of course, he's done this before. Taken off with his newest one. Always lasts a few months before he goes back to his wife and kid."

"Does the wife just take him back?"

"Yeah. Tina isn't the sharpest knife in the drawer."

"So where do you fit in?"

"Nowhere anymore," Justina mumbled.

"You were traveling with them, weren't you?"

"Hunter's my cousin. He's really the only family I have left. He can be out there sometimes, but he's always been there for me —until now."

"You two are close?"

"We were. Of course, he's a control freak. Has to get his own way. He's been like that since he was a kid, which is why they'll be going to Oregon if that's where he wants to go."

"I know lots of people who have to have their own way."

"It's the other thing that drives me nuts sometimes," Justina said.

"Other thing?"

"He tries to get people to believe he has certain…well, powers."

"Powers?" The woman frowned.

"He likes to come off all mystical. Claims he hears voices—sees spirits and stuff. I tell him he's full of it, but people like Claire eat it up."

"You mean like seeing ghosts? Talking to the dead?"

"Yeah, pretty much."

"And you don't think he can?"

Justina began to laugh. "No. Absolutely not. It's Hunter's con. Works for him. He's made a few bucks from it over the years. Funny thing, I think he's starting to believe the con."

"I suppose if you tell a lie often enough, you begin to believe it's true."

"Exactly." Justina nodded.

"Now what?"

Justina stood up and faced the motel room. "Sounds like those two have calmed down. I suppose it's time I go in there and say my piece. See what happens."

"So you might go with them to Oregon?"

"I don't think so. But I suppose I need to give Hunter a chance."

"I'll be going too." The woman stood up.

"Yeah, probably best if you don't stick around. Hunter's not too crazy about strangers."

The woman nodded, then turned from Justina and began to walk away. She paused briefly, turned, and watched Justina go into the motel room.

HUNTER HAD JUST GOTTEN out of the shower and stood between the two beds, drying off, when someone knocked on the motel room door. Wrapping the towel around his waist, he grabbed some money off the nightstand.

Claire, who had been napping on one of the beds, woke up and rolled over, rubbing her eyes as she watched Hunter answer the door.

He handed the pizza delivery boy a handful of crumpled one-dollar bills before snatching the pizza box from the teenager's left hand and slamming the door shut. He'd given the delivery boy just enough to pay for the pizza with nothing extra to cover a tip.

"It took them long enough!" Claire sat up in the middle of the bed. She had taken a shower before Hunter and now wore an over-sized white T-shirt. It fell to her midthigh. "I'm starved."

Hunter tossed the pizza box on the bed where Claire had been napping. She grabbed it and quickly opened the box. Hunter sat on the edge of the bed and helped himself to a slice of pizza.

"You promised me steak," Claire said as she took a bite.

"When we get to Oregon. I promise. I'll buy you a big steak." Hunter shoved half the slice into his mouth and bit down.

"I still can't believe you let Justina leave." Claire scooted backwards on the bed and leaned against the headboard, stretching her legs out in front of her as she ate pizza.

"I wasn't thrilled at first, but now that I think about it, it works out better this way. We'll catch up with her in Oregon. I want to fly, and this way I only had to buy two tickets."

"Well, at least we're flying, and we don't have to drive. I still wish we could go to Vegas."

"If you're going to keep nagging me, baby, I can just leave you here."

"You wouldn't really do that, would you?" Claire asked with a pout.

"Try me. One more word about Vegas and I cash in the ticket I bought you, and you're on your own. Then you can get that steak you've been whining about. I'm sure they have a dumpster behind Sizzler. You're a resourceful girl, shouldn't be too hard to wrestle scraps from the rats."

"You'd leave me here without any money?"

"The moment you become more trouble than you're worth, yes."

"But the money, it isn't just yours."

"Isn't it? What exactly did you do for it? Justina and I did all the dirty work while you just stood there watching. And don't think for a moment you're innocent in all this. The courts won't care who killed that woman. You're just as guilty as we are."

"Don't leave me here! Please, Hunter! I won't say anything more about Vegas."

Hunter didn't respond immediately. Instead, he stared at Claire, his expression unreadable. Finally, he said, "Then finish eating and get ready for bed. We have a big day ahead of us. I need to get us each some new clothes, a decent suitcase, and we need to do something with your hair."

"My hair?" Claire absently twisted a lock of damp hair between her fingers.

"When we show up at that B and B, the last thing I want is for them to know we've been living on the road."

"Are you really sure about this?" Claire reached over and grabbed a second slice of pizza.

"You nagging me about Vegas again, Claire?"

"No! Honest…just that…" Claire took a bite and chewed for a moment before finishing her thought. "I just don't really understand why we have to go to the B and B. Plus it's so close to…well, you know."

"It is a sign, Claire, I told you. The moment I found that notebook, I just knew."

"But don't you think the owners of that B and B have already been through the house? If there are other hidden treasures, wouldn't they have found them already?"

"They don't have my gift, Claire. The moment I read the notebook I knew—I knew that's where I need to go. You'll see. You'll thank me. Hell, when we're finished, you can have steak every night if you want!"

"It's just that…" Claire said with a pout.

"Just that what?"

"It's not that far from Tina."

"It's not all that close either. So what do you care anyway?"

"She's your wife." Claire nervously chewed her lower lip.

"I told you. I'm with you now."

"Then why don't you just divorce her?"

"Why would I want to do that?"

"We can't get married if you're still married to her."

"Don't start that again. I told you, I'm never going to get

married again! Once is enough. And if I divorce Tina, then she can get married again."

"Would that really be so bad?"

"I told you I'm not going to have the mother of my kid sleeping with some other guy!"

"What makes you think that isn't happening now?"

"Tina wouldn't dare." Hunter angrily grabbed another slice of pizza.

"When we stay at the B and B, how will we check in?"

"Don't tell me you care what they think?" Hunter began to laugh. Claire blushed and shook her head. "If it makes you feel any better, I made the reservation for me and my wife."

"I still feel kind of funny about going back there."

"Why? No one will remember us."

"But still…"

"It's a sign. None of this is a coincidence. There are no coincidences. We are meant to go back."

"What about Isabella?"

"What about her?" Hunter frowned.

"That's where she's from."

"So?"

"Have you talked to her about going there? What does she say?"

"Let me worry about Isabella." Hunter stood up and went to the nightstand. Pulling open its drawer, he removed the local phone book. He tossed it on the bed next to Claire. "You worry about finding a local beauty shop. We need to make a good impression."

SEVEN

Thursday morning, Walt stood at the doorway to the Red Room and watched as Danielle changed the bedsheets.

"You could have Joanne do that," Walt suggested.

"If you'll remember, Joanne is gone until next week. I didn't know we'd be having any guests when she asked for the time off. Really didn't expect any reservations after Labor Day."

With a wave of his hand, Walt summoned a thin cigar. It was already lit. "Are you sure you're up to this, Danielle?"

"Not really, but what else can I do? I've already accepted the reservation."

"You could call and cancel it. Tell him the house has plumbing issues."

Danielle tossed the bedspread over the bed. "Not a bad idea—if I had his phone number."

"Didn't he leave one?"

"I guess I need more work on Reservation Taking 101." Danielle leaned over the mattress. She ran her palms over the bedspread, smoothing out the wrinkles. When she finished, she sat on the edge of the mattress and looked at Walt.

"You're going to mess up the bed." Walt took a puff from the cigar.

"She can't be dead, Walt. She just can't be," Danielle whispered.

In the next instant, Walt was seated next to Danielle on the bed, the cigar no longer in his hand.

"I know she's like family to you." Walt spoke in a soothing tone.

"I just buried my last family member. I can't do this again. She's like my sister."

"I know." Walt studied Danielle's delicate profile. Wisps of dark hair escaped her once tidy fishtail braid.

"My parents are gone...I never had any brothers or sisters... Aside from Cheryl and her brother, I never had any cousins...never knew my grandparents..."

"You know that is the second time you've said something like that," Walt interrupted.

Danielle looked up into Walt's blue eyes. "What do you mean?"

"That you didn't know or have any grandparents. What about your grandmother? You told me she was the first spirit you encountered."

"You're right." Danielle sighed. "I just meant I never knew my mom's parents and can't remember my dad's father. Other kids seem to have grandparents."

"But you did have a grandmother."

"Yes, you're right. And she was a special grandmother. But they are all gone now. My parents, grandparents, cousins...all of them, even my husband, Lucas. Although, I suppose Lucas basically checked out of my life when he got a girlfriend."

They were quiet for a moment when Danielle laughed ruefully.

"What is it?" Walt asked.

"I sound like a big old whiny baby—as if this is all about me. But it isn't. It's about Lily. And I need to do something to help her and not spend my time feeling sorry for myself."

"You're entitled to feel sad."

"Maybe. But I shouldn't sit here having a pity party. Especially with you."

"Why do you say that?" Walt frowned.

"I had my parents for longer than you had yours."

"I suppose we don't miss what we never really had."

"Aren't you even a little bit anxious to move over to the other side to be reunited with those you've lost?"

"I'm not ready to give up what I have here," Walt said quietly.

"That's what I'm worried about." Danielle turned to face him, her expression serious.

"What do you mean?"

"You told me earlier I didn't have to lose Lily. That she could just stay here."

"She could."

"I don't think spirits are supposed to stay earthbound indefinitely. I believe there is something beyond this, somewhere where spirits are supposed to go…to continue on their journey. Like with Cheryl. She knew it was time for her to move on. She didn't even show up for her funeral."

"Do you want me to leave?" Walt's voice was barely a whisper.

Danielle did not answer immediately. Finally, she said, "No. That's my problem. I don't want you to leave. I don't want Lily to leave. But I can't be responsible for holding either one of you back."

"Let me worry about myself. When the time is right for me to move on, I'll go. I promise. As for Lily, I think maybe she's right."

"Right how?" Danielle asked.

"She's adamant about not being dead. And there is the matter of the reflection."

"What do we do?"

"Figure out some way to help Lily reconnect with her body—before it's too late."

"That's assuming it really is out there somewhere." Danielle stood up.

When she went downstairs fifteen minutes later, she found Lily in the library, standing over the desk, reading the morning newspaper.

"Can you please turn the page for me?" Lily asked when Danielle walked into the room.

"Have you tried harnessing your energy?" Danielle asked.

"Last night Walt tried to show me how. But it just doesn't work for me. I can't move anything—can't pick anything up. If I am dead, I must have been a bad person because this is definitely hell. Talk about taking for granted simple things, like being able to pick up a newspaper or turn a page."

"The upside, you don't seem to have a problem moving through walls or sitting on chairs." Danielle walked over to the desk and began turning the page.

"Which is a good thing, since I'm now doorknob challenged, and I can't imagine just floating around indefinitely!" Lily looked down at the newspaper. "One more page, please. I was reading the article about that local woman they found."

"I started reading that this morning but got sidetracked."

After Danielle turned the page, Lily pointed to a photograph excitedly. "That's where I was!"

Danielle looked at the picture and read the caption. "It's where they found Isabella Strickland."

"That's the rest stop I pulled into on Monday! I recognize it! It's not far from Palm Springs."

Danielle picked up the newspaper and looked at the photograph. "Are you sure?"

"Yes. I'm starting to remember more."

Lily pointed to the vehicle in the picture. "I even recognize that car! It was there when I pulled in. I remember noticing it because my sister has a car just like it. It's a Tahoe. Same color and make."

"According to the article, that's Isabella Strickland's car. That's how they initially determined who she might be. Before her uncle identified her."

"She wasn't alone."

"What do you mean?" Danielle set the paper back down on the desk.

"When I pulled into the rest stop, it was empty—except for one car. That one. I did a double take because it looked just like my sister's car. There were a few people standing around it. Three, maybe four. I'm not sure exactly."

"Men? Women?"

"A couple of women for sure. One I wasn't so sure about. Could have been a guy, I suppose. I really didn't look that close. I didn't park near them."

"This is really strange. Are you sure?"

"Yes." Lily looked down at the newspaper. "What day did they find that woman's body?"

"According to the article, on Monday evening—Labor Day."

"Well, that's pretty creepy." Lily cringed. "They must have done something to her after I left."

"Or…when you were still there…"

"Why do you say that?" Lily frowned.

"What do you remember after pulling into the rest stop?"

"Well…" Lily pondered the question for a moment. "I remember parking. Thinking I was glad I'd left so early."

"Why?"

"It was early in the morning, and there weren't many cars on the road. I wanted to leave early to miss the Labor Day traffic."

"What do you remember after parking?"

"Walking to the restroom. Going to the bathroom. And then…" Lily frowned, trying to remember something.

"What is it?"

"I don't know. It kinda gets fuzzy from there. I think I heard someone shouting, but I can't remember what exactly. My next real memory is walking up to Ian's house."

"Lily, whoever left Isabella Strickland near that rest stop must have done it while you were there. If you heard someone screaming, maybe that's what you heard—someone attacking her. My guess is you're still out there."

"Are you saying my poor body is lying in the desert by that rest stop?"

"That's where they put Isabella. Since her car was the only one there, I don't think anyone thought to look for another body."

"Oh my god…do you think I'm still alive?"

Before Danielle could answer the question, Lily ran out into the hallway and looked into the mirror.

"I still have a reflection!" Lily shouted from the hallway.

"What is going on?" Walt asked as he walked down the staircase. He found Danielle stepping out of the library and Lily jumping up and down in front of the mirror.

"We know where I am!" Lily shouted, turning to Walt. "But we need to hurry up and find me before…oh my god…wild animals! Who knows what sort of damage has happened to my poor body by now!"

"What in the world is she talking about?" Walt asked Danielle.

"We think we may know where Lily's body might be. And if we're correct, we need to find it as soon as possible. Before it's too late."

Walt followed Danielle back into the library as she explained what Lily remembered and then showed him the newspaper article on Isabella Strickland.

"If this is true," Walt said as he studied the paper, "I wonder what Isabella Strickland might be able to tell us."

"She's in a coma, according to the article. I don't think she can help us."

Walt set the newspaper back down and looked up at Danielle. Lily was still in the hallway, admiring her faint reflection in the mirror. "What are you going to do?" he asked.

"We need to get someone to search the area immediately."

"Are you going down there?"

"That would take too long, and I don't know the area. I was thinking I could hire someone—maybe a private detective from Palm Springs."

"Sounds like a good idea. And I agree, you better hurry. If Lily really is alive and her body was dumped out with Isabella Strickland in the desert, who knows what condition it's in now." Walt picked up the newspaper again and started reading the article.

"But if it's not there, then whoever attacked Isabella may have taken Lily. Maybe one of the people responsible was driving Lily's car when it was in the accident."

"Did you read this entire article?" Walt asked.

"No, why?" Danielle looked down at the newspaper in Walt's hand.

"Because you might be onto something. According to the article, Isabella's car was broken down at the rest stop. They speculate in the article that she may have asked the wrong person for help, and whoever it was attacked her."

"Or whoever she was traveling with."

"True. But the point I was making, if Isabella's car was broken down, then maybe whoever was standing by her car when Lily drove into the rest stop—"

"Took Lily's car."

"Exactly." Walt nodded. "Lily said it was the only other car in the rest stop, and according to the article, it was broken down."

"Okay, I need to get online and see who I can hire to go search the area for Lily."

"If she's not there, then maybe they'll find some clues that can help us figure out where they took her," Walt suggested.

"Part of me hopes they took Lily and that she's safe somewhere. If she was left in the desert like Isabella…it's been a few days now. That can't be good."

EIGHT

C laire gazed out the side window of the Cadillac as they drove northwest on Highway 26. She glanced at Hunter and said, "I hope it wasn't a mistake to take an expensive car."

With both hands on the steering wheel, Hunter looked over at Claire and then looked back down the highway. "Jail time's the same for an economy car as it is for this one. Might as well drive in style."

"I hope its owner is taking a long vacation."

"I told you it was fate. Justina forgot to take the plate with her, so even if the owner returns today, he won't be able to find his car until after we ditch it."

Claire absently ran her fingers through her recently styled hair. "I hope you're right."

"Stop that," Hunter snapped, his eyes darting in her direction.

"What?" Claire frowned, looking over at Hunter.

"You've messed up your hair. Fix it."

Claire flipped down the sun visor and looked in the mirror. "I hate my hair like this," she grumbled. "I look like someone's mother." Using her fingers, she attempted to straighten her hair.

"You're messing it up more! Can't you do anything right?"

"I don't know why you're being so mean lately!" Stifling a sob, she flipped the visor back up and slumped back in her seat, looking away from Hunter.

"Don't start crying on me. You'll screw up your makeup."

"You never used to be like this. I thought you liked the way I look!"

"We have a part to play. You know that."

"I know. I get to pretend to be your wife," Claire said with a pout.

"My bride. I told them we're on our honeymoon."

"I wish it really was our honeymoon."

"Last I heard, polygamy isn't legal in this state." Hunter laughed.

"Since when do you care about the laws?"

"Fine, let's get married."

Claire turned in her seat and faced Hunter. A hopeful smile replaced her glum expression. "Are you serious?"

"As long as I don't have to screw with a divorce, why not?"

"But that wouldn't be a real marriage!" Claire slumped back in her seat, her smile gone.

"I can't please you. Why do you care how real it is in the eyes of the law? I'm with you, not Tina, aren't I?"

"I suppose…" Claire glanced down at her left hand and the engagement ring and wedding band she wore. Hunter had purchased them at Kmart before they left California. The diamonds were glass. After inspecting the fake wedding set, Claire reached down and picked up her purse off the floor by her feet. Opening it, she retrieved a gold and sapphire bracelet and began fastening it on her right wrist.

Hunter glanced over and scowled. "What are you doing?"

"Just putting on the bracelet."

"Take it off!" he snapped.

"Why? You want them to think we have money, and I bet this bracelet is the real deal." She glanced briefly at her left hand. "Unlike this engagement ring."

"I said take it off! Someone might recognize it."

"It's just a bracelet! I'm sure there are other women who have one just like it."

"We're not going to blow this by some stupid bracelet. I knew I should have sold it with the other stuff."

"Fine…" Claire said with a pout as she snatched the bracelet off her wrist and shoved it back in her purse. "I still don't understand why we have to go through all this."

"I thought you'd be happy to have new clothes."

"Sure, if you would've let me pick them out. I look like a freaking librarian."

"You look respectable."

"You didn't cut your hair." Claire looked over at Hunter, who now wore his long hair pulled back into a ponytail.

"So? Lots of classy dudes have long hair. And you have to admit, I look good in these clothes."

"Better than I look in mine," Claire said glumly.

"You look fine. Trust me, dressed like this, driving this car, Boatman will think we're just a couple enjoying a quiet honeymoon. They won't be watching to make sure we don't steal the silver."

"Who is Boatman?"

"She's the one who owns the bed and breakfast."

"Well, I hope you're right about that place. I hate to think we wasted all the money on these clothes—the airline tickets—just to stay in some stupid seaside inn. At least in Vegas there would be stuff to do. And there I could wear clothes I actually like!"

"WHERE'S DANIELLE?" Walt asked when Lily found him in the attic on Friday morning.

"She's at the market, getting some last minute things for the guests."

"How are you doing? Having any luck harnessing your energy?"

"No. I've given up. I think in this state—"

"As an undead?" Walt interrupted.

"Not sure I like the sound of that." Lily cringed. "But, yeah…I suppose the undead sorta sums it up. I don't think it's possible."

"We could give it another try."

"Actually, I'm here to ask you about something else you do."

"What's that?" Walt studied Lily's expression.

"You know how you visited my dreams?"

"Umm…yes…about that. I suppose that may seem rather intrusive, but you see—"

"No, that's okay. I understand. It was the only way you and I could actually talk—communicate. I'm okay with it. In fact, I was hoping you could try that little trick on someone else."

"What do you mean?"

"Isabella Strickland."

"Isabella Strickland? From what I understand, she's in a coma."

"Right. But that's sort of like being asleep. If you could somehow jump into her dreams, maybe you could talk to her, find out what happened back at the rest stop. Maybe she saw me."

"That's an interesting idea..." Walt considered the suggestion. Waving his hand, a lit cigar appeared between his fingers. "I'm not sure it's possible. I've only done it with you."

"You remember how you did it, don't you?"

"I suppose. The first time was the day you both arrived in Frederickport. That night—actually, after Danielle left here for the second time. I started thinking about you both, remembering how you each looked, thinking what I would ask you about Danielle if you could hear me, when suddenly I was in your dream. I wasn't sure what was going on. I tried it a second time, focusing just on you —after you two moved into Marlow House—and it just worked."

"Then you could do it with Isabella!"

"I've never seen her. I don't know what she looks like."

"There was a picture of her in the newspaper."

"True, but it wasn't a very clear photograph." Walt took a puff off his cigar.

"What if I could get a better picture of her?"

"I suppose I could try."

"Or you could go to her. We know where she is." Lily grinned.

"No, Lily, I can't leave Marlow House."

"I thought Dani said you're free to go now, but you choose to stay."

"It's not that simple. If I leave Marlow House, I may not be able to come back."

"You did before. Dani told me."

"That was different, Lily. You don't understand. As long as I decide to stay on this plane—not to move on to the next level—I can't leave this house. Not even to go outside. I thought you understood that."

"Then a photograph will have to do."

Danielle arrived home from the market a few minutes later. Lily and Walt were still upstairs. She had just finished putting away the groceries when someone rang the doorbell. At first, she wondered if it was her guests arriving early, but it turned out to be Ian. She hadn't seen him since Wednesday evening.

"Your guests haven't arrived yet?" Ian asked when Danielle opened the door. His golden retriever, Sadie, followed him into the house.

"Not yet. They're supposed to be here sometime this afternoon."

Wagging her tail, Sadie pressed her wet nose into Danielle's open hand before racing off down the hall and up the stairs, looking for Walt.

"I don't know why she insists on going upstairs whenever we come over." Ian shook his head and closed the door behind him.

"She's okay. Sadie isn't any trouble. There's probably a mouse up there," Danielle lied.

"I suppose..." Ian followed Danielle into the parlor. "Have you heard from Lily's mother? I was going to call her...but then..." Instead of finishing his sentence, Ian took a seat on the small sofa and leaned back, staring up at the ceiling.

"Looks like you haven't slept." Danielle took a seat on the chair next to him.

"Have you heard any news? Have they made a positive identification?"

"I spoke to Lily's mother late last night. She said they hope to have it by Monday."

Ian looked up at Danielle. "She still convinced it's just a formality?"

"Pretty much." Danielle let out a sigh and then said, "I hired a private investigator."

"You did?" Ian sat up on the couch.

"I'm holding on to hope it wasn't Lily in the accident—that someone stole her car. If that's the case, then I really don't want to wait around until Monday for the dental records. Because if Lily is alive somewhere, we need to find her."

"I spent all day yesterday on the phone," Ian explained. "Calling people I know around Palm Springs. I even called a PI I once worked with—to hire him to look for Lily."

"You hired someone too?"

"After I told him the story, he made a few calls, called me back and told me to save my money, that it was Lily in the car."

"How does he know that?"

"I don't think he knows for certain. But after talking to the cops he felt he knew, thought I was wasting my time."

"Jerk," Danielle muttered.

"He did promise to make some more inquiries. Not really sure what that meant. I think he just wanted to make me feel better. In fact, that's the reason I came over. I wanted to see if you'd watch Sadie so I could fly down to Southern California and poke around myself. I can't wait until Monday. Like you said, if that wasn't Lily in the accident, we can't be waiting until Monday to go looking for her."

"The private eye I hired didn't seem to have a problem taking my money."

"Do you know if he's any good?"

"I have no idea. I hope so."

"I still want to go down there. I can't just sit here. It's driving me crazy."

"Where are you going to look?" Danielle asked.

"Figured I'd start at the motel. Follow the route Lily most likely took when going home. What's your PI doing?"

"Kinda the same thing." Danielle failed to mention the fact she had told the private investigator to search the area around the rest stop where they had found Isabella Strickland. She wasn't sure what the PI thought about her request, but considering what he was charging, she figured he'd happily check out any of her hunches, regardless of how outlandish they might seem.

"Will you watch Sadie?" Ian asked.

"No problem. If this is what you really want to do. But my private investigator will be going over the area."

"Better two people looking instead of one." Ian stood up.

"I better give him a call and tell him about you coming down. Otherwise, if your paths cross, he may think you had something to do with her going missing and then start looking in all the wrong places."

"You should probably give me his name so I don't jump to the same conclusion if someone mentions him making an inquiry."

"Do you want to contact him?" Danielle asked nervously.

"I don't think that's necessary. I'd rather we each do our own search."

Danielle was relieved to hear Ian didn't want to join forces with the private investigator she had hired. She wasn't sure how she could explain her detailed instructions to the PI to search the area around the rest stop where they had found Isabella Strickland.

NINE

The golden retriever charged up the stairs leading to the attic. By the time Sadie reached the second floor, both Walt and Lily heard her coming. Walt opened the attic door without the pretense of using his hand. The door flew open while he and Lily stood a few feet away.

For a moment, Lily forgot her body was only an illusion, making it impossible to pet the dog. When Sadie entered the attic, Lily reached out and her hand moved effortlessly through Sadie's head. When it did, Lily quickly jerked back her hand.

"Not sure I would ever get used to that…hope I don't have to." Lily grimaced. Sadie ran through Lily and then Walt, and then doubled back, racing through them several more times in greeting.

A few seconds later Lily whistled for Sadie, who continued to run in circles. Hearing the command, Sadie sat down and looked at Lily.

"I assume you being here, girl, means Ian's downstairs. Let's go say hello!"

When Lily got downstairs with Sadie, she found Danielle at the front door, hugging Ian.

"Keep in touch. I promise to take good care of Sadie," Danielle said as their brief hug ended.

"I will. You're one of the few people I trust with her. I know you'll take good care of Sadie."

"Where's Ian going?" Lily looked anxiously from Danielle to Ian.

Ian knelt down on one knee and ruffled the fur on Sadie's shoulders. "Goodbye, girl."

Wagging her tail, Sadie nuzzled Ian and licked his face.

"Where is Ian going?" Lily asked impatiently.

"Did you get your airline ticket yet?" Danielle asked, trying to ignore Lily.

"I'm on standby. But I need to hit the road." Ian stood up and gave Sadie a final pat before heading out the front door.

"Fly safe!" Danielle called after him before shutting the front door.

"Where's Ian going?" Lily repeated.

"He's going to California to look for you."

"Look for me? I don't understand. I thought you hired that PI to look for me."

"I did, Lily." Danielle turned from the front door and began walking down the hall to the kitchen, Lily at her side. "But Ian's going crazy just doing nothing."

"He doesn't believe I was the one killed in the car accident, does he?" Lily smiled at the thought.

"He doesn't want to believe it. And until the dental reports come back, none of us will know for sure. If your hunch is right—if that reflection we see in the mirror is an indication that your body is still alive, then I'm all for Ian looking for you along with the PI I hired."

"About that PI, when this all gets worked out, I promise to repay you for whatever he cost."

Danielle shook her head. "Don't be silly." She walked into the kitchen and began putting the dishes away from the dishwasher.

"I'm serious. I heard what he's costing you. You shouldn't have to pay for it."

Plate in hand, Danielle paused a moment and looked at Lily, who now sat up on the kitchen counter, watching her. "Lily, have you forgotten I'm a very rich woman now? I can afford to pay the private investigator. There's no reason for you to pay me back. I want to do it."

"No. I don't want to be the kind of friend that takes advantage of you. I refuse to be a user."

Shaking her head again, Danielle set the plate she was holding in the cupboard and resumed emptying the dishwasher.

"You're hardly a user. You're practically family—heck, you are family. The only family I have. I can't think of any better way to spend my money. And let's not forget, I never did anything to earn it in the first place."

"That's not true. You were a good niece to your aunt Brianna. That's why she left you the money and not Cheryl."

"Perhaps. But still, it's not like I worked for it. And let's not forget the inheritance from Cheryl. I certainly didn't do anything to earn that!" Danielle pulled the basket of clean silverware from the dishwasher and dumped it on the counter.

Lily watched Danielle organize the silverware before putting it in a drawer. "I wish I could help you put the dishes away."

"Me too. Still no luck harnessing your energy?"

"No. But I had an idea this morning. I bet Isabella Strickland knows what happened to me. She was there at the rest stop."

"She probably does. But until she comes out of her coma—and according to what I've read, that doesn't look promising—she's not going to be of much help." Danielle finished putting the silverware away. After closing the drawer and dishwasher, she turned to face Lily.

"She may not need to come out of her coma to help us." Lily jumped off the counter; her feet landed on the floor.

"What do you mean?" Danielle asked.

"If Walt can jump into her dreams, like he did with me, they could have a little chat."

"Do you think people dream when they're in comas?" Danielle asked.

"I read once on the Internet that people in comas dream."

"You know what they say—if it's on the Internet, it must be true." Danielle grinned.

"Well, it's possible!"

"Actually, you have a good idea. A really good idea."

"You seriously think so?"

"I do. When's he going to try?" Danielle asked.

"He needs a better picture of her, something to focus on. He's not really sure how it all works, but when he did it with me the first time, he focused on how he remembered my face."

"There was a picture in the paper," Danielle suggested.

"It was kind of washed out and out of focus. I promised him I'd find a better one."

"How are you going to do that? You can't even pick up a photograph if you find one."

"I thought maybe you could find a more recent picture of her," Lily suggested.

"Where? I can't very well knock on her uncle's door and ask him if he has a recent photograph of his niece."

"What about the Internet?" Walt asked when he appeared a second later.

Danielle and Lily turned to Walt and chorused, "The Internet?"

"Sure. Danielle seems to find everything on there." Walt smiled.

"I suppose..." Danielle muttered.

"Facebook!" Lily blurted out. "Everyone has a Facebook page. We need to see if she has one—with a profile picture better than the photograph in the paper."

"She might have a Facebook page." Danielle considered the suggestion. "Of course, it will depend on her privacy settings."

"Privacy settings?" Walt asked.

"When people set up Facebook accounts, they have privacy options—so they can decide who can see the photos they post. Since we're not her Facebook friends—assuming she has an account—then we may not be able to see any of her pictures."

"We won't know for sure until we check!" Lily said excitedly.

"Okay, let's go look now." Danielle led the way to the parlor, where she had left her laptop computer. She sat at the desk while Lily and Walt stood behind her, anxiously waiting to see what she'd find. It took less than ten minutes for her to log into Facebook and find Isabella's Facebook account.

"That's the same picture they used in the newspaper article," Lily said when she saw Isabella's profile picture. She sounded disappointed.

"I think this one is better. It's a little clearer than the one in the paper," Danielle said.

"Are there any other pictures?" Lily asked.

Danielle navigated through Isabella's Facebook account, moving the mouse on the desktop. "Yes, but none seem to be of her. Photos of the area mostly. Interesting..."

"What?" Lily asked.

"Under her work, says she's a writer," Danielle said.

"What does she write?" Walt asked.

"Doesn't really say. I sort of got the impression she was basically a trust fund girl," Danielle said.

"She's a bit of a hotsy-totsy," Walt noted as he peered over Danielle's shoulder. "I might be able to work off that photograph."

"Humm, so you won't mind hijacking her dream?" Lily teased.

"If this works out, maybe I'll have Danielle find me photographs of other attractive women. Gets a little boring cooped up in this house sometimes."

"Well, thanks," Danielle said dryly.

"Oh...I didn't mean you're not a doll!" Walt glanced from Danielle to Lily. "Both you and Lily are very attractive...I just meant..."

"Oh, save it, Walt." Danielle stood up and faced the pair. "I won't be pimping for you."

"Pimping?" Walt frowned.

Lily laughed and pointed to the computer monitor displaying Isabella's profile picture. "Focus, Walt," Lily said. "If you're able to get some useful information from Isabella Strickland, I'll happily find you all the photos of current sexy starlets you can handle."

"I didn't mean that how it sounded," Walt muttered as he sat down at the desk and looked at the computer.

"Well, I hope not," Danielle said. "The idea of a ghost stalking pretty women while they sleep is just—well, a little creepy."

"Do you have to call me a ghost?" Walt grumbled. He looked at the picture of Isabella Strickland.

"I forgot. You prefer spirit," Danielle retorted.

"Oh, come on, Danielle, don't be such a prude. Imagine if you had the power to pop into someone's dream, wouldn't you be tempted to try—just for the fun?" Lily grinned.

"Oh brother, you better be alive, Lily, because if you aren't, I have a feeling you'd be getting into all sorts of mischief as a gh...spirit."

"I'm not dead—yet. And, Walt, when I finally get reunited with my body—which I will—please come visit me in my dreams, because I'll miss our chats."

"Thank you, Lily, I appreciate that." Walt flashed Danielle a smug look, to which she countered by rolling her eyes. "I think you ladies should leave me alone while I focus on Miss Strickland. I don't think this is going to work with you two in the room."

"Okay. Thanks, Walt." Lily turned to the door.

"Behave yourself," Danielle teased. She looked down at Sadie curled up under Walt's feet. "Come on, girl, you come with us. Walt needs to focus."

Sadie looked up at Danielle.

"Go on, Sadie, she's probably right. I need total concentration."

The golden retriever looked from Walt to Danielle and then reluctantly stood up and followed Danielle and Lily from the parlor. Danielle closed the door behind them.

"I hope this works," Lily said, anxiously looking back at the closed door.

"Me too." Danielle paused a moment and then asked, "Walt does know what to ask her, doesn't he?"

"Yes, we discussed all that."

Before Danielle could respond, the doorbell rang.

"Is that your guests? I thought they weren't supposed to arrive until later this afternoon."

"They aren't." Danielle walked to the front door. "They must be early."

When Danielle opened the front door a moment later, she was surprised to find Officer Joe Morelli standing alone on the front porch.

"Officer Morelli?" Danielle said with a frown, surprised to find Joe at her door. He wore his uniform, and in his hands, he held his baseball cap, its Frederickport Police Department insignia partially visible.

"Can't you at least call me Joe?" he asked in a soft voice.

TEN

D anielle considered his question for a moment and then asked, "Joe, what can I do for you?"

"I was hoping I could come in for a moment so we can talk."

"This really isn't a good time. I have guests arriving this afternoon, and I still have some things to get ready." Danielle glanced over her shoulder at Lily, who stood quietly listening.

"Please, Danielle. Can you just give me ten, fifteen minutes?"

Reluctantly, she opened the door wider and stepped aside, letting him into the foyer.

"You in trouble with the law again?" Lily teased.

Trying to ignore Lily, Danielle shut the front door and looked at Joe, waiting for him to say what was on his mind. Absently, she tucked strands of hair, which had escaped from her braid, back behind her ear.

"Wow, does that boy look lovesick!" Lily noted.

"Maybe we could talk in the parlor?" Joe glanced to the closed parlor door. Nervously his hands fidgeted with the brim of his baseball cap.

"He still wants you, Danielle. Yep, that boy is heartsick."

Danielle closed her eyes briefly, trying to shut out Lily. Looking at Joe, she said, "No, not the parlor. Let's go into the library." Instead of waiting for him to reply, she turned and headed down the hallway, leaving Joe to follow in her wake.

"He really is good looking," Lily said as she walked by Danielle's side, glancing over her shoulder at Joe. "He has that macho Italian thing going for him."

"Hush," Danielle whispered under her breath.

"I bet he's going to beg you again to forgive him. He looks so sad, I almost feel sorry for him."

"Lily, please stop," Danielle whispered as she walked into the library. When Joe followed her into the room, Danielle waved toward the sofa, silently offering him a seat. Before she knew what was happening, he tossed his cap on the sofa, walked to her, and placed his hands on her shoulders, looking seriously into her eyes.

"I wanted to say how so very sorry I was to hear about Lily," he said solemnly.

Danielle's eyes widened and she stepped back abruptly. Joe dropped his hands from her shoulders.

"He knows..." Lily said. "Wow, news travels fast. I wonder how he found out."

"I'd like to know that too," Danielle said.

"Excuse me?" Joe asked with a frown.

"Umm...I meant I'd like to know how you found out about Lily."

"I saw it on her Facebook page," Joe explained.

"Facebook page?" Danielle glanced from Joe to Lily.

Lily shrugged. "People must be posting about my death on Facebook. We need to look at it. I'm curious what people are saying about me."

"Lily was one of my Facebook friends," Joe explained.

"You were Facebook friends?" Danielle's eyes darted to Lily.

"In all fairness, he accepted my friend request before all that mess with Cheryl. I considered deleting him. But I wanted to see what he was up to. I knew you weren't one of his Facebook friends, so I figured I'd let you know if I read anything interesting on his page."

"Danielle, I know how close you two were. I wish you would've called."

"Lily is not dead," Danielle said.

"I don't understand? What about all those things they're posting on her page?"

"I haven't read her Facebook page."

"But you obviously know..."

"I know her car was in an accident, and someone was killed. But the identity of the driver hasn't been confirmed. As far as I'm concerned, Lily is still out there, alive someplace."

"Oh, Danielle," Joe said sadly. Stepping toward Danielle, he reached out for her hand. Abruptly she stepped back, avoiding his touch. Dropping his hand, he shook his head wearily.

"Stop looking at me like that!" Danielle snapped.

"What do you mean?"

"Yeah, Dani, what do you mean? He's just trying to be comforting. I think it's sweet."

"Like I'm broken," Danielle said, ignoring Lily's comment. "It was nice of you to come over here and offer your sympathy, but it's premature. I prefer to believe Lily is alive. And until the accident victim is positively identified, no one knows for sure."

"I didn't know I was looking at you that way." Joe took a deep breath.

"It's just that I think it's premature to think the very worst."

"I'm surprised they haven't made a positive identification yet. When are they supposed to know?"

"Her mother said Monday, maybe. There was some mix-up with the dental records."

"I understand you wanting to hold on to hope. But, Danielle, it doesn't look good. You've been through so much already. I'm worried about you."

"I'm fine," Danielle insisted.

"You have to admit, Dani, it is rather sweet, the way he wants to take care of you." Lily plopped down on the couch. Putting her feet up on the sofa, she watched the pair.

"How's Ian. Does he know?"

"Yes. And he's like me, holding on to hope that Lily wasn't in the car."

Joe looked down at Sadie, who sat by Danielle's side. "Where is Ian? Is he here? In the parlor?"

"The parlor?" Danielle asked.

"Since Sadie's here, he must think Ian is too. And since you didn't want him to go into the parlor, he must think Ian's in there," Lily surmised.

"Ian went out of town. I'm watching Sadie," Danielle explained.

Joe didn't reply.

"He looks a little jealous," Lily observed. "I wonder if he

thinks you and Ian have something going on now. After all, you two did run into Joe the other day when you had breakfast together."

"Joe, it was thoughtful of you to come over today and offer your condolences. Yet, like I said, Ian and I prefer to hold on to hope that Lily is still alive. But in the meantime, I do have a business to run, and my guests are going to be arriving shortly, and I have a million things to do."

Instead of leaving, Joe walked to the couch and started to sit down.

"Hey, watch out!" Lily shouted from her place on the sofa. Unable to get out of the way fast enough, Lily found Joe's body covering hers as he sat down. Surrendering the sofa to Joe, Lily rushed to Danielle's side and shuddered. "Eww, that was sort of creepy!"

"Always freaks me out when Sadie does that with Walt," Danielle said under her breath, just loud enough for Lily to hear.

"Excuse me?" Joe asked.

"Umm, nothing." Danielle shook her head as if trying to clear out the cobwebs. "But like I said, I really need to get ready for my guests." Danielle's eyes darted from Joe to the open door leading to the foyer.

"I'm a little surprised you're taking reservations, considering everything."

"Well, to be honest, I had the reservation before I heard about the accident." Reluctantly, Danielle sat down on a chair facing Joe.

"Maybe it would be a good idea if you found them someplace else to stay," Joe suggested.

"I can't do that. Plus, it's their honeymoon."

"I'm sure you could find them someplace to stay, it's the slow season, vacancies all over town, and it's not like you need the business."

"He may be sweet, but he is kind of a buttinski," Lily noted.

"If I intend to make a success of the bed and breakfast, I certainly can't turn away customers."

"Danielle, with everything that's happened, I really don't understand why you still want to operate Marlow House as a bed and breakfast." He leaned back and studied Danielle.

"Why do you say that?"

"For one thing, you don't need the money."

"That may be true, but I can't very well sit around the rest of my life and…and do what exactly?"

"I just don't understand a bed and breakfast—letting strangers into your house. You're a single woman, living all alone. It's not safe."

"You didn't seem to have a problem with me turning this place into a bed and breakfast when we first met."

"That was before…" Instead of finishing his sentence, Joe picked up his cap and began fidgeting with it.

"Before what?"

"It's just that so much has happened since you moved to Frederickport. I worry about you here alone with strangers. It wasn't as bad when Lily was here."

"What do you mean?"

Joe looked into Danielle's questioning eyes. "Lily could keep an eye on things. Make sure you were okay."

"You mean keep an eye on me? What, like a child?" Danielle told herself to stay calm.

"Oh. My. Gawd." Lily choked out. "He really has no clue who you are!"

"No, not like a child. But, Danielle, you're vulnerable. Especially now with what you're going through with Lily. As it is, you've had a rough summer, and now with your inheritance, you'll be a target for every fast-talking scammer out there. Opening your home to the public just doesn't seem like the smart thing to do, considering everything."

"Ah yes, my summer," Danielle said angrily, standing up again. "And who helped make my summer so memorable? You arresting me—at gunpoint—was certainly the highlight."

"You were about to bash in Clarence's head."

"I was not about to bash in his head. It just looked that way. And anyway, considering he tried to kill me, I think I had every right to defend myself."

"I didn't come over here to argue with you." Joe stood up and fitted the baseball cap on his head. "I wish you'd understand I'm just trying to help you. It's what I've always wanted to do…help you. I care about you."

Danielle took a deep breath and closed her eyes for a moment. Once again calm, she looked at Joe. "I believe you. I think you do care about me."

"I do. I just want what's best for you," he insisted.

"But the problem with that, you think you know what's best for me. But you don't. How could you? You don't even know me."

"You believe that," Joe said wearily, walking to the door. "But I know you better than you think."

Danielle didn't respond. Instead, she silently walked with Joe to the front door, Lily by her side.

When they got there, Joe turned and looked somberly at Danielle. "I hope you're right about Lily. I hope she's alive and comes home. But if she doesn't, I want you to know I'm always here for you. If you need anything, please call me."

"When I have news about Lily, I'll let you know." *So I can say I told you so.*

"Thank you. I would appreciate that." He glanced briefly at the closed parlor door and then looked back at Danielle. "When you see Ian, tell him I was asking about him. This must be rough on him. I know how much he cared about Lily."

Before Danielle could respond the front door bell rang. Without hesitation, Joe reached for the door and opened it. Standing on the front porch was a well-dressed, thirtysomething couple.

ELEVEN

Silently, Hunter grabbed Claire's left hand, holding her in place. He knew instinctively she was ready to bolt. He couldn't blame her. The last person he expected to greet them at the door of Marlow House was a uniformed policeman.

Part of him wanted to turn tail and put some distance between him and the cop, yet he hadn't come this far to throw it all away by overreacting.

A young woman appeared at the doorway next to the officer. Giving the cop a gentle nudge with her hip, she pushed him out of the doorway, making room for Hunter and Claire to enter. "You must be the Stewarts," she greeted them. She looked at the officer and back to Hunter before saying, "He was just leaving."

Judging by the woman's appearance, Hunter wondered if she was the housekeeper—dressed in worn faded denims and a powder blue shirt. Her dark hair was pulled back into a fancy braid, but wayward strands had already made their escape. Glancing down, he noticed she was barefoot, and he couldn't imagine the housekeeping staff running around shoeless.

"Yes, yes, we are." Hunter looked from the woman to the cop. "Have you had some sort of problem?"

"Problem? No, no problem at all. I'm Danielle Boatman, your host at Marlow House. This is Sergeant Morelli. He was just leaving."

"You know where I am if you need me," Sergeant Morelli told the woman before giving Hunter and Claire a brief nod and smile. He made his way down the walkway toward the street.

"I'm Hank Stewart, and this is my wife, Claire."

"Nice to meet you. Please, please come in." Danielle stepped away from the doorway.

Releasing hold of Claire, Hunter moved his hand to her lower back and gave her a little shove toward the doorway as he picked up the suitcase sitting by his feet on the front porch. Together they walked into Marlow House. Danielle closed the door behind them.

"You'll have to excuse how I'm dressed," Danielle said with a blush. "I expected you a little later."

"We got here sooner than I expected. I hope it's all right." Hunter flashed Danielle his most charming smile. "And you look fine, Ms. Boatman. Doesn't she, darling?"

Claire, dressed in a conservative linen suit, responded with a silent nod as she glanced around the foyer, her eyes wide. "This sure is an old house, isn't it?"

"Yes, over a hundred years," Danielle said proudly. "It was built in 1871."

Claire let out a low whistle and said, "Wow, that's old." She looked at Danielle and asked, "It does have a bathroom, doesn't it? I mean, we don't have to go outside to use the toilet, do we?"

"Of course it has a bathroom, darling." Hunter grabbed Claire's hand again and gave it a tight squeeze.

Claire yanked her hand from Hunter's hold and glared at him. "I was just asking," she said under her breath.

"Let me show you to the library. You can wait there while I get your room ready. It will only be a few minutes," Danielle suggested.

She led them to the library. She left Hunter and Claire there while she went upstairs.

"Maybe the next time you have something stupid to say, just don't," Hunter snapped.

"I don't think it was stupid. This house is frickin' ancient. How was I to know if it had an indoor toilet?"

"Do you honestly think she could run this place as a bed and breakfast without indoor plumbing?" Hunter asked.

"How am I supposed to know? I've never been to a bed and breakfast before." Claire plopped down on the sofa and looked around. "You think she's read all these books?"

"I doubt it." Hunter took a seat next to Claire and looked around. "I bet these were all here when she inherited this place."

"I wonder why that cop was here."

"She sure seemed anxious to get rid of him," Hunter said.

"I was glad to get rid of him myself. You don't think he was here because of us, do you?"

"I don't see how that's possible. I thought for a moment there you were going to take off when he opened the door."

"You didn't have to grab my wrist so hard."

"Don't be such a baby." Hunter leaned back on the sofa and looked around the room. "I didn't see his car parked out front when we drove up. Did you notice a cop car on the street?"

"I wasn't paying any attention."

"I'd think you'd notice a cop car!"

"Well, you didn't notice one either."

"Yeah, well, I was looking for this house and driving. You were just sitting there. The least you could do is pay attention to the area. From what I remember, there were a couple cars parked up the street at the neighbors'. Maybe one was a cop car."

"So why do you think he was here?" Claire asked.

"I just hope she's not sleeping with the guy. We don't need him hanging around here."

"She called him Sergeant Morelli. Didn't call him by his first name," Claire reminded him.

"That doesn't mean anything. We just don't need a cop nosing around."

"So what do we do now? Do we start——"

Hunter grabbed Claire's wrist, giving it a squeeze. "Quiet!"

Claire jerked her hand from him. "Stop doing that! You're going to bruise me."

Hunter took a deep breath then asked, "Do you smell that?"

Claire sniffed the air. "Smells like someone was smoking in here. I hope that means we can smoke in our room. I'm getting tired of having to go outside to have a cigarette."

Hunter stood up and closed his eyes. "Someone is here with us…"

"What?" Claire sat up straight and stared at Hunter. "Who's here?"

"I feel a presence…"

"I hate it when you do that. Freaks me out."

"No reason to be afraid, Claire. He's here to help us."

"It's a he?" Claire anxiously watched Hunter, who was walking around the room, his arms stretched outward, as if he was trying to touch something.

"Whoever it is, he's been here a long time…"

"Are you telling me this old house is haunted?" Claire warily glanced around.

"Are you surprised?" Hunter stopped walking and looked at Claire. "Didn't I tell you a man killed himself in the attic? I bet it's him."

"The dead guy? He's still here?" Claire jumped up.

"Yes, I'm certain it's him. From what I remember in the article, his last name was Marlow, like the house."

"And his first name?"

"First name? I don't remember…" Hunter closed his eyes and said, "Spirit, tell me your name."

Hunter stood there a few minutes, his eyes closed, saying nothing as Claire watched. Finally, he opened his eyes and said, "Marvin. His name is Marvin. Marvin Marlow."

"Marvin Marlow? That's kind of a dorky name."

"Please, Claire, you're going to offend the spirit, and we need his help!"

"Oh, I'm sorry." Claire sat back down on the sofa.

"According to what I read about this place, Marvin Marlow's death was ruled a suicide; he hanged himself in the attic. But the current owner, Danielle Boatman, has been telling the story that he was murdered."

"You mean he was murdered; he didn't kill himself?"

"No." Hunter shook his head. "Marvin Marlow killed himself. That's why his spirit is so conflicted—why he's trapped here."

"You said he was going to help us?"

"Yes, Claire. He's going to be our guide."

WHEN DANIELLE RETURNED to the library, she found Walt leaning against the edge of the desk, smoking a thin cigar, watching the Stewarts. Sitting next to him on the desktop was Lily, her ankles casually crossed.

"You have a couple winners here," Walt said with a chuckle when Danielle walked into the room.

"Walt's right, Dani. I don't think you should let them stay," Lily said.

Trying to ignore Walt and Lily, she smiled at her guests. "Your room is ready. Would you like to go up now and see it?"

Claire started to stand up, but Hunter motioned for her to sit down. He turned to Danielle and said, "Ms. Boatman, I think there is something you need to know about your house."

"Yes, Mr. Stewart? What's that?"

"It's inhabited by a spirit—a very troubled spirit," Hunter said in a serious tone.

"A spirit?" Danielle glanced over to Walt, who responded with a shrug.

"I told you, you shouldn't let them stay," Lily said.

"Do you understand what I'm saying, Ms. Boatman?"

"Not really. When you say spirit, what exactly do you mean?"

"In layman's terms, Ms. Boatman, your house is haunted. You are sharing your home with a ghost."

"A ghost?" Danielle's eyes darted to Walt and Lily and back to Hunter.

"Oh, don't be afraid, Ms. Boatman," Claire said, standing up. "Hu...I mean Hank knows all about spirits and stuff...he's gifted."

"Really?" Danielle raised her brow. "And you say this house is haunted?"

"Yes, but there is no reason to worry. As soon as we give the spirit what he needs, he'll be able to leave, to move on. I can help you do that. It's what I do."

"You mean like *Ghostbusters?*" Danielle couldn't help but giggle.

"You know I hate the word ghost," Walt scolded.

"Please, Ms. Boatman, don't make light of the situation."

"I'm not...really...I'm just surprised," Danielle said, suppressing more giggles. "Where is this ghost right now, do you know?"

"Why, he's over there," Hunter said as he pointed to Walt and Lily.

No longer finding humor in the situation, Danielle cleared her throat and asked, "Are you telling me you can see him?"

"It doesn't work like that," Hunter said with a laugh. "People can't actually see spirits. That's a bunch of media hype. When communicating with spirits, it's on a different level, something I don't expect you to understand."

"I say it's a lucky guess," Walt said. "He smelled the cigar smoke."

Silently, Danielle considered Walt's suggestion before asking, "Mr. Stewart, is there just one spirit, or do you think there could be more than one?"

"More than one? Why would you think that? Did someone else die in this house?" Hunter asked.

"No...not that I know of...I was just curious...umm...you mentioned you could get rid of the spirit; exactly how do you do something like that?"

"First, you need to stop spreading lies about him," Hunter explained.

"Lies?"

"I read your brochure on Marlow House. You wrote how one of the previous owners died in the attic. You claimed it was murder and not a suicide."

"Yes, that's true. At the time it happened, the police assumed it was suicide. But I did some research and discovered he was murdered."

"No, Ms. Boatman, he killed himself. He wasn't murdered. I can understand that the story of a murder might be more titillating for your brochure, the mystery and all. But he needs the truth to come out. He wants people to know he killed himself."

Danielle looked at Walt and said, "He does, does he?"

"Is that true, Walt?" Lily asked with a laugh. "You have to admit, this guy is amusing...and somewhat creepy."

Walt shrugged. "I told you they were winners. The guy gets a whiff of my cigar smoke and he takes off on some wild tangent."

"But what about the other thing, Walt?" Lily asked.

"I'm afraid you're wrong, Mr. Stewart. Walt Marlow was murdered in the attic. In fact, his autopsy verifies that."

"Walt Marlow? It wasn't Walt Marlow who died in the attic, it was Marvin Marlow."

"Marvin Marlow?" Danielle frowned.

"Yes, Marvin Marlow. The man you wrote about in your brochure."

"No, his name was Walt Marlow. You must have confused the Walt Marlow story with someone else's."

"Not unless two men died in your attic," Hunter insisted. "Marvin must have been his nickname. Or perhaps it was his given name, and he went by Walt."

"Where exactly did you get the name Marvin?"

"The ghost told him," Claire spoke up.

"The ghost told him?" Danielle asked, glancing from Claire to Hunter.

"Yes. The minute we walked in here, Hank could feel the ghost. He's gifted. When he asked the ghost for his name, he told him. I know it's hard to believe, but my husband is always doing this sort of thing."

"This is where it gets kinda weird, Dani," Lily said. "Tell her, Walt."

"I was just kidding around," Walt insisted. "I had no idea he could hear me. When he asked me what my name was, I just said…Marvin."

TWELVE

After Danielle showed the Stewarts to their room, she went back downstairs and shut herself in the parlor with Walt and Lily.

"You told him your name was Marvin, and he heard you?" Danielle asked after she shut the door.

"I don't know if he heard me. It could have been a coincidence." He paced the room, a lit cigar in his hand.

"Yeah…right." Danielle sat down on the couch and looked at Walt.

"It was just weird," Lily said as she sat on the sofa next to Danielle. "When they first walked in the house, I got the yuckiest feeling. Bad feng shui."

"Not thrilled he seems to have some sort of psychic powers. He actually started talking to you guys, asking for names?"

"He was talking to Walt—not me!"

"I still say it's some strange coincidence," Walt insisted.

"Tell me what happened, Lily," Danielle said.

"After you left them in the library, they started talking about Joe. They didn't seem too thrilled to be greeted by a cop. I don't get a good feeling about them, Dani. Maybe you should ask them to leave."

"A lot of people feel intimidated around the police. I got the impression they were concerned there was a problem, like Joe was here because I called him about a break-in or something."

"No, I don't think so." Lily shook her head. "But then Walt lit up his cigar and that Hank dude immediately noticed."

"Everyone can smell the smoke," Walt reminded them.

"Which is why you probably shouldn't smoke around the guests," Danielle said.

"Smoking is one of my remaining pleasures. As it is, I agreed not to smoke in your room. But ban the library? I think not."

"After he smelled the smoke," Lily continued. "The guy started telling his wife that he felt a presence, that there was a spirit in the room. And then he went on to say it was the guy who died in the attic. He remembered Walt's last name by something he'd read about the house but couldn't remember his first name, so he asked."

"It was amusing. The way he walked around the room as if going into some trance. He started asking me to give him my name. So, well, I said Marvin."

"Marvin?"

"I certainly didn't expect him to hear me. Still not sure if that's what really happened."

"He must have some psychic powers if he picked up on that name," Danielle said.

"I don't know, Dani." Lily shook her head. "I'll confess I was stunned when he told his wife the spirit's name was Marvin right after Walt said it. But then all that other stuff he said was just plain goofy and not even close to the truth."

"What do you mean?" Danielle asked.

"He started saying Walt was stuck here because he really had committed suicide, and that Walt wanted Hank to help him."

"You mean Marvin." Danielle snickered.

"There was also that other thing," Walt recalled. "He told his wife I was going to be his guide. Just exactly what is that supposed to mean?"

"I suppose we should go hang out in his room and see what else we can learn," Lily suggested.

"No. Neither of you are to go into their bedroom."

"Why?" Lily asked.

"Do I have to remind you they're here on their honeymoon? They may be odd—and he probably has some psychic power, although I don't think it's as strong as he thinks—but they deserve their privacy."

"Oh yeah, it is their honeymoon. I really don't wanna watch that." Lily cringed.

"It may be their honeymoon, but I think I should keep an eye on them," Walt said.

"That's fine, but just don't do it when they're in their bedroom with the door closed."

"Maybe you should have Joe run a check on them," Lily suggested. "I really don't get a good vibe. The moment they walked in the house, a shiver went up my spine."

"Oh yeah, like I'm going to ask Joe for a favor! And considering his lecture earlier today about not letting strangers in this house, I don't think I want to go there."

"I suppose it will be okay, with Walt here. I'm afraid I won't be of any help."

"Perhaps it's a good sign he didn't sense your presence," Danielle suggested. "Might be another indication you're having an out-of-body experience. If he has limited psychic powers, he probably can't pick up on you."

Danielle abruptly turned her attention to Walt and said, "I almost forgot, what happened with Isabella?"

"It didn't work," Lily said sadly.

"I drew a total blank. Maybe it only works after I've seen someone in person. I can try again later if you'd like."

"It's too bad you can't move around like Cheryl did," Lily said sadly. "That way you could just go to where she is."

"I'm sorry, Lily. I'm afraid I don't have the ability to wander at will like Cheryl did."

"Maybe I could slip into Isabella's dream and talk to her. Do you think that might be possible?" Lily suggested. "I'm pretty sure I can get to her house easily. After all, I did get here from California."

Walt considered the idea for a moment. "I don't know. You haven't been able to harness your energy to move objects. But then, if you really are still alive and experiencing some out-of-body experience, perhaps it's impossible for you to harness your energy in that way. However, going into someone's dream takes a different level of concentration, so maybe it is possible."

"You think I can do it?"

"Perhaps," Walt murmured.

"I say give it a try," Danielle said.

"Okay, I'm going to!"

"When, now?" Danielle asked.

Lily considered the question a moment. "I don't want to rush this…"

"Do you really think you should be wasting time, considering everything?" Walt asked.

"It's just that I need to think about what I want to ask her. And I thought maybe you could go over the whole thing with me again. You know, what I might expect, how to talk to her."

"Fine," Walt agreed.

"I know this sounds crazy, but do you think you could drive me over there, Dani, in the morning? I don't remember exactly how I got here from California, and well, if I just take off by myself, I'm not sure I'll actually get to where I need to go."

"Sure, after I serve the Stewarts their breakfast. I could drop you off on my way to Marie's."

"You're going to Marie's tomorrow?" Lily asked.

"I promised her last week, before I made the Stewart reservation, that I'd stop by before noon on Saturday. When Adam was cleaning out her attic, he found more pictures of Brianna. She wants to give them to me."

"I forgot about the Stewarts. Are you sure you want to leave them alone in the house?" Lily asked.

"Walt will be here. I'm not worried about it."

JOE MORELLI SAT at his desk, going over some reports, when Brian Henderson walked into the office. Looking up, Joe set his pen on the desktop and asked, "When did you get back from Portland?"

"About ten minutes ago." Brian sat down in one of the two chairs facing Joe. Dressed in his police uniform, Brian removed his cap and tossed it on the empty chair next to him. "Did I miss anything exciting today?"

"Not really. But I stopped by Danielle's."

"How's the crazy Miss Boatman doing?"

"Come on, Brian, she just lost her best friend." Joe leaned back in his chair.

"Sorry. I guess that wasn't called for, considering the circumstances. How is she doing?" Brian was much older than Joe—old enough to be the younger officer's father.

"She's in denial," Joe said with a sigh.

"What do you mean?"

"She doesn't think it was Lily in the car accident."

"Didn't they already make a positive identification?"

"Apparently not. There was some mix-up with the dental records."

"If it wasn't Lily in the car—then where does Boatman think Lily went? Doesn't she think it's a little odd that she's simply dropped out of sight—at the same time her car is involved in a fatal car crash with a female victim?"

"I didn't say she was being rational. I said she was in denial."

"Rational does not seem to be Boatman's strong suit."

"Come on, Brian, that's not fair."

"Oh please, Joe. I know you have a thing for the woman. Something I don't understand. I know she's attractive, but hell, the woman is a fruitcake."

"You don't know her like I do. She's really very sweet and bright."

"And she talks to imaginary people and has a violent streak."

"Clarence was trying to kill her. I can understand how she reacted in the heat of the moment."

"She also has impulse-control issues. Need I remind you of her cousin's suitcase? You don't need a woman who throws a tantrum every time things don't go her way. Not unless you don't mind a girl-friend who gets pissed and then burns your clothes."

"Even if I wanted to start dating her again, that won't happen. She's made it perfectly clear she can't forgive me for believing she had something to do with her cousin's death."

"Maybe she didn't have anything to do with Cheryl's murder, but she still isn't someone I'd want to get close to. Consider yourself lucky you dodged that bullet."

"I suppose." Joe sighed.

They were interrupted by a knock at the office door. The door opened and the woman from the front desk popped her head in and said, "Susan Mitchell from the bank's here and wanted to talk to the chief, but he's not in. Do you think one of you could talk to her?"

"Sure, send her in," Joe said.

A few moments later Susan Mitchell entered the office, carrying a manila envelope.

"What can we do for you, Susan?" Joe asked, pointing to the

empty chair for her to sit down. Brian immediately picked his cap up from the chair, making room for Susan.

"I was wondering if you were working on the Isabella Strickland case?" she asked.

"It really isn't in our jurisdiction," Brian told her. "They found her in California, and I know the authorities down there are working on the case. Of course, we'll be cooperating."

"I went to see Isabella, but Stoddard didn't want to let me in to see her."

"I understand she's still in a coma," Joe said.

"Yes, she is. But still, we've been friends forever. He finally let me in but would only allow me to stay for a few minutes."

"How did she look?" Joe asked.

"It was awful. Those monsters almost killed her. Her poor head is all bandaged. I practically didn't recognize her...if it wasn't for her tattoo...it's just that she looked so helpless, and Isabella never seemed helpless to me. I hated seeing her like this. They need to catch whoever did this to her."

"Unless she wakes up, they may never find out what happened," Brian said.

"According to Stoddard, she wasn't raped."

"We heard that," Joe said with a nod.

"If it wasn't a sexual assault, it must have been a robbery," Susan insisted.

"From what I understand, there hasn't been any unusual activity on her credit cards, and her car was left at the rest stop," Brian explained.

"Yes, but this wasn't on her," Susan said as she removed an eight-by-ten photograph from the envelope and slapped it on the desk in front of Joe.

Joe picked up the photograph and examined the picture. It was a close-up of Isabella Strickland showing off a matching necklace and bracelet. "I don't understand?" he asked, handing the photograph to Brian.

"I took that picture of Isabella about a week before she went missing. I printed it out from my computer this afternoon. I wanted you to see it."

"What are we looking at exactly?" Brian asked.

"Isabella commissioned a jeweler in Portland to make that necklace and bracelet. It's kind of hard to see, but the clasp looks like a dragon, similar to her tattoo.

"She stopped over at the bank to show it to me, and I took the picture. I know it's valuable, and from what I understand, it wasn't on her when they found her. I asked Stoddard about it, and he said he's never seen it before. I have to assume whoever tried to kill her took the necklace and bracelet. Maybe that's why they tried to kill her. The authorities should check pawnshops. It could be a clue."

"She may not have been wearing it when she went missing," Brian suggested.

"Oh no." Susan shook her head. "Isabella designed the set herself. She told me she was never going to take it off."

"If that's so, don't you think it's a little odd Stoddard didn't recognize it?" Joe asked.

"Not really. I don't think they saw each other that often, and I doubt she showed it to him before she left town," Susan explained.

"Can I keep this?" Joe nodded to the photograph in Brian's hand. "I'd like to send this to the authorities in California working the case. Could be a lead."

"Yes, thank you!" Susan stood up. "I was hoping you'd say that."

When Susan left the office, Brian glanced at the photograph one final time before tossing it on the desk. He looked at Joe and said, "Between the Missing Thorndike and now this, I've come to believe expensive jewelry is nothing but a liability."

THIRTEEN

"The Stewarts sure seemed happy to have the house to themselves this morning," Lily said as Danielle pulled out of the driveway.

"It's their honeymoon, what do you expect?"

"Of course, the joke is on them. I imagine Walt will be watching their every move."

"Just as long as he doesn't watch them in their bedroom."

"I wonder if Mr. Stewart will pick up on Walt again. If he does have some sort of psychic power, I wonder why he can't see him."

"I think everyone has psychic powers. Just some people are more sensitive than others. For whatever reason, most people seem to be able to smell Walt's cigar smoke. You did, Joanne did, even Cheryl did when she was alive. So for Mr. Stewart to pick up on it, that's not surprising."

"True. But *Marvin*."

"When you were a kid, Lily, didn't you ever play the game where someone thinks of a color and you try to guess it?"

"Yeah, but what does that have to do with it? You think he guessed at the name, like Walt suggested?"

"No. But sometimes when people play that game—sometimes the answer is not a random guess but something they picked up telepathically."

"You think that's what happened?"

"It could be." Danielle glanced over at Lily in the passenger seat. "Put your seatbelt on."

Without thought, Lily attempted to grab the seatbelt. It slipped through her hand. She looked up at Danielle and scowled. "Funny."

"Sorry." Danielle giggled. "I couldn't resist."

"You have a rather peculiar sense of humor about all this." Lily slumped back in the seat and looked ahead.

"It's probably a coping mechanism." Danielle added with a chuckle, "Plus, it was sorta funny."

"I hope I'm able to communicate with Isabella," Lily said after a few moments of silence.

"Me too."

"What if something horrible has happened to my body?"

No longer finding levity in the situation, Danielle said, "I have to believe it's in relatively good shape. Otherwise a reflection wouldn't be attached to your spirit."

"But that's all speculation. None of us knows for sure. We don't even know what the reflection means. You admitted you've never encountered an out-of-body experience."

"Sometimes, all we can do is believe."

They were silent for a few moments before Danielle asked, "Lily, do you still feel as if you're alive? That you aren't dead?"

"Walt told me that when you explained to him he was dead, everything fell into place. It suddenly made sense to him. He knew instinctively you were telling the truth, and he wasn't surprised. It was as if he always knew but couldn't quite grasp what that was. But for me, I have this strong pull...toward life. It's hard to explain. But yes, I still feel as if I am alive...someplace."

"Ian called me last night," Danielle said.

"He did? How is he? Did he get a flight?"

"Yes. He got into Palm Springs late last night. Gave me the name of the motel he's staying at. Said he would call me later this afternoon. I wish I could tell him what I know. But then he would start looking at me like Joe does."

"You mean lovesick? I hope not! I may be temporarily out of commission, but I've got dibs on Ian!" Lily grinned.

"No. Not lovesick. Joe looks at me like I'm broken—like I'm a candidate for the looney bin."

"Joe also looks at you with...longing. I sorta feel sorry for him. After all, Dani, it's not entirely his fault. He has every reason to believe you maliciously ruined Cheryl's clothes, that you hit her, that you tried to kill Renton when he was already unconscious, and that you seemingly talk to imaginary people. In spite of all that, he's still interested in you. He sees the real you, but it gets lost with all that other stuff in the way."

"I don't want to talk about Joe." Danielle pulled the car over to the curb and stopped. "Here we are." They looked up at the Gusarov Estate. Wrought-iron fencing surrounded the massive home.

"Okay, we won't talk about Joe. But I will say one last thing on the subject. Personally, I think he has a tendency to be a little too controlling. I don't see you with a helicopter boyfriend who tries to take care of you in that way. But I don't think you should be so angry with him."

"Duly noted. Meet me out here when you're done. I should be back within the hour."

"Okay. Wish me luck!" Effortlessly Lily moved outside. Standing by the car, she gave Danielle a wave before turning and running through the gate toward the Gusarov mansion.

"DANIELLE! I wasn't sure you were going to make it!" Marie said when she answered the door five minutes later. Still spry at ninety, the elderly woman led Danielle into the living room. Sitting on the sofa reading the newspaper was Marie's grandson, Adam. When the two women walked into the room, he set the paper on his lap and looked up.

"Really? I said I'd be here this morning." Danielle glanced over at Marie's grandson. "Morning, Adam."

"How are you holding up, dear?" Marie clutched Danielle's arm, looking into her face.

"We're really sorry to hear about Lily," Adam said from the couch. He picked up the newspaper from his lap and tossed it to the coffee table. Leaning back, he studied Danielle.

"You heard? How?" Danielle looked from Marie to Adam.

"Joe dropped by Adam's office yesterday afternoon and told him. Why didn't you call me, dear?" Marie asked, leading Danielle to a chair and giving her a little push to sit down. Obediently, Danielle sat.

"Joe's a regular busybody," Danielle grumbled under her breath.

"I can't believe you didn't call me!" Marie sat down on the chair next to Danielle.

"I didn't want to say anything yet, because we don't know for sure. I didn't want to upset you needlessly."

"What do you mean you don't know for sure?" Adam asked. "I thought Lily's car was in an accident; the driver was killed."

"Yes, but the body hasn't been identified yet, and Lily would never speed. Whoever was driving the car was going over a hundred miles an hour down the freeway. Lily would never do that."

"If it wasn't Lily in her car, where is she?" Marie asked.

"I don't know. I just wish they would hurry up and ID the body so they'll know to look for Lily."

"When are they supposed to do that?" Marie asked.

"We're hoping by the first of next week."

"Where was the accident at?" Adam asked.

"Outside of Palm Springs. Not far from where they found Isabella Strickland," Danielle said.

"Isabella Strickland…another senseless tragedy." Marie sighed. "I've known the family since they first settled in Frederickport. Such a shame. Adam used to date Isabella. For a while there I hoped…well…"

"Yes, Grandma is always trying to get me married off," Adam said under his breath.

"Have you seen her since they brought her home?" Danielle asked Adam.

"No. I haven't seen much of Isabella since we stopped dating. That was about a year ago. I heard she was in a coma, so I really don't see the point."

"She did stop in to check on you after they dropped the charges for Cheryl's murder. That was considerate of her. You should go see her," Marie said. "Make sure she's all right."

"Grandma, we know she isn't all right. She's in a coma. She wouldn't even know I was there," Adam said impatiently. He glanced over at Danielle, rolled his eyes, and shook his head.

"What was she like?" Danielle asked, curious about the woman who might know what happened to Lily.

"Isabella? I suppose if I could sum her up in one word, it would be—flighty."

"How so?" Danielle asked.

THE GHOST WHO WASN'T

"Adam, that's not nice! And with that poor girl lying there in that coma!" Marie scolded.

"It's true, Grandma. You know it. Isabella would come up with some crazy idea and just go for it—without thinking it through."

"I thought that's what you liked about her," Marie said. "You said she was an adventurous spirit."

"Yeah, I said that. But I got a little tired of her adventures. And by the looks of it, her last one didn't work out too good for her, did it?"

"What kind of crazy things would she do?" Danielle asked.

"Let's see..." Adam considered the question. "Well, right before we broke it off, she got involved with this crazy cult and decided to leave them all her money when she died. Her uncle flipped out."

"Yes, Stoddard was furious about that," Marie agreed.

"Her estate includes fifty percent of the family business. Stoddard was not thrilled with the prospect of that particular future business partner."

"I can understand. But did he really expect to outlive his niece?"

"I suppose he was thinking of his own children. Not that he has any, but I heard wife number three is expecting," Adam explained.

"We've heard that before," Marie scoffed. "I don't think Stoddard is capable of fathering a child."

"So he knew about her will?" Danielle asked.

"Sure. Isabella doesn't keep things like that quiet. He was furious. But she refused to back down. We stopped seeing each other around that time. But from what I've heard, she never changed the will. In retrospect, that might be one smart thing she did."

"Why do you say that, Adam?" Danielle asked.

"Think about it; if she dies now, Earthbound Spirits inherits her estate, and Stoddard gains a new business partner. He won't even have a majority share. As it is right now, Isabella signed an agreement a few years back giving him control over the business. She can revoke the agreement at any time. But with her in a coma she can't do that," Adam explained. "And as long as she's alive, Earthbound Spirits can't inherit."

"That's odd. When Isabella left town this last time, according to Ian, her uncle was going around town complaining about Isabella just taking off—as if she was in some way shirking her duties with the family business," Danielle said.

"Who knows why Stoddard does anything." Adam shrugged. "I don't think Isabella's ever been involved with the business."

"I happened to look at her Facebook page. She listed her occupation as writer," Danielle said.

"Oh yes, she's so talented," Marie said. "In high school she won a number of writing contests. I think she even got one of her stories published in a magazine."

"Isabella is a talented writer," Adam agreed. "But calling it her occupation is stretching it, to say the least."

"So she doesn't do it professionally?" Danielle asked.

"No. Isabella always loved writing stories. She never learned to type, never wanted to. Wrote everything longhand in notebooks. But after writing a story, she'd move on to the next story without even trying to find a publisher."

"Lot of people self-publish these days," Danielle said.

"True. But like I said, she doesn't know how to type—doesn't use computers. She does have an iPad, which is probably how she set up her Facebook account. Isabella isn't someone who'd go through the trouble of publishing herself. She doesn't have the patience. And frankly, she doesn't need the money."

Marie stood up. "I'm going to check on the coffee. I put on a fresh pot just before you arrived."

"Let me do that," Adam said, preparing to stand.

"No, you stay there and keep Danielle company."

"I am really sorry about your friend," Adam said when Marie left the room. "I hope you're right. Do you have any idea where she might be?"

"Not really. Ian went down to Southern California to see what he could find out."

"So Ian thinks she's alive too?"

"We're hoping." Danielle smiled weakly. "I still can't believe Joe told you about her. You said he stopped by your office yesterday?"

"Yes. It was right before I was getting ready to go home. Right before five."

"That was after he stopped at Marlow House. I told him I didn't think it was Lily in the car. I don't know why he couldn't wait until we learn more before he starts telling people."

FOURTEEN

I t took Lily just a moment to go from the street where Danielle had dropped her off to the front door of the Gusarov Estate. She wasn't certain how she got there exactly—had she run, walked or floated? Preoccupied with her plan to infiltrate Isabella's dream, she pushed the question from her mind and headed to the front door. It was closed. She suspected it was locked. She would be surprised if it wasn't protected by some sort of alarm security system. Yet she didn't have to worry about that.

Effortlessly, Lily moved through the front door and found herself standing in the massive foyer of the Gusarov Estate. Its ceiling went up two floors. Glass and steel surrounded Lily. The interior had the same industrial feel as the house's exterior.

The sound of footsteps coming down the hallway in Lily's direction echoed through the foyer. Without thought, Lily looked for a place to hide. Before she could duck behind the curtains covering the large window adjacent to the front door, a maid appeared. The woman, neatly dressed in a white and black uniform, walked past Lily, oblivious to her presence.

As Lily watched the maid pull open the curtains, her attention was drawn to the keypad between the door and window. It was for the alarm system, and by the looks of it, it was not armed.

"Hello, can you hear me?" Lily couldn't resist asking.

The maid, now humming a tune, pulled a dust rag from her apron pocket and began wiping down the foyer's small table.

"Hmm, I guess not. Too bad, I hoped you could point me to Isabella's room."

Lily watched the maid for a few moments before taking off to explore the house. She expected to encounter more of the housekeeping staff on the first floor, but so far, the only one she had come across was the maid in the foyer. There was no one in the kitchen or in the laundry room or the billiard room, theater room, dining room, or living room. Each room was immaculate, and if Lily didn't know better, she would assume no one lived in the house.

The last room she came to was what appeared to be Mr. Gusarov's study. She assumed the silver-haired man sitting behind the desk was Stoddard Gusarov, and the attractive twentysomething woman behind him, rubbing his shoulders…was that his wife?

"I wish she didn't have to stay here, Todd," the young woman said as she massaged his shoulders. "When we were married, I never considered a stranger would be living with us."

"Darling…" Stoddard reached up and patted one of her hands. "I told you, she has to stay until she makes her new will."

"I still don't understand how you plan to do that!" The woman intensified the massage, digging into Stoddard's shoulders with vigor.

"Darlene, not so rough!" Stoddard snapped. "Your nails are lethal!"

Darlene took a deep breath and gentled the massage. "But then you'll send her away?"

"Yes, I told you I would. I've already located a sanitarium in Canada that will suit our needs. Of course, we can't send her right away. She'll stay here a while after she changes the will. After a month or so, then we can have her moved. I don't want people to start asking questions."

"A month or so?" Darlene groaned. "It would be a lot easier if she just died. Paying for a private sanitarium is going to cost us a fortune."

"What a witch!" Lily gasped. "Poor Isabella."

"I agree, it would be. If we're lucky, that might happen after the will is changed."

"You want her dead too? Your own niece?" Lily said angrily. She wished she had learned to harness her energy because she wanted nothing more than to smash a hard object over their heads.

"You know, Todd, if you send her to a private sanitarium, there's always the chance that she could recover. Then what do we do?"

"I've thought about that. But with what I'm paying, she'll never get beyond the sanatorium walls."

"Wouldn't it be easier if we…just say…slipped a pillow over her face?"

"Darlene!" Stoddard looked over his shoulder. "You want me to kill her?"

"She's practically brain dead anyway," Darlene insisted.

"I know, but kill her?"

"Do you realize how much trouble we'll be in if someone finds out?"

"Yes, I know," Stoddard said solemnly.

"Will you at least consider it? It doesn't have to be painful. You would be doing her a favor."

"Some favor," Lily scoffed. "You people are nuts! I'm going to find Isabella, and then I'm going to see what I can do to get her out of this house!"

Lily abruptly left the room. Had Stoddard and his wife, Darlene, possessed Danielle's gift, they would have seen what appeared to be a trail of smoke leading from the study up the stairs to the second floor.

Once upstairs, Lily went from room to room, searching for Isabella. Like the rooms downstairs, each was immaculate, reminding Lily more of an upscale hotel than someone's home.

"Where is everyone?" Lily asked aloud. "I can't believe they have just one maid."

She was about to go through a door to another room when it opened. A man dressed in white stepped into the hall and closed the door behind him. He started down the hall, away from Lily.

"Ah, jackpot!" Lily said. "If I'm not mistaken, you're a male nurse, which means our patient is in that room."

A cellphone in the man's pocket began to ring. He paused a moment to answer it. "Я сказал тебе не называть меня на работе."

"Whoa, what language is that?" Lily asked, watching the man disappear down the hall as he continued his cellphone conversation.

When the man turned a corner and was no longer in her sight, Lily moved into the room. Once inside, she paused a moment and looked around. It reminded her of a hospital room. Along the right wall was a hospital bed, and in it was a woman. She slept on her right side, her back to Lily.

"They certainly didn't scrimp on anything." Lily glanced around. "If I hadn't overheard that conversation downstairs, I'd assume—by the looks of this decked-out hospital room—that your uncle is doing all he can to take care of you."

Lily shook her head in disgust and slowly approached the bed. Looking down, she said, "Oh, poor Isabella."

The woman in the hospital bed wore a blue-gray gown. A bedsheet and a blanket covered the lower portion of her body. Bandages covered the top of her head while wisps of reddish hair peeked out from the bandage. She was hooked up to an assortment of tubes, and an electric monitor near the bed kept track of her vitals.

Random beeps and chirps coming from the monitor broke the room's eerie silence. Stepping closer to the bed, Lily looked down, the woman's back still to her. Lily's gaze moved over the body. She reached out to touch the sleeping form but paused a moment and then pulled back her hand.

"Isabella, I need to do this. I hope I can for both our sakes. If you can help me, then it will be easier for me to help you. I'll find some way to get you away from here. Your aunt and uncle don't have your best interest at heart. Well, at least I assume those people downstairs are your aunt and uncle. She looks young enough to be your kid sister. Why do some men do that, marry girls young enough to be their daughters?"

Lily closed her eyes and tried to focus, remembering all that Walt had taught her about going into a person's dream. She stood there a few moments, her eyes closed, and nothing happened. Finally, she opened her eyes and looked down at the woman in the bed.

"Maybe I need to be looking at your face. I have a feeling the reason Walt couldn't jump into the dream is because the photograph we were using wasn't a good likeness. I can tell, even from this angle."

Lily started to move around the bed but paused. She couldn't help but notice the deep, red jagged scratches along the woman's exposed left shoulder, undoubtedly the result of being dumped on the harsh desert floor and left to die.

"I hope they're taking care of that," Lily said, leaning closer to the injured area. "It looks a little infected."

While taking a closer look at the shoulder, she noticed a horse-shoe-shaped scar on the woman's forearm.

"That's funny," Lily murmured, her head cocked to one side in curiosity. "I have a scar just like that...in the same place." She leaned closer. "Weird, I even have a freckle in the middle of the scar, just like you. Odd." Lily shook her head and made her way around the bed, her eyes sweeping over the unconscious body.

Once on the other side of the bed, Lily looked down. A bandage wrapped around the comatose woman's head, covering her eyes and skull. Her face, from her nose to her chin, was visible.

Lily stared down and frowned. "Wow, Isabella, you have an uncanny resemblance to my sister. If I didn't know better, I'd swear it was Laura lying in this bed."

Leaning closer to the bed, Lily studied the woman's face. "You don't look anything like your picture. I can't believe how much you look like Laura...of course, Laura doesn't have red hair. I'm the only one of the kids with red hair..."

Before Lily could get back to her task at hand and focus on jumping into Isabella's dream, the door opened, and in walked the man who had left earlier. He wasn't alone. With him was a woman dressed in a white nurse's uniform. She carried clean bed linens while he carried a tub of water. The two chattered away in the same foreign language Lily had heard the man speak earlier.

"Is that Russian?" Lily asked after a moment of listening to the exchange. She didn't expect an answer.

Lily watched as the female nurse set the linens down on a chair. As the pair scurried about the room, Lily surmised they were preparing to give Isabella a sponge bath and then change the bed linens.

"Dang, I need to be alone to do this right! Can't you give her a bath some other time?" Lily stomped her foot in exasperation. The pair continued on, oblivious to Lily's presence.

Lily glanced at the clock on the wall. "I suppose I'll just wait until you're done. I have time. Or maybe I'll go ahead and give it a try and jump on in."

Lily stepped back from the bed as the female nurse pulled the sheets and blanket from the mattress, dropping them to the floor. With help from the male nurse, she rolled the patient over so that she was on her back. Lily silently watched.

The male nurse gathered the sheets from the floor and deposited them in a nearby hamper as the female nurse began unfastening the hospital gown.

"I feel like a voyeur," Lily said. "I really don't need to watch them bathe you." Lily was just about to turn around, putting her back to the hospital bed, when the nurse pulled off the hospital gown, exposing to Lily's view the nude body of the woman in the hospital bed.

Something inside Lily snapped. She stood frozen, staring at the familiar body. She moved closer, standing at the foot of the bed, looking down.

"Holy crap!" Lily cried out. "I know now why you look so much like my sister. But you aren't my sister—you're me!"

FIFTEEN

Sadie sat in the middle of the upstairs hallway, watching Claire and Hunter. The pair went from room to room, trying to open each door.

"I'm not surprised they're locked," Hunter said. "But I suspect what we're looking for is in the attic. After all, that's where they found that necklace."

"Oh, I get it now." Walt leaned against a wall and watched. "You two are treasure hunters. Is this even your honeymoon?"

"It's a little insulting she locked all the doors," Claire grumbled. "After all, most of these are guest rooms. It's not like anyone's staying in them."

"Or maybe it's that Danielle isn't completely naïve," Walt said.

"Let's go check out the attic," Hunter suggested.

By the time Hunter and Claire made it to the attic, Walt was waiting for them, standing in the corner by a stack of boxes.

"At least the attic door wasn't locked," Claire said as she looked around, Sadie at her side. "This place is fairly clean. If anyone hid something up here, don't you think Boatman would have found it already?"

"Not if she didn't know about it. Or where to look. I doubt she knew what Isabella did." Hunter slowly walked around the room. He touched the paneling and checked for loose boards.

"You know what I don't understand?" Claire asked.

"No, what?" Hunter leaned down to look at a section of floorboard.

"Didn't you say this Boatman chick is rich? Didn't she inherit a bunch of money?"

"Two inheritances," Hunter said. "According to the newspaper article, one from her aunt and one from a cousin."

"We are talking rich, millions, right?"

"Yes, millions. Why?"

"Don't you think it's a little odd she made us breakfast today? If I inherited buckets of cash, I sure wouldn't rent out rooms to strangers and make them breakfast. How stupid is that?"

"I also question her reasoning, but I wouldn't call her stupid," Walt said to deaf ears.

"Rich people tend to be eccentric," Hunter explained with a shrug. He stood at the window, fidgeting briefly with the spotting scope. Putting his right eye to the scope's eyepiece, he looked across the street and into Ian's front window.

"Interesting," Hunter murmured.

"What?"

"Wonder if our host is some sort of peeping tom. She has this pointed to the house across the street. I can see right inside."

"Here, let me see." Claire rushed over to Hunter's side and took his place at the scope.

Feeling bored, Walt waved his hand and summoned a lit cigar. He took a puff and leisurely exhaled.

"There it is again!" Hunter cried out, grabbing hold of Claire's forearm.

"What?" Claire asked, no longer looking through the scope.

"Can you smell that? The spirit is back." Hunter let go of Claire.

Claire took a deep breath. "I want a cigarette."

"Later, Claire." Hunter looked around the room.

Claire started for the door. "I'll be right back. I'm going back to the room to grab a cigarette. You want one?"

"We can't smoke up here. Boatman made it very clear we have to smoke outside, on the patio, not inside the house."

Claire stopped walking and looked back at Hunter. "He smokes inside."

"I don't think she can control that. We don't want to do anything that might get us kicked out. Stay here. Don't leave."

"Okay, fine," Claire grumbled. "So now what?"

In response, Hunter walked to the center of the room, outstretched his arms, and closed his eyes. "Marvin Marlow, can you hear me. Please give me a sign!"

"You remind me of a carny barker when you do that." Walt snickered.

"Please give me a sign!" Hunter repeated.

Feeling mischievous, Walt pushed the top box off the stack. It fell to the floor with a loud thump. Claire jumped and let out a squeal; Sadie barked, and Hunter stood mute, his eyes wide.

"You didn't really expect me to answer you, did you?" Walt snickered, taking a puff off the cigar.

"What was that?" Claire asked nervously.

"It has to be Marvin Marlow. He's here. He's reaching out to me."

"I'd rather think it was a little earthquake," Claire said, her eyes darting around the room.

"No. It wasn't an earthquake. I can feel his presence. He's reaching out to me."

"I don't like this." Claire glanced to the door, considering a quick exit.

"No, Claire," Hunter said when he saw Claire was about to bolt. "I want you to stay here with me."

Reluctantly, Claire stayed put.

"Marvin, I understand you're trapped here. I can help you."

Arching his brow, Walt said, "You slay me!"

"You're the spirit that died in the attic, aren't you? Knock once for yes, two for no."

"Parlor games? Okay, I can play." Walt flashed a smile and then knocked twice on the wall: two distinctive knocks.

By Hunter's stunned expression, it was clear to Walt the man hadn't expected the knock. Claire let out another scream, preparing to run from the room, yet Hunter grabbed her arm again, holding her in place. Sadie began to bark.

"There is nothing to be afraid of," Hunter insisted, yet he didn't sound convinced.

"Stop barking, Sadie," Walt scolded. "You know better than that." Sadie immediately stopped barking. She lay down on the floor, her tail wagging. She peeked up at Walt, yet didn't bark again.

"I can help you cross over to the other side, Marvin," Hunter promised.

Claire frowned and thought, *I thought two knocks meant no.*

"What if I don't want to cross over?" Walt asked, leaning casually against what remained of the stack of boxes. "And stop calling me Marvin. I was teasing you, you dumb palooka."

"You must come to terms with your suicide. I know you're angry that Danielle Boatman has changed your story."

"I didn't kill myself. You need to read the updated version of Marlow House history." Walt wondered how the man could get everything wrong, yet picked up on the fake name he threw out.

"You have to make amends to free your soul so you can move on," Hunter insisted.

"Amends? For what? For a suicide that didn't take place?"

"Tell me where you hid the diamonds, and I'll make sure they're returned to the rightful owner."

Claire started to question Hunter about returning the diamonds, but he quickly silenced her.

"Aha…now we're getting somewhere! You are on some sort of treasure hunt. Diamonds, you say? What diamonds?" With a wave of Walt's hand, the thin cigar disappeared.

"Marvin, knock twice if the diamonds are still here and once if they've been moved."

Instead of knocking, Walt stood and watched.

"Is he still here?" Claire asked in a whisper.

"I'm not sure." Hunter sniffed the air. "I can barely smell the cigar smoke."

"I can't smell it at all anymore," Claire said.

"Marvin, we don't have to talk about the diamonds. Knock once if you're still here," Hunter said as he sniffed the air.

"What are you up to?" Walt asked, eyeing the couple curiously.

"He's not here," Hunter said with conviction.

"Are you sure?" Claire looked around uneasily.

"If we smell cigar smoke, we'll know he's in the room. No smoke, he left."

"Are you sure?" Claire didn't sound convinced. "I don't like the idea of ghosts. I don't know how you can do it, Hunter. It freaks me out."

"Claire, when we're here, you need to call me Hank. Even when we're alone."

"Why?"

"Because I don't want you to slip. While we're at Marlow house, we are Mr. and Mrs. Hank Stewart."

"Fine," Claire said begrudgingly. "Can I please go have a cigarette now?"

"Go ahead, but smoke outside on the back patio off the kitchen."

"Okay. But I think it's stupid. You coming with me?"

"No, I'm going to explore the attic, see if I can find any loose boards. From what I read, they found the necklace in a hiding place in the wall. Chances are, there's more than one hiding place up here."

Claire gave Hunter a quick kiss before leaving the attic. Walt looked down at Sadie. "Sadie, go with her. Keep an eye on her. Let me know what mischief she gets into downstairs."

Sadie jumped up from where she was lying on the floor and dashed out of the room after Claire.

———

WHEN CLAIRE REACHED her room's door on the second floor, Sadie was by her side. Before opening the door, Claire looked down at the dog.

"You look like a purebred. I bet we could get some major cash for you."

Sadie looked up innocently, her tail wagging.

Claire opened the door and walked into the room. Sadie started to follow her in, but Claire roughly pushed her back with a knee. "I don't need your dog hair in here." Claire slammed the door shut, leaving the dog alone in the hallway.

That dog is so stupid, she'd be easy to take, Claire told herself as she grabbed her purse and began rummaging through it for her pack of cigarettes. *If we can't find someone willing to pay big cash for her as a pet, there's always Jimmy. He pays good bucks for bait dogs.*

Claire found her pack of cigarettes and lighter and was about to toss her purse on the bed when she spied the sapphire and gold bracelet.

"I don't know why I can't wear this," Claire said as she picked up the bracelet and tossed her cigarettes and lighter on the bed with her purse. She admired the piece a moment, holding it up so that the sunshine streaming through the window made the stones glisten. Without thought, she fastened it on her right wrist. Standing at the foot of the bed, she held her wrist out, admiring the bracelet.

"This is so much nicer than the crappy fake engagement ring and wedding band," Claire said to the empty room.

Instead of taking the bracelet off, she grabbed the cigarettes and lighter and left the room. Sadie was waiting for her in the hallway. She followed Claire downstairs to the kitchen and outside to the back patio.

When Claire finished her cigarette, she decided to do some sleuthing downstairs before Danielle returned home. She'd love to be the one to find the diamonds for Hunter. Maybe that way he would finally divorce his wife, and they would marry for real. Claire decided to begin with the parlor first.

Sadie lay down in the middle of the room and watched Claire inspect the paneling, looking for loose boards. After about thirty minutes, Claire plopped down at the desk.

"This is silly," Claire announced to the empty room. She glanced down at Sadie. "But the day doesn't have to be a bust." Claire laughed. "I think I'll give Jimmy a call." Under her breath she mumbled, "Stupid dog."

Sadie raised her head and cocked it to one side. Without warning, she stood up, dashed from the room, down the hallway and up the stairs to Walt.

Claire paid little notice to Sadie's departure. Instead, she admired the bracelet on her wrist, turning her hand from side to side, watching the stones sparkle. To her surprise, the bracelet fell off, landing in her lap.

"What the…" Claire said as she started to pick the bracelet up. Yet Hunter barged into the parlor before she did. Claire froze, her hand covering the bracelet on her lap.

"What are you doing in here?" Hunter asked, glancing around the room.

"I was checking out the paneling, looking for loose boards."

"It would make this a lot easier if we could get Marvin Marlow to tell us where he hid the diamonds. I'm going to the library to see if I can make contact with him again. I want you to come with me."

"Okay. I'll be right there." Claire smiled innocently. "I need to go to the bathroom first."

"Hurry up," Hunter said as he left the room.

Claire snatched the bracelet from her lap and stood up. Her outfit didn't have any pockets, and she'd left her purse upstairs. Glancing around for somewhere to temporarily stash the bracelet, she spied an antique copper teapot sitting on a curio shelf across the room.

"I'll come back for you later," Claire whispered as she dropped the bracelet in the teapot.

SIXTEEN

Danielle pulled the car up next to the sidewalk in front of the Gusarov Estate and put it in park. Lily was nowhere in sight. Danielle was just getting ready to turn off the ignition when Lily appeared in the car, sitting in the passenger seat.

"Drive down the street," Lily ordered.

"What do you mean?"

"Just drive down the street; I'll tell you when to stop."

Danielle drove a half a block when Lily ordered her to pull over and park the car near a wooded area between the street and the ocean, adjacent to the Gusarov Estate.

"What's going on, Lily? Were you able to communicate with Isabella?"

"Isabella wasn't there."

"Have they moved her?"

"It wasn't Isabella in the hospital bed—it was me!"

Danielle swung around in her seat and stared at Lily.

"I found my body, Danielle. No wonder I returned to Frederick-port—my body is here!"

"Are you sure?"

"I feel a little foolish that I didn't recognize myself immediately, but my head is all bandaged. Stupid me, I kept thinking how much Isabella looked like my sister. It didn't dawn on me that I was looking at myself."

"Are you sure? I remember from Isabella's picture, she was also a redhead. Maybe she just looks like you."

"What, are you saying all redheads look alike?"

"No, but—"

"And they cut my hair! They hacked it off like a boy!"

"It doesn't make sense; why would Stoddard Gusarov identify your body as his niece? Is it possible he really thinks you're Isabella? If that's the case, at least we know you'll be getting the best of care while they have you."

"Why in the world would you say that? They were talking about killing me!"

"Killing you?"

"Yes, the aunt said something about putting a pillow over my face."

"No, that doesn't make sense." Danielle shook her head. "According to Adam, Isabella revised her will and left her estate to some cult—the estate includes half of the family business. There is no way Stoddard would hasten her death."

"Well, that explains what else I heard. They talked about Isabella changing her will—and then killing me!"

"So they actually believe you're her?"

"It sounded that way. But I don't know how that's possible. I don't think I look anything like her picture. Aside from the hair color."

"What do we do now? I can't very well call the police. Like Joe would believe me!"

"He would believe a picture."

"What do you mean?"

"Do you have your cellphone with you?" Lily asked.

"Sure. Why?"

"We go back to the house, sneak up to the bedroom where they have me, and you take my picture. Then we can show that picture to the police."

"And how am I supposed to get in the house? I'm sure it has an alarm system."

"It does, but I noticed it was disarmed. And there is a back door we can use, it takes us up the back stairs. It wasn't locked. I can go in first and make sure the coast is clear."

Danielle took a deep breath then said, "Okay. Let's do this." As she took the key out of the ignition, she turned to Lily and asked, "Why did you want me to drive down the street?"

"Well, I figured if I talked you into breaking into the Gusarov house, it wouldn't be a great idea to be parked right in front of it."

Danielle locked her purse inside the car and tucked her phone and keys into her back pocket. Instead of walking back down the street, Danielle and Lily entered the wooded area and raced toward the rear section of the Gusarov Estate.

Lily went inside first while Danielle hid behind some trees near the back door of the house.

"It's safe to come in," Lily said when she returned a few minutes later. "Gusarov and his wife are in the kitchen, eating, and the maid is in there too. There are two nurses, but they're in a room down the hall from where they have me, playing cards. Looks like they just started their game, so hopefully they'll be there a while."

"Yeah, hopefully," Danielle mumbled under her breath as she followed Lily into the house. Together they raced up the back stairs, Lily leading the way. The two managed to slip into the hospital room unnoticed.

Once in the dimly lit room, Danielle hesitantly approached the bed. She looked down at the sleeping woman. Ever so gently, she reached down and touched her face, turning it slightly in her direction. It was Lily.

"Oh my god, you're right," Danielle said in a hushed whisper. "It's really you!" Tears filled her eyes.

"Can you believe it? They cut my hair!"

"Oh, Lily, you look beautiful!" Danielle said with a sniffle. "I wonder what would happen if you could simply reconnect with your body?"

"No, not while it's here. I don't trust them."

"But if you came to, you could tell the nurses who you are."

"I don't think that would work."

"Why?"

"I don't think they speak English. Not sure what they were speaking, but it wasn't English, Russian maybe."

"Perhaps they're bilingual. I can't imagine Gusarov would hire someone he couldn't communicate with."

"Umm...Gusarov, isn't that Russian?" Lily asked.

"So? It doesn't mean he can speak Russian."

"I can't take the chance. What if they only speak Russian? They won't be able to help me. And if I could communicate with them, how do I know they would?"

"Okay, let's do this and get out of here." Danielle walked toward the window.

"What are you doing?" Lily asked.

"It's kind of dark in here," Danielle said as she started to pull back the curtain, letting in the sunlight.

Just as Danielle finished opening the curtain, the bedroom door flew open.

"Oh crap," Lily mumbled.

Before Danielle could react, the two nurses rushed into the room, charging straight for her.

"I thought you were supposed to stand guard!" Danielle cried out as she attempted to run in the opposite direction.

"You have to take the picture, take the picture!" Lily called out hysterically.

Danielle did not have sufficient time to pull the phone from her back pocket and snap the picture. Her attempts at dodging the nurses failed, and before she knew what happened, both of her arms were seized—one by the male nurse and one by the female nurse. As they dragged her from the room, down the hall and to the staircase, they talked excitedly to each other in a foreign language.

Halfway down the stairs she noticed five people standing in the foyer, looking up the staircase at her and the two determined nurses. Two of the people she recognized—it was Joe and Brian from the local police department. She felt an instant sense of relief. Maybe this wasn't how she wanted to handle the situation, but it would work. Once Joe had a look at Lily, this would end.

"Danielle, you're the one who broke in?" Joe said when Danielle reached the landing.

"Why aren't I surprised?" Brian said under his breath.

Danielle tried to pull away, but the nurses continued to grip her arms.

"You can let her go," Joe told them. Stoddard repeated Joe's instructions in Russian, and they released her.

"You know this woman?" Stoddard asked.

"I'm afraid I do," Joe said with a sigh.

"I don't know why you're here, but I'm happy to see you!" Danielle said, rubbing her forearms, still stinging from the rough handling.

"The silent alarm went off. Since we were in the neighborhood, we took the call."

"And here I thought the alarm hadn't been set," Danielle said under her breath as she glared at Lily, who flashed a sheepish grin.

"Breaking into houses now, Ms. Boatman? What is it, the thrill? You certainly don't need the money," Brian said as he removed his handcuffs from his belt.

"Wait, I can explain!" Danielle said in a panic. "It's Lily, they have Lily up there! It's not Isabella! It's Lily!'

"What is she talking about?" Darlene asked.

"I'm afraid Danielle has been under considerable stress since her best friend was killed," Joe said, looking at Danielle with pity.

"That doesn't give her an excuse to break into our home!" Darlene snapped. Stoddard wrapped his arm around his wife and glared at Danielle.

"Please, Joe, just listen to me! Go see for yourself. If it's not Lily in that bed, then go ahead and arrest me. Throw the book at me if you want. But please, just go look!"

"You honestly believe I wouldn't recognize my own niece?" Stoddard asked.

"All I know is that's Lily upstairs."

"That's ridiculous," Darlene scoffed.

"I want you to arrest her," Stoddard demanded. "And I want a restraining order against her. She's not to come near my niece again."

"Perhaps I could just go look in on Isabella," Joe said.

"Are you suggesting this woman may be telling the truth?" Stoddard asked incredulously.

"Can I speak with you alone for a minute, Stoddard?" Joe asked.

Stoddard nodded, and the two men walked away from the others.

"Danielle isn't dangerous, she's just a little—well, a lot of things have happened to her. She's the one who owns Marlow House."

"Her cousin was the one Clarence killed?"

"Yes. And Lily is her best friend. She was killed in a car accident. They have the body, but Danielle refuses to believe the truth. If I could just see Isabella and have something to tell Danielle so she'd give up this notion."

"I don't suppose her friend has a tattoo."

"Lily? Not that I know of. Ahh…Isabella. Right. She has that tattoo on her right arm. A dragon, wasn't it?"

"I'll take you up but only you. And only if I can go in the room first and make sure Isabella is modest. I want her treated with respect."

"Of course, Stoddard. I understand."

"This doesn't look good," Lily whispered to Danielle after listening in on Joe's private conversation.

Danielle frowned at Lily, afraid to ask her anything for fear Brian would overhear her seemingly talking to an imaginary friend.

When Joe and Stoddard reached the bedroom door leading to Isabella's hospital room, Stoddard entered first. Lily lay on her back. Hurriedly, Stoddard rolled her over onto her stomach, careful not to unhook any tubes. Very gently, he turned her head so that her face was looking away from the door. He then rolled up the right sleeve of the hospital gown, exposing the tattoo. Before letting Joe into the room, he closed the curtains and rearranged some of the lighter pieces of furniture, making it difficult to walk around the bed in order to get a closer look at the woman's face.

Stoddard opened the door. "You can come in now. But I think this is all ridiculous."

It took Joe's eyes a moment to adjust to the dimly lit room. Walking toward the bed, he saw it immediately—the tattoo on the woman's right arm. With his attention focused primarily on the exposed arm, he glanced toward the face. From his angle, all he could see was a bandaged head and wisps of shortly cut red hair. Isabella wore her red hair short.

"That's definitely Isabella," Joe said, looking back at the tattoo. "It seems to be peeling."

"Yes. I'm afraid she got a little sunburned in the desert. We're lucky it wasn't in the dead of summer when they dumped her out there. Or it would be worse."

"I'm sorry I put you through this," Joe said as he turned from the bed.

"No!" Lily cried out. "You didn't even look at my face!"

"I'd like to have that woman arrested," Stoddard said as they walked down the hallway. "But I'd be happy if I just never see her again. I don't want her returning."

"Don't worry, Stoddard, I'll take care of it," Joe promised.

Danielle could hear Lily coming down the staircase, and by her words, it was obvious Joe failed to identify the body correctly.

"Those crazy people tattooed my arm!" Lily shouted to Danielle when she reached the first-floor landing. "I have a freaking dragon tattoo on my arm! He didn't even look at my face!"

"You didn't even look at her face!" Danielle glared at Joe.

"Interesting how you already know I didn't find Lily up there. If you honestly believed that was your friend upstairs, I'd expect to be greeted with something like *I told you so*—not some excuse as to why I didn't find her," Joe said angrily.

"I take it that was Isabella upstairs?" Brian said as he reached for Danielle's wrists, handcuffs in hand.

SEVENTEEN

Alone in the interrogation room, Danielle wearily rested her head on the desktop. Pillowing her head on her folded arms, she thought of Lily, who had stayed back at the Gusarov Estate to keep an eye on her body. Danielle wasn't sure how that was going to help.

Joe and Brian had refused to stop at the car so she could retrieve her purse, and they had confiscated her cellphone and keys. Even if they had let her keep the phone, she wasn't sure who she would call. Ian was in California, and Joanne was out of town on vacation.

The door opened. She lifted her head briefly and opened her eyes. Joe walked into the room and closed the door behind him. Taking a deep sigh, Danielle sat up straight and looked at Joe, who was now sitting down across the table from her. In his hands was a manila folder. He dropped it on the desk.

"So am I under arrest? Do I get to make my one phone call?"

"Stoddard doesn't want to press charges."

"Well, that's generous of him, considering he's kidnapped my best friend."

"It wasn't Lily, and you know it." Joe picked up the folder and began shuffling through the papers.

Danielle looked at the folder in Joe's hand. "What's in there?"

"Your file."

"I have a file?"

In response, Joe closed the file and set it on the desk. When Danielle reached for it, he pushed her hand away.

"If I'm not under arrest, does that mean I can go now?"

"I said Stoddard doesn't want to press charges. Not that you can leave quite yet."

Danielle glanced over to the two-way mirror. "So tell me, who's listening in on us? Brian, the chief? The whole gang?"

"You've quite an attitude for someone who's just been caught breaking and entering."

"And you don't think it's a bit odd that I'd break into someone's house? It's not like I need the money. Last I heard, I'm quite rich."

"I'm not sure what you're up to."

"I told you. Lily is in that house. If you would have taken just a minute to get a good look at her face, you would know I'm telling the truth."

"I told you it was Isabella. I recognized the tattoo."

"Right. The tattoo. Like two people can't have the same tattoo."

"I don't remember Lily having one."

"She doesn't. Or she didn't. They obviously tattooed her so people like you would believe she's Isabella."

"Do you hear how you sound, Danielle?"

"Well, tell me this, what condition was the tattoo in? Did it look like it had been there a long time?"

"It was hard to tell, the skin was peeling."

"Aha! A fresh tattoo! They always do that after a couple days."

"No. Stoddard explained she got sunburned in the desert."

"Now do you hear yourself?" Danielle snapped.

"What is that supposed to mean?"

"Of course Stoddard is going to come up with some plausible excuse for the tattoo peeling. Did you happen to look at her other arm? It was scratched up, but it wasn't peeling."

"Danielle, I think it would be a good idea if we put you under observation for a few days."

"What? Are you crazy? No, wait—you don't have to answer that. You think I'm crazy."

"I just think you've been under a lot of stress lately. And breaking into Stoddard's house like that, insisting he has kidnapped Lily, the fact that you don't see how that makes you look convinces me you need help."

Danielle closed her eyes for a moment and told herself to count to ten and calm down. When she opened her eyes again, she looked into Joe's. "I have guests staying at Marlow House. You can't just lock me up while they're all alone over there, wondering where their host has disappeared to. Plus I'm babysitting Sadie."

"I suppose you should have considered that before you broke into Stoddard's home."

Danielle studied Joe's expression for a moment. The brown eyes she once found warm and friendly now seemed judgmental. "You never can give me any slack, can you?"

"I think the fact you're not sitting in a cell right now disproves that."

"I'd like to make my phone call," Danielle said abruptly.

Joe studied her for a moment. "Fine, I'll let you make one call."

"I'd like to make it on my cellphone."

"Okay." Joe stood up and pulled Danielle's cellphone from his pocket. He set it on the desk. "One call. I'll be back in ten minutes." He picked up the manila file and headed to the door.

Hesitantly Danielle picked up her cellphone and stared at it. Looking up, she watched Joe leave the room, closing the door behind her. She glanced over to the two-way mirror and wondered who was watching her.

"I don't want you holding her for observation," the chief told Joe a moment later when he entered the office next to the interrogation room. Brian stood with the chief by the window, watching Danielle. They'd turned the sound off. "I think you should cut her loose."

"But we caught her red-handed!" Brian said.

"And Stoddard refuses to press charges. He had me on the phone the minute you left his house. He doesn't want this in the press. And I can't blame him. He's dealing with enough right now, with Isabella's attack and the coma. He just wants us to make sure Danielle doesn't bother her again," the chief explained.

"Then shouldn't we hold her for observation?" Joe asked.

"You forget, Danielle Boatman is a very wealthy woman, and she can make our lives miserable if she puts her mind to it. She's probably calling some high-priced lawyer right now," the chief explained.

"I don't know, she's just staring at that phone," Brian noted as he watched Danielle. "She looks as if she's about to cry."

"Maybe that's a good thing," the chief said. "Shake her up a bit.

She did get caught breaking into a house. Just because Stoddard doesn't want to press charges now, doesn't mean he won't…let's say, tomorrow."

"I thought you said he was emphatic about not pressing charges?" Joe asked.

"Well, we don't have to let Danielle know that! Maybe the way to keep her in line—and away from the Stoddards' estate—is to let her believe possible arrest is just around the corner."

"How is that helping her?" Joe asked. "If she's put under observation, she might get the help she needs."

"She's not your responsibility," Brian said.

"Brian's right, Joe. The girl has some emotional issues, but it really isn't your problem. Stoddard refuses to press charges. I'm not going to hold her. I want Brian to wrap this up. You're too emotionally involved."

"What do you want me to do, Chief?" Brian asked.

"Wait until she makes the call. Give her a little time to stew. Then go back in there, lead her to believe Stoddard may press charges. When she leaves here, I want her feeling grateful she's not in jail. And hopefully, she'll realize it's in her best interest not to bother Isabella's family again."

"Since we're going to let her go anyway, can I turn the sound back on and listen to who she calls?" Brian asked.

"No," the chief said. "We'll turn the sound back on after she makes her call."

"This is not going to help Danielle," Joe said.

"That isn't our problem," the chief countered.

"THEY'RE CUTTING YOU LOOSE!" Lily said when she popped into the interrogation room a few moments later. Danielle looked up in surprise and then glanced at the two-way mirror.

"They're watching you," Lily explained, "but they have the sound turned off. The chief said to leave it off until you make your call."

Threading her fingers together, Danielle lowered her head and rested the bridge of her nose against her hands, obstructing her mouth from the view of the men watching in the next room.

"Are you sure?" Danielle asked.

"Stoddard refuses to press charges. He was adamant. If he had caught you breaking in, I don't think he would have called the police. The only reason the cops were there was because you set off the silent alarm."

"I thought you said it wasn't armed."

"It wasn't. Someone must have turned it back on."

"They're going to let me go after I make the call? Why even have me make a call if they're planning to cut me loose?"

"Joe wants you put under observation."

"Yes, he told me that. I am crazy, you know."

"But the chief is afraid of your money."

"My money?"

"Sure. You can afford the best lawyers to go after them if they don't dot all the i's and cross all the t's. Isabella's uncle refuses to press charges, so there's nothing to hold you on."

"That still doesn't explain why they're allowing me to make a call instead of just letting me go."

"He's trying to play some mind game with you so you'll stay away from Isabella."

"If Isabella was really in that house, there wouldn't be a problem." Danielle peeked up at the window.

"After you make the call, the chief is having Brian come in and play bad cop with you. He's afraid Joe is too emotionally involved."

"I guess I better make that call. You say they won't be listening?"

"They said they wouldn't. But I'll go over there, and if they turn on the sound, I'll let you know." Lily disappeared.

Danielle dropped her hands and sat up straight. She picked up the cellphone and began to dial. When the party answered the phone, she said, "Hello, this is Danielle Boatman."

"Danielle? This is a surprise."

"I wondered if you would like to make a quick hundred bucks."

"Why, sure. What do you need?"

"Could you pick me up in about five or ten minutes at the police station and then drive me over to where my car's parked on the south side of town, about a half a block from the Gusarov Estate."

"The police station? Are you okay?"

"They have me in that lovely room with the two-way mirror; what do you think?"

"I'll be right there."

Danielle turned off her phone and set it on the desk, waiting for Brian.

"Miss Boatman," Brian said when he entered the room.

"Officer Henderson," Danielle said primly, folding her hands on the desktop.

"You got yourself into quite a mess this time, didn't you?" He sat down across the table from her.

"If Joe would have actually looked at the woman's face, he would have seen it was Lily and not Isabella."

"So Lily has a tattoo just like Isabella? Tell me, did they use the same tattoo artist?"

"Lily never had a tattoo—until someone gave her one to help her pass as Isabella. Of course, you would know that had Joe just taken a moment to look at her face—like he promised!"

"The thing is, Miss Boatman, you can't just go around giving in to whatever delusion you might be under. There are consequences for your actions. If Stoddard Gusarov decides he wants us to arrest you, I don't think any of your high-priced attorneys will be able to get you off. You will be serving some time. It might only be six months—but do you think you'd really be up to that? Six months can be rough for someone like you."

"Oh, I don't know," Danielle said calmly. "My defense would be that he was holding Lily—I don't think he'd want that sort of publicity. You seem to forget I've a marketing background, and you'd be surprised what sort of publicity my money can buy."

"Even if Stoddard doesn't press charges, we could hold you over for observation," Brian threatened. "Only mentally unstable people see ghosts."

"Ghosts?"

"Your friend is dead, Ms. Boatman. If you think you saw her at the Gusarov Estate, then you've seen a ghost."

EIGHTEEN

"I think we can let Ms. Boatman go home now," the chief said when he barged in the interrogation room the next moment. Startled, Brian stood.

Danielle glanced from Brian to the chief. Smiling, she picked up her cellphone and said, "Thanks, Chief. I'll need my keys, please. Joe took them when he took my phone."

"Certainly," the chief said. "If you wait here a moment, I'll have him bring them to you, and he can drive you to pick up your car."

"No, that's not necessary. I just want my keys."

"No problem, Ms. Boatman, Officer Morelli will take you to your car." The chief looked at Brian and said, "Brian, would you come with me?"

"What was that all about?" Brian asked when he and the chief were alone in the hallway.

"You weren't accomplishing anything in there. She obviously knows Stoddard doesn't want the media attention."

"Does that mean we let her harass Stoddard just because she's got money?"

"No, we arrest her if she breaks the law again."

DANIELLE ANXIOUSLY PACED the interrogation room, waiting

for Joe.

"Did you bring my keys?" she asked the moment he walked through the doorway.

"Yes. I'll take you to your car."

"Please give me my keys."

"I said I'd give them to you. Let's go. I'll take you to your car first."

"Why won't you give them to me now?" Danielle said angrily.

"I don't know why you're getting upset." His tone of voice reminded Danielle of a parent trying to calm an irrational child—which only heightened her irritation.

Tucking her phone in her jeans' back pocket, she put out her hand. "Just give me my keys, please. The chief said you would."

"And I will when we get to your car."

"How do I know that? You also said you'd look at the woman in the hospital bed to see if it was Lily. But you didn't even look at her face!"

"Please, let's not go into that again."

"Give me my keys!"

Reluctantly, Joe dug the key ring from his pocket and handed it to Danielle. She snatched it from his hand and pushed her way past Joe to the door.

"Where do you think you're going?" Joe asked, trailing behind Danielle.

"That's really none of your business, Sergeant Morelli," Danielle said as she walked down the hall toward the front area of the police department. She pushed her way through the doorway leading to the public waiting area.

"You're being ridiculous. Let me drive you to your car," Joe said, following her to the door.

Danielle stopped in her tracks and spun around, facing him. "Just how am I being ridiculous?"

"For one thing you're acting like a stubborn child, insisting on walking to your car when I'm willing to take you."

"That is so typical of you, Joe Morelli, jumping to conclusions." Danielle took hold of the door leading to the street.

"What is that supposed to mean?" Joe asked.

"You assume I'm refusing a ride from you because I'm being stubborn and childlike. Not once do you consider maybe I don't need a ride."

"I know you're capable of walking. Not sure what you're trying to prove, but it's a long walk from here."

"Once again—jumping to conclusions. I don't need your ride because I already have one." With that said, Danielle stepped outside to the sidewalk.

Joe followed Danielle outside and watched as she walked down the sidewalk, not looking back. To his surprise, a car pulled up and stopped. Danielle got into the car.

"Adam Nichols? That's who she called? Not her attorney?" Joe mumbled to himself.

"Thanks for doing this," Danielle said as she got into the car.

"I have to admit, I'm surprised you called me," Adam said from the driver's seat.

Danielle buckled her seatbelt and looked back at the police station, where Joe stood, still staring at her. She glanced from Joe—to Adam. It seemed just yesterday she thought Joe might be the one, the one to replace the void after Lucas. He was handsome, honest, caring—while Adam was the epitome of the stereotypical used-car salesman—slick, smooth, not quite honest—yet it was Adam she had turned to.

"Yeah, maybe I need to broaden my acquaintances in Frederickport," Danielle said dryly, leaning back in the seat.

"That might be a good idea." Adam laughed as he sped off.

"I can either give you a check, or we can stop at the ATM after I pick up my purse," Danielle suggested.

"I don't want your hundred bucks."

"You don't?"

"Nah, I'd rather know what kind of trouble you got yourself into this time."

Danielle considered his request for a moment, then realized the story of her escapade was probably already circulating through the station, and by tomorrow would be buzzing through the local coffee shops.

"I broke into the Gusarov Estate."

"Whoa, the Gusarov Estate? Why would you do something like that?"

"I'll tell you...but you'll think I'm crazy."

"I don't think you can say anything to make me think you're crazier than I already do."

Danielle laughed. "I'm not sure how to take that."

Adam shrugged, waiting for her explanation.

"They have Lily."

Adam frowned. "What do you mean?"

"They didn't find Isabella at that rest stop—they found Lily. She's the one in the coma, not Isabella."

"How would that even happen?"

"I'm not sure, but I have a theory. Lily was on her way home; she pulled into that rest stop. Someone attacked her, stole her car, and left her for dead in the desert."

"But they identified her body before Stoddard saw her."

"No, I don't think so. Not a positive ID. They found Isabella's car abandoned at the rest stop with her purse inside. They assumed the unconscious woman was Isabella, and when they showed her picture to Stoddard, he verified the identification."

"Do you know that for sure?"

"No, it's just a theory. But the woman in the coma, that's Lily. I saw her myself. I was going to take her picture so I could show the police, but they caught me before I could."

"How did they catch you?"

"I set off the silent alarm. I had just opened the blinds so I'd have enough light to take the picture when the two nurses walked in. They jumped on me and dragged me downstairs."

"Did you try to explain?"

"What, that Lily was the woman in the coma and not Isabella?"

"Yes."

"Kinda hard to do, they didn't speak English."

"Russian?" Adam asked.

"Why do you say Russian?"

"Because Stoddard speaks Russian."

"Russian was my guess. By the time they got me downstairs, Joe and Brian were there, with Isabella's aunt and uncle. Joe wouldn't listen to me, but he finally agreed to look in on her."

"And then?"

"Apparently Isabella had a tattoo on her arm."

"Yes, a dragon tattoo. She got it when we were going together."

"They've tattooed Lily's arm. When Joe went into the room, he saw that first and never really looked at her face. He thinks it's Isabella. He's wrong."

"I have one question."

"What?"

"How did you happen to break into the house in the first place?"

Danielle chewed her lower lip, considering his question. "Adam, everything I've told you is true. I understand if you don't believe me. I wish I could tell you why I happened to check out the house, but I can't."

"Joe admitted he didn't have a good look at her face?"

"Half of her head is covered in a bandage, and they've cut her hair. He looked at the tattoo and only saw Isabella. He pretty much said I was insane to imagine Stoddard would do something like that —have Lily tattooed."

Adam let out a snort. "Joe can be clueless."

"What do you mean?"

"I could see Stoddard doing something like that—the tattoo—if it suited his purpose. But my only question—where is Isabella?"

"I don't know." Danielle shook her head. "That was her car at the rest stop."

"You don't think Isabella was the one driving Lily's car, do you? The one killed in the accident?"

"I don't know. Do you think it's possible?" Danielle asked. "You knew Isabella. I didn't."

"Well…" Adam pondered the question a moment. "If whoever was driving that car was the one who left Lily in the desert, then it wasn't Isabella. Isabella could be a little flaky sometimes, but she was never mean or cruel. She would never hurt anyone. It wasn't in her nature, which is one reason she got sucked into that screwy cult."

"Do you believe me, Adam?"

"It's an interesting story. What are you going to do now?"

"I'm not sure."

They pulled up beside Danielle's car a few minutes later. As Danielle unhooked her seatbelt she said, "I'd still be happy to give you that hundred bucks."

"Nah, if Grandma ever found out, she'd bust my chops."

Danielle opened the door and stepped out of the car. "Thanks again, I really appreciate it."

"No problem, and, Danielle—"

"Yes, Adam?"

"I liked Cheryl. I'm really sorry about what happened to her. I don't think I ever told you that."

"Thanks, Adam. She liked you too."

NINETEEN

W hen Danielle got into her car, Lily was waiting, sitting in the passenger seat.

"I wondered where you went," Danielle said under her breath as she closed the car door. She waved to Adam before he drove off, and then she slipped the key into the ignition.

"I wanted to check on my body before we went home." Lily looked out the window to the Gusarov Estate.

"Let's get outa here and go home. After I get something to eat, we can figure out what to do next." Danielle turned the key and started the engine.

"We have three days, Dani. I'll be okay for three days, but we have to do something before Wednesday," Lily announced, still gazing out the passenger window at the house where her body was being held. The car pulled away from the curb and headed north, back to Marlow House.

"Wednesday? What is Wednesday?" Danielle asked.

"They're moving me on Wednesday, out of the country. Our break-in has really freaked out Isabella's aunt and uncle. They don't believe they've heard the end of you. I think the fact you have money makes them uneasy."

"Why are they doing this? Did you find out?"

"When I first listened to their conversation, I thought Isabella was upstairs. Not me. They kept talking about Isabella changing her will. I assumed they thought she was going to come to and they'd convince her to revise it. But I don't think that's what they were talking about."

"What do you mean?"

"I think they intended to have a fake will prepared and lead people to believe she'd changed it when she came out of the coma. But Gusarov feels that's too risky now. He says they need to revise their plan. They intend to move me out of the country—to a private hospital in Canada. They want to get me out of Frederickport and away from you before you try something again. He's contacted the hospital, and the soonest they can take me is Wednesday."

"What about the will?"

"They've decided to create a new will—one supposedly written six months ago—that leaves everything to Gusarov. They're planting it at her place, and when he sends over a crew to clean out her house, they'll find it."

"What do you mean clean out her house?"

"I got the impression no one's been in it since she disappeared. When they talked about the house, Gusarov's wife mentioned selling it, but he said it would take some legal wrangling for him to be able to sell Isabella's house, and even if he could, he didn't want to. He'd rather make a show of taking care of it—so it would be there for Isabella when she recovered and came home."

"What a nice guy." Danielle snorted.

"At least they're no longer talking about holding a pillow down on my face."

"Did they say anything about Isabella? Where is she? Do they know where she is?"

"They never said. But if they're doing this, they must believe she's not coming back."

"Maybe you should stay and see what else they say."

"It wouldn't do any good. Apparently, we gave Gusarov's child bride a migraine. She took some aspirin and is lying down. No talking between those two. And it seems the staff only speaks Russian—even the maid. So nothing to pick up there."

"At least we have until Wednesday."

"I was a little surprised how you used your one phone call—Adam?"

"You told me they were going to cut me loose, so I didn't see the point in calling an attorney. And I figured I'd need a ride back to my car."

"But Adam?"

"When I was sitting there deciding who to call, I realized I don't have any real friends in Frederickport. Oh, I've met a few people but none I consider friends—other than Ian and Marie. And if Adam hadn't come forward with that video of his, I might be serving time for my cousin's murder."

"Does he know why you were at the police station?"

"Yes. I told him you're the one at the Gusarov Estate, not Isabella."

"And he believed you?"

"I'm not sure. But I found out something interesting at Marie's. It seems Adam used to date Isabella. They broke up about a year ago."

"Really? Humm…But you don't know if he believed you?" Lily asked.

"He didn't discount me. We discussed where Isabella might be—assuming you were in that hospital bed. We discussed one possible scenario—that Isabella was the one who took your car and that she was the person killed in the accident. After all, you drove your car to the rest stop, and it looks like someone else drove it out—while Isabella's car was abandoned there."

"I never really considered that."

"Adam says he doesn't see that happening. Claims Isabella would never hurt anyone. I can't see her doing it either. I mean why? The woman was rich. If she had car trouble, she'd simply ask you for help, she wouldn't hit you over the head, take your car, and dump you in the desert. Makes no sense at all."

"Makes more sense that someone stole Isabella's car—and when they needed a new one, they took mine."

"That's what I'm thinking too. And if someone left you for dead, I would assume they did the same to Isabella, since she hasn't resurfaced."

"There is one thing that doesn't make sense, Dani."

"What?"

"The way Isabella's aunt and uncle are behaving, it's as if they already know she's dead—or not returning. How do they know that? Are they someway connected with whoever left me in the desert?"

"Why have them dump you in the desert and then claim the

body? I can't believe they planned that. They had no way of knowing the cops wouldn't use fingerprints to ID you—which they obviously didn't for some reason, or you wouldn't be in Frederickport."

"It's probably a good thing I'm in an altered state right now—or I'd be getting a headache!"

"When we get home, we'll discuss this with Walt and figure out what to do. And if all else fails, we'll resort to plan B."

"We have a plan B?"

"Yes. I just thought of it. We storm the Gusarov Estate and take you."

"How do we do that? As you can see, I have no Walt-like powers."

"True. But I could probably round up some local mercenaries—with the help of Adam—to storm the fort."

"Ahh…friends in low places."

"And enough money to pay them with." Danielle smiled smugly.

"Have you forgotten how Adam and Bill bungled the break-in at Marlow House? And we didn't do such a terrific job ourselves today."

"Okay…you have a point. Perhaps I'll rethink plan B."

***

JOE ENTERED the break room and found the chief sitting with Brian, having coffee.

"You back already?" the chief asked.

"I didn't take her." Joe filled his coffee cup and then sat down at the table. "Apparently she used her one phone call on Adam Nichols. He picked her up."

"Are those two getting chummy?" Brian asked. "I wonder if something is going on there."

"I remember when she couldn't stand him. Insisted he broke into her house." Joe shook his head in disgust and then took a sip of coffee.

"Boatman has a penchant for telling tall tales," Brian said.

The chief set his mug down on the table and looked from Brian to Joe. "I think you're both reading her wrong."

"What are you talking about?" Joe asked.

"Brian seems to think she's some sort of fruitcake—"

"She is," Brian interrupted.

"And you see her as this vulnerable broken creature who's not wholly responsible for her actions."

"It's just that she's been through a lot," Joe said in defense.

"Poor little rich girl." Brian snickered.

"What—you think just because she has money means she can't have issues?" Joe asked.

"Hell no. That woman has a boatload of issues!"

"Like I said, I think you're both wrong," The chief picked up his mug and downed the rest of his coffee.

"How so?" Joe asked.

"She seemed pretty rational to me today. Now that I think about it, she always has. We need to remember she was completely innocent in her cousin's disappearance and murder. As for her attack on Clarence, can't say I wouldn't have been tempted to finish the job myself if he had tried to kill me."

"Are you saying you think that's Lily and not Isabella up at the Gusarovs'?" Brian asked incredulously.

"No, of course not. If Joe says it's Isabella, that's good enough for me. But I do wonder what Danielle Boatman's up to." The chief stood up and went to get more coffee.

"What do you mean?" Brian asked.

After filling his cup, the chief turned to face Brian and Joe. He took a sip of the coffee and then said, "She doesn't come across to me as a fruitcake or vulnerable. From what I know about her, she was doing well before she inherited Marlow House. I did a little checking, and the marketing firm she started with her late husband was well respected and profitable. She made a tidy little sum when she sold it. She's no dummy. And frankly, I don't think she's some fragile wimp. But she is up to something, and I'd like to know what it is exactly."

"You don't think she believes it's Lily at the Gusarovs'?" Joe asked.

"Do you?" the chief countered.

Joe considered the question a moment then said, "I did when I first arrived on the scene. Not that I believed her, but I thought she believed it."

"But you changed your mind?" the chief asked.

"When I came back downstairs, she immediately knew I hadn't found Lily and started giving a reason for it—saying I hadn't looked at Lily's face. It was as if…" Joe paused a moment, trying to frame his thought. "It was as if she knew I wouldn't find Lily and was working off a script. But she screwed up and delivered her lines too early. She should have waited until after I said I hadn't found Lily upstairs before she accused me of not looking close enough."

"So you think she's up to something too?" the chief asked.

"I suppose. But I don't know what."

"Either way, I still say she's a fruitcake," Brian grumbled. "And don't forget, according to her cousin, Boatman thinks she can communicate with the dead."

"That was when she was a troubled kid," Joe argued.

"Maybe a troubled kid then, fruitcake now," Brian said.

"If she was just your average run-of-the-mill fruitcake, it wouldn't be an issue," the chief said. "But she's the type that can get herself into all sorts of trouble—send us running in circles—while having more than enough money to pay whatever lawyers she needs to bail her butt out. What bothers me, I don't think she's some eccentric we have to deal with. She strikes me as a clever young woman who we shouldn't underestimate. And frankly, I think both of you have done that."

"What do you want us to do?" Joe asked.

"A little digging. I want to find out what sort of connection she has to the Gusarov family or any of their business interests. Did she have any kind of a relationship with Isabella or with anyone in Stoddard's circle? See if she has anything to do with that group Isabella supposedly left her estate to, Earthbound Spirits. If the rumors are true, I bet they're anxious to find out how Isabella is doing. If she dies, they'll be coming into a significant fortune. There has to be some reason Boatman broke into that house, and I don't believe it's because she thought Lily was being held there. No, that makes no sense at all. She's playing us with all this Lily nonsense. She is up to something, and I want to know what. Find out."

TWENTY

"I suppose I need to call Ian. But what do I tell him? How am I going to explain why I happened to break into the Gusarov Estate?" Danielle asked Lily as she pulled into the drive at Marlow House.

"I've been wondering about that myself." Lily gazed out the window, considering the day's events.

When Danielle got out of the car a few moments later, she pulled her phone from her back pocket and looked at it. "Speaking of the devil."

"What do you mean?" Lily stood outside the car by Danielle.

"Looks like I missed a call from Ian. He left a message." Looking closer at the phone, she said, "Dang, I must have accidently turned the sound off when I called Adam." She turned the phone's volume up, then placed it by her ear and listened to Ian's message.

"Are you going to call him back?" Lily asked when Danielle finished listening.

"No. It seems poor Ian has the flu. He just called in to see if I've heard anything from your mom or the private investigator I hired. He's going to try to get some sleep and he's turning his phone off for a while. He'll call later."

"Is he at the motel?"

"That's what I assume." Danielle quickly checked her other messages. "There's nothing from the PI I hired."

"Not surprised since you sent him on a wild-goose chase. He's obviously not going to find my body anywhere near the rest stop."

"I'll need to redirect the PI. Maybe see if he can find anyone who saw the people driving Isabella's car."

"Hey, I just noticed the Cadillac isn't here," Lily said as they walked into the kitchen at Marlow House. They found Walt inside, waiting for them.

"Where have you two been? It's been hours!" Walt demanded.

"We found my body!" Lily said excitedly. "It wasn't Isabella Strickland they found at the rest stop, it was me!"

"Then why are you here?" Walt asked.

"Where are the Stewarts?" Danielle asked as she tossed her purse, keys and phone on the kitchen counter. "I really don't need them walking in on me talking to myself."

"I don't think that's their name. But they went out to dinner."

"Is it that late? No wonder I'm hungry." Danielle opened the refrigerator and looked inside. "What do you mean you don't think it's their name?"

"I'll explain, but you first," Walt insisted.

Danielle made herself a quick sandwich and then joined Lily and Walt at the kitchen table. She told Walt about their day, beginning with what Lily found at the Gusarov Estate, what she'd learned at Marie's, and how she'd been arrested.

"That explains why I couldn't jump into Isabella's dreams. Either she wasn't sleeping at the time—or—"

"She's dead," Danielle finished for him.

"Yes. But it was daytime when I tried to jump into her dream. So it doesn't necessarily mean she's dead."

"I suppose you could try a little dream jumping tonight when she might be sleeping. If she's alive, I'd like to find out where she is —and what she has to do with Lily being taken by her uncle."

"I'll try," Walt said.

"Umm...where's Sadie?" Danielle asked Walt as she glanced around the room.

"She's with the Stewarts."

"She's what?" Danielle screeched.

"When they left to grab something to eat, the woman told Sadie she could go with them."

"And you let them take her?" Danielle could feel her blood pressure rise.

"Oh, settle down, it'll be all right. I figured Sadie could keep an eye on them. When she gets back, she can let me know what she's learned about those two."

"I don't like it, Walt. I don't like it at all. We don't even know those people. Ian trusted me to take care of Sadie! And I trusted you!" Danielle felt like crying.

"She'll be fine," Walt insisted.

"You said they went out to dinner. Why would they take Sadie to dinner with them? None of the restaurants around here allow dogs."

"I figured they were going to grab something to eat and go down to the beach."

"I suppose that's possible. It's been pretty warm today. Would be a good evening for a picnic," Danielle said begrudgingly.

"What did you mean when you said you didn't think Stewart was their name?" Lily asked.

"I don't believe they're newlyweds. They're treasure hunters," Walt said. "The minute you left, they started going through the house, looking for hidden treasure. They tried all the bedroom doors, and when they couldn't get in there, they searched the attic."

"And you let Sadie leave with these people?" Danielle found herself getting angry again.

"Only because I knew they were coming back. The woman— Claire—seemed to like Sadie. I didn't see any harm." He then added with a laugh, "And what did you want me to do, levitate Sadie to the ceiling so they couldn't take her?"

"I'm sure Sadie will be all right," Lily said. "Walt, do they think you were some jewel thief or something, stashing your loot here?"

"For some reason they seem to believe I hid diamonds in the house."

"Diamonds? I wonder where they got that idea," Danielle asked.

"Well, that's the odd part. They mentioned something about Isabella knowing they were here."

"Isabella? Certainly not Isabella Strickland?" Lily asked.

"I doubt it. I think the name is just a coincidence," Walt said.

"Although, it could be Isabella Strickland," Danielle said thoughtfully, her brows drawn into a frown.

"Why do you say that?" Walt asked.

"Adam and Bill broke into Marlow House, looking for treasure. And Adam used to date Isabella Strickland."

"But I never took any diamonds," Walt said. "Adam and Bill were looking for the Missing Thorndike, which I had taken. But I never took anything else."

"You forget, the Missing Thorndike had diamonds. And if you think about it, they had been removed from the necklace—twice," Danielle reminded him.

"Yes, but the first time I had nothing to do with it. Eva's husband took those diamonds, and no one knows where they went. And the second time—well, that was this past summer, and we all know those are now in the necklace, back in the safety deposit box at the bank."

"True. But I'm just saying stories get started and taken out of context. It's possible they're here because of something Isabella told him—because of something Adam told her. Marie mentioned Isabella stopped by to see Adam after his release."

"His release?" Lily asked.

"After he was arrested for Cheryl's murder," Danielle explained.

"Oh…"

"I really don't feel like dealing with treasure hunters right now. We need to focus on Lily. Maybe it would be best if I found the Stewarts—or whoever they are—someplace else to stay. I can use the excuse we're having plumbing issues or something."

"I don't think they'll go willingly," Walt said.

"Maybe you can convince them," Danielle suggested.

"Hank Stewart, or whatever his name really is, doesn't seem to be afraid of me. If anything, he gets quite excited when he thinks I'm present. And apparently, the cigar smoke means I'm in the room. If he doesn't smell it, I'm not there."

"Oh really?" Danielle rolled her eyes. "I hate to say this, but I should have listened to Joe and cancelled their reservation before they arrived."

"I think they're back," Lily said after she heard sounds coming from the front of the house.

Danielle walked to the doorway and looked down the hallway to the front door. The Stewarts had just come in. But there was no Sadie.

"Where's Sadie?" Danielle called out as she walked down the hall toward her guests.

"Sadie?" Claire asked with a frown. "Who's Sadie?"

"The dog. Sadie. The golden retriever."

"I have no idea where your dog is," Claire said.

"She was here when we left to grab some dinner," Hunter said. "Did she get out?"

"You took her with you. Where is she?" Danielle panicked.

"I have no idea where your dog is," Claire said as she walked past Danielle.

"Don't say anything," Walt silenced Danielle as Claire and Hunter made their way upstairs to their room.

Danielle glanced at Walt. She looked as if she were about to cry.

"I'm going upstairs with them. I'll see what they say about Sadie."

"I'm going with you," Lily said. "If they hurt Sadie, I want you to crush them, Walt!"

"Why would she say we took the dog with us? Do you think someone saw us?" Claire asked as she entered the bedroom with Hunter and closed the door.

"Nah. She just jumped to that conclusion because the dog wasn't here. No one saw us. Hell, there's nothing she can do. And she'd be pretty stupid to accuse a guest of taking the dog. Like where exactly does she think we took the mutt? All she has to do is talk to the guy at Pier Café and know we ate there. And no one saw us with a dog. Nah, she was just hoping we took it. I bet she's down-stairs wondering how the mutt got out."

"You don't think anyone saw us drop her off at the cemetery, do you?"

"Wasn't anyone around. I just hope your friend comes through with the money he promised."

"He will. Said he'd stash the money at the cemetery when he picks the dog up tonight. He wouldn't cheat me. He knows it would be too easy for me to turn him in. I know where he holds his dog fights."

"Seems like good money to pay for a dog that's not going to last very long. But hell, if he's willing to pay, I'll take the money!"

"Oh my god! They're going to use Sadie as a bait dog!" Lily gasped.

"Bait dog?" Walt frowned.

"Dog fights, Walt. These scum—they train poor animals to fight, and they use dogs like Sadie as bait dogs. They usually wrap tape around their muzzles so they can't defend themselves and then throw them in a pen with a couple fighting dogs to be torn apart."

"What have I done?" Walt moaned.

"They said the cemetery? It sounds like they've left Sadie at the cemetery for the guy to pick up. Hopefully he hasn't come yet. I'm going to tell Danielle. You stay here and listen to what they say. Whatever you do, restrain yourself. I don't care what you do to them later, but we need to pay attention to whatever they say about where they've taken Sadie—and the man who they sold her to."

"Danielle hates cemeteries," Walt said.

"I know. But she'll go for Sadie. Unfortunately, Dani needs to go now—alone—and leave us here to see what else we can find out. And if you hear anything she needs to know later, I'll go down to the cemetery and tell her."

Lily found Danielle downstairs in the library, pacing.

"Did you find out anything?" Danielle asked when she saw Lily.

"It's not good, but I think Sadie is okay for now. But you have to hurry."

"What did they do?"

"They've sold her as a bait dog."

"Oh my god! Dog fighting?"

"Yes. But whoever they sold her to couldn't pick her up right away, so they've left her at the cemetery. My guess, she's tied up down there."

"Cemetery? I don't do well at cemeteries." Danielle groaned.

"I know. I'm sorry, but you don't have any other choice."

"Did they say where in the cemetery? That's not a small place."

"I don't know. They just said cemetery and the guy was coming tonight. Walt's still in there with them, listening to what they have to say. If they say anything that might be helpful, I'll come down to the cemetery and find you. I wish I could go with you, but I need to stay here in case they say anything more."

"Okay. I'm going to leave now." Danielle grabbed her phone from the counter and put it in her back pocket. She then grabbed her purse and keys.

"Good luck, Dani."

Before Danielle opened the door, she looked back at Lily. "Well, there is one upside to going to the cemetery."

"What's that?"

"If there are any spirits around, I'll ask them if they've seen a golden retriever."

TWENTY-ONE

Danielle parked her car on the road alongside the older part of the cemetery. If the Stewarts had left Sadie for someone to pick up later, she couldn't imagine they'd do it in the newer section and risk running into visitors. The original section of the cemetery tended to be quieter. She had visited it not long after moving to Frederickport. It was where she had met Walt's wife, Angela, the woman who had conspired to kill him some eighty-plus years before. Danielle wondered if Angela was still here under house arrest.

Getting out of her car, Danielle slammed the door shut and took a deep breath as she looked at the cemetery with its lush green lawns and standing headstones. She loathed graveyards. Under normal circumstances she'd be dreading the spirits she might run into, yet because of Sadie, she was actually hoping to meet one who might help her find Sadie before it was too late.

Stepping onto the lawn, she began walking away from the street and deeper into the cemetery while calling out, "Sadie! Here, girl, can you hear me?" She didn't expect Sadie to come running toward her. She assumed the dog had been tied up somewhere, but she hoped Sadie might bark if she heard Danielle calling for her.

"It is you!" a woman's voice called out. Danielle turned to the right and saw Angela Marlow sitting atop her impressive headstone, her bare legs crossed as she playfully wiggled her toes. Angela wore the same fringed minidress she'd been wearing the first time Danielle had met her. She reminded Danielle of a flapper.

"I see you're still here." Danielle approached the headstone.

With a dramatic sigh, Angela said, "Still under house arrest." While fluffing her blond curls with one hand, she asked, "How is Walt? I hear through the spirit grapevine he's still haunting Marlow House."

"I don't have time to chat. I'm looking for a dog," Danielle explained in a rush.

"A dog? Funny place to look for a dog. Although, a couple walked by here not long ago walking a dog."

"A golden retriever?"

Angela shrugged. "I don't know. A big yellow dog. I don't know what kind."

"Which way did they go?"

"It doesn't matter. They came back this way, got in a car and drove away. I tried to talk to them, but they couldn't hear me. You're the only one who can hear me. At least, the only one who's alive." Angela looked down at her toes and wiggled them again. "I have nice feet, don't you think so?"

"The couple with the dog, you say they came back this way and got in a car, did they have the dog with them then?"

Angela looked up at Danielle. "No. No, they didn't."

"Which way did they go with the dog before they came back to their car?"

"You never answered my question. How is Walt?"

"Please, Angela, this is very important. I need to find the dog before something terrible happens."

"Then answer my question, and I'll tell you. You don't know what it's like to be trapped here day after day and only get to talk to a few dreary souls that pass through. No one seems to stick around."

"I promise I'll come back and chat with you. But please, tell me where they took the dog!" Danielle said anxiously.

Angela stubbornly crossed her arms and shook her head. "No. You have to talk to me first."

"Okay, what do you want to know? Oh yeah, about Walt, yes, he is still at Marlow House," Danielle said impatiently.

"Why is he still there? I heard he could leave if he wants."

"He's not ready to move to the next level."

Angela narrowed her eyes and studied Danielle. "Is he staying for you?"

"For me?"

"You need to remember, Walt is a married man. I am still his wife."

"Umm—okay—first, Walt and I—what you are insinuating—not really possible. And even if it was, you tried to kill him! And the last time we talked, you didn't even want to be called Angela Marlow, you told me you wanted to be called by your maiden name."

"Well, I've changed my mind," Angela said with a pout. "I figure if I have to be stuck here, maybe Walt could stay with me. Keep me company. He's not bad to look at, from what I remember."

"How about we make a deal? You tell me where they took my dog, and I'll have a talk with Walt and convince him to come stay with you. I bet he'd love to!" Danielle lied.

"You will? Honest?" Angela hopped down off the headstone.

"Yeah—sure—now please!"

"They took the dog this way. Come on, I'll show you."

Angela took Danielle deeper into the cemetery. Although there were a couple hours of daylight left, the afternoon clouds had gathered overhead plus the mature trees in this section of the graveyard blocked much of the sunlight. The afternoon temperatures had been in the eighties, yet walking through the shaded area, it felt much cooler.

"What's back here?" Danielle asked.

"Some of the old family crypts. Not where I'd want to spend my eternity."

Danielle let out a whistle and called out, "Sadie." She heard a bark come from the right, and then she heard what sounded like a second bark, this one muffled.

"That's her!" Danielle took off running in the direction of the sound. The minute she turned the corner around several trees, she came upon a man fastening a muzzle on Sadie—who was doing her best to wiggle away.

"Let go of my dog!" Danielle shouted, racing in Sadie's direction. She came to an abrupt stop when the man pointed a gun at her. He stood about ten feet away, holding Sadie on a short leash, the tight muzzle firmly on the dog's mouth.

"Who are you?" the man demanded.

Danielle swallowed nervously, glancing over at Angela, who looked curiously at the unfolding scene. "Do something," Danielle whispered, nodding toward the gun.

"What do you expect me to do?" Angela asked. "If he was driving a car, I might be able to get it to stop running. But he doesn't seem to be driving a car right now."

"Just give me my dog. You don't want to shoot me over a dog," Danielle said nervously.

"Who were you talking to just now?" he asked.

"Just the ghosts hanging out in the graveyard."

"Funny girl." The man yanked on Sadie's leash, trying to calm her down. "This is my dog. She got away earlier."

"So why are you pointing a gun at me?" Danielle asked weakly.

"You looked like you were gunna take my dog. I don't like people screwing with my things."

"She isn't yours. Her name is Sadie. She belongs to a friend of mine."

"I thought you just said it was your dog," the man said with a laugh.

"I'm taking care of her."

"Doesn't look like you're doing a very good job of it."

"Just give her to me. You don't want to shoot someone over a dog."

"I don't know about that. Shot people for a hell of a lot less. You willing to get shot for a dog?"

Danielle glanced around nervously, trying to get her bearings. The man stood in the shadows. He wore a dark hoodie sweatshirt and jeans. With the hood pulled up over his head, it was impossible to make out his features. He was maybe six feet tall with a stocky build. Even if he didn't have a gun, he could easily take her. Should she manage to get away, she wouldn't be able to give much of a description, aside from height and clothing. He could be black or Irish for all she could tell.

"This is the most interesting afternoon I've had in a long time," Angela said cheerfully.

"I want you to lie down," the man ordered.

"Excuse me?"

"I want you to lie down, face down. I don't want you looking at me when I come over there. I'm going to tie you up. You should be thankful. I could just as easily kill you. And then I'm leaving with my dog."

"Please, please don't take Sadie!"

"Shut up and get down on the ground!" the man said angrily.

"What is going on here?" a woman's voice asked.

Danielle glanced toward the voice. A petite woman with short red curls stood next to Angela.

"That man over there is stealing the dog. And he plans to tie the woman up—or shoot her if she doesn't do as he says," Angela explained.

"Is that right?" the woman said angrily.

"I said get down on the ground!" the man ordered as he wrapped the leash around a tree, holding Sadie in place so he could take care of Danielle.

"Umm...do you think you can help me?" Danielle asked the woman.

"So you can see me?" the woman asked brightly.

"Yes, yes, I can."

"Who are you talking to?" The man looked around, waving his gun.

The redhead flashed Danielle a smile. In the next moment, she was standing next to the man. She picked up a rock and effortlessly brought it down on his skull. He fell unconscious to the ground, his head bleeding.

"I did it!" the woman said excitedly. "I actually did it! I picked up the rock!"

"I wish I could do that!" Angela said longingly.

Danielle rushed to Sadie, removing the muzzle and untying her from the tree. Excitedly, Sadie jumped on Danielle and repeatedly licked her face, her tail wagging. The redheaded spirit used the leash to tie up the unconscious man.

"I don't know how to thank you," Danielle said as she took her cellphone out of her back pocket.

"You're the first person I've found who can actually see and hear me."

"If you wouldn't mind, I'd really like to call the cops and get them down here before this guy wakes up."

"Sure, no problem. Maybe when they're gone, we could have a little talk?"

"Not until I finish talking to her!" Angela said in a pout.

"I promise I will talk to both of you—but first, the police."

"I HAVE to give it to you, Boatman, you sure as hell aren't timid when it comes to bashing a man over the head," Brian said as he checked the vitals of the unconscious man.

"Is he alive?" Joe asked.

"Yeah. Lucky for him Boatman didn't try for a second round, like with Clarence."

By the sound of the moans coming from the man in the hoodie, it was obvious he was regaining consciousness. His movement continued to be restricted by the ropes binding his hands.

"So tell us again what happened," Brian ordered.

"I'm sorta surprised to see you two," Danielle grumbled. "Figured you both would have gone home by now."

"You saying you waited to knock this guy out until after you thought we were off duty?" Brian asked.

"No, but...I'm just surprised to see you again."

"What happened here, Danielle?" Joe asked.

"This guy tried to steal Sadie. He had her in a muzzle." Danielle pointed to the muzzle lying on the ground. "And he pulled that gun on me." She pointed to the gun Joe was putting in an evidence bag.

"Any idea why he'd want to steal your dog?" Brian asked.

"He was going to use her as a bait dog. He's into dog fighting."

"How do you know that?" Brian asked as he hauled the man to his feet and unfastened the ropes.

"She's lying!" the man spat. "I found her dumb dog running loose and just tried to get her on a leash. I didn't know if she was going to bite me, so I put a muzzle on her. When she found me with her dog, she started freaking out. She's crazy!"

"Danielle, why do you think he's into dog fighting?" Joe asked.

Danielle looked at the man and then at Joe. She couldn't very well tell Joe that Walt had eavesdropped on the Stewarts' conversation, but she couldn't risk Joe letting the man go.

"He told me," Danielle calmly lied.

"He told you?" Brian frowned. "Why would he tell you something like that?"

"Because..." Danielle stared into the eyes of the man who had just minutes earlier been holding her at gunpoint. "Because he intended to kill me. He told me he was going to kill me and then use Sadie as a bait dog. He even described how his dogs would tear her up."

"You lying bitch!" the man exploded. "I wasn't going to kill you! I told you I was just going to tie you up! But I should have killed you!"

TWENTY-TWO

D anielle sat with Sadie on the sidewalk a few feet from the parked police car and wondered if Walt and Lily were worrying about her. She had expected Lily to show up by now. Danielle looked down at her lap where Sadie rested her chin. The dog clung to her side as if she instinctively knew she'd just been saved from grave danger.

In the police car, the man who'd tried to steal Sadie sat in the backseat in handcuffs while Joe and Brian talked to another officer. Danielle gently stroked Sadie's fur and glanced toward the cemetery. She could see Angela sitting atop one of the headstones, watching, and next to her was the redheaded woman who'd been her savior.

The woman looked at Danielle and smiled. It was then that Danielle saw it. It was the smile. Danielle knew who the woman was —or who she had been. It was Isabella Strickland. She recognized her from the Facebook profile picture. She had so many questions for Isabella, but they would have to wait until the police officers left the cemetery.

Glancing over toward the huddle of officers, Danielle stood up when she saw Joe coming in her direction.

"We found his van parked on the other side of the cemetery," Joe told Danielle when he reached her side. "There were three dog crates in the back. One with a black lab and another with a pit bull. I'm pretty sure they're stolen. Someone reported a black lab stolen earlier today over at Astoria. The third crate was empty. Probably for Sadie."

"What are you going to do? Are you taking him in?"

"Yes. We have more than enough to charge him with. He won't be making bail tonight. He doesn't have a permit for the gun, which isn't surprising because with his priors he wouldn't be able to get one."

"Priors, do they include dog fighting?"

"Yes. He's not from Frederickport, but we're working with the officers where he lives. They're searching his place right now."

"I don't understand people like that. Terrifies me to think what could have happened to Sadie." Danielle looked down at the golden retriever sitting at her side. She stroked Sadie's head.

"I still don't understand how you ended up here tonight."

"I told you. I got home and Sadie wasn't there. I went looking for her and ended up here."

"How do you think Sadie got out?"

"I have guests staying at Marlow House. They must have let her out. But it's not like Sadie to wander off."

"She might have gone looking for Ian. Dogs are like that." Joe reached down and gave Sadie a pat. "How did you happen to stop at the cemetery to look for her?"

"I don't know…" Danielle tried to come up with a logical explanation. "Figured she likes to chase squirrels sometimes, she loves wooded areas, and the cemetery has lots of interesting smells for a dog."

"You might want to point out to her some of the no dogs allowed signs posted throughout the cemetery," he teased.

"I will. I'll have a little talk with her," Danielle said in mock seriousness. She glanced over at the police car and noticed Brian talking to the prisoner through the car window.

"So you'll stop by the station tomorrow?" Joe asked.

"Yes, I promise. Thanks for not making me go tonight." Danielle looked back to the police car and noticed Brian walking in their direction.

"Ms. Boatman, our prisoner insists you aren't the one who hit him over the head with a rock. He says someone was with you," Brian said when he reached them.

"Just me and Sadie," Danielle said.

"According to the prisoner, he heard you talking to someone."

"I pretended to talk to someone. I didn't want him to know I was alone."

"How is it exactly you managed to hit him when he was holding a gun on you?" Brian asked.

"I got him to believe someone was with me. He got nervous, and when he turned his back for a moment, I managed to hit him with a rock I had in my hand. He never saw it coming," Danielle lied. "I'm sure he won't admit that. He's not going to want his friends to know an unarmed woman got the best of him."

"I suppose you're right," Brian mumbled, yet he didn't sound convinced.

"If you'll excuse me, I think I'll put Sadie in my car until we're ready to go. Will it be much longer?"

"No, about ten more minutes. But if you want to leave now, that shouldn't be a problem. I think we have everything from you," Joe said.

"I'll wait until you leave, just in case you need to ask me anything else." The truth was, Danielle wanted to talk to Isabella after the police left.

Danielle's car was parked a hundred yards or so down the street from the police car. When she opened the backseat to let Sadie in, she was surprised to find Lily sitting in the car. Sadie barreled into the backseat and greeted Lily, her dog body easily walking through what appeared to be Lily's body. Danielle glanced up the street at Joe and Brian. The two cops were talking with each other and weren't looking in her direction. She slipped in the car and closed the door.

"I'm so happy to see Sadie is all right!" Lily said. "Oh my god, Walt was beside himself!"

"What are the Stewarts doing?"

"They're still in their room. Walt's in the hallway, keeping an eye on them in case they decide to go anywhere or snoop around the house."

"So he's no longer in their room? I figured Walt would realize I'd rescinded the ban on spying on them in their room, considering everything."

"Oh, he understands that. But they were getting—well, all honeymoony—and Walt didn't want to watch. So what happened?"

"I'll explain everything when I get home. But I need you to go back to Marlow House and tell Walt Sadie's okay."

"When are you coming home?"

"After I talk to Isabella Strickland. I found her. Or should I say, she found me."

"Isabella is here?"

"She's dead, Lily. Her spirit is in the cemetery. She's the one who helped me get Sadie." Danielle glanced up and saw Joe walking in her direction. "I can't explain any more. Joe is coming this way."

"Drat. I'd like to stay and talk to Isabella. Please find out what she knows about me." Joe was almost to the car. "But I understand. Walt and I will keep an eye on the Stewarts," Lily said as she disappeared.

Danielle opened the car door and stepped out, leaving Sadie in the backseat.

"Animal Services just picked up the two dogs," Joe told Danielle when he reached her car. "The tow truck's hooking up the van right now. They'll be taking it to impound."

"I hope they throw the book at him."

"You're probably anxious to get home. It's been a long day," Joe said as he opened the driver's door for Danielle.

"It has been a little crazier than most," Danielle said dryly. She glanced over at the cemetery and could see Isabella watching her. Reluctantly she got into the driver's seat and sat down. Joe shut the car door and leaned down, looking through the open window at Danielle.

"I'm really sorry about Lily. I really liked her. I know you wanted that to be her today. I wish it was."

"I don't want to get into that now, Joe."

"Fair enough. I'll see you in the morning."

"Okay." Danielle grabbed her purse off the passenger seat and pretended to rummage for her car keys. Joe gave her a goodbye nod and turned, walking back up the street. Danielle watched as Joe got in the police car with Brian and the prisoner. She gave them a quick wave as they drove by her car, heading back to the police station.

The sun would be setting within the hour. Danielle hoped her business in the cemetery could be resolved before then. She got back out of the car. Before closing the door, she gave Sadie a little whistle. The golden retriever leaped over the back of the seat and out of the car on the driver's side. Danielle slammed the car door shut. Together Danielle and Sadie walked to Isabella Strickland.

"You came back, thank you!" Isabella said when Danielle returned.

"No, thank you for helping us," Danielle countered. She glanced over to the headstone where Angela had been sitting. She was nowhere to be seen.

Danielle looked back to Isabella and said, "You're Isabella Strickland, aren't you?"

"How did you know?" Isabella asked in genuine surprise.

Silently, Danielle studied Isabella. On closer inspection, she realized there were a number of similarities between her and Lily. The two women were shorter than she was, and Danielle was not a tall woman. They shared a similar body type—busty yet petite—small sexy packages. They each had red hair, yet Isabella wore hers short while Lily's was a riot of curls falling down her back—or at least it had been until someone had cut Lily's hair.

Danielle hadn't noticed a resemblance between Lily and Isabella when she'd looked at the Facebook profile picture. That picture had enabled Danielle to recognize Isabella. However, while looking at her in person—if one could call looking at a ghost in person—Isabella did look a little like Lily. It wasn't the eyes or forehead. Their foreheads were nothing alike. There was something about the nose and mouth, which explained to Danielle why Joe believed Lily was Isabella. She doubted he would have made that mistake had Lily's head not been bandaged.

"I recognized you by your picture in the paper. Your uncle has my friend Lily—he's telling everyone she's you."

"She's alive, then?" Isabella asked.

"Yes. But in a coma."

"I'm so relieved!"

"You know about my friend Lily, don't you?" Danielle asked.

"I thought they killed her. But after they dumped her body, I could see she was still alive. But just barely. I knew she would die if someone didn't find her right away."

"What happened to Lily? What happened at the rest stop?"

"I can explain that later, but now you have to help me."

"Help you how?"

"I'm dead," Isabella explained.

"Yes, I sort of figured that out."

"Angela told me you can see people like us. People like me."

"Not always. I don't really know how it works."

"I've been trying to find someone who can help me. I've found a few like me, but they're of no help. Other people I ran into, like that man who had your dog, he couldn't see me. Considering what kind of person he was, I'm glad."

"Did you also see the people who brought my dog here?" Danielle asked.

"No, I'm afraid not. Will you help me?"

"What do you need?"

"I need to show you where they put my body. It can't stay where they put it. I'm not comfortable there."

"Where is your body?"

"Come, I'll show you." Isabella motioned for Danielle to follow her through the cemetery.

"It's going to be dark soon." Danielle glanced around uneasily. "Umm...okay..."

"I thought about having you take the police to it when they were here, but I didn't think that would work."

"You want your body found so you can have a proper burial?" Danielle asked as she and Sadie followed Isabella through the trees, walking toward the older section of the cemetery.

"That and I want my friends to know I'm dead. Everyone believes I just took off. But I've been here all along. And if my uncle is telling everyone your friend is me, then everyone thinks I'm still alive."

"Your body is here at the cemetery?" Danielle asked.

"Yes."

"I suppose that's fitting," Danielle muttered under her breath.

TWENTY-THREE

I sabella led Danielle to a stone crypt. By its appearance, Danielle guessed it was as old as the cemetery. There was still enough light out to make out the crypt's inscription. Danielle took a closer look.

"This is a Marlow family crypt," Danielle said in surprise.

"Yes. Frederick Marlow and his wife are in there. He founded this town, you know. Their son and daughter-in-law are in there too. And me. But I don't belong in there."

"By the size of this crypt, I wonder why Walt Marlow's body isn't in here. It's buried over by Angela's grave. You met Angela."

"Yes, I know who she is. She told me. I don't know why Walt isn't in the family crypt, but I certainly don't belong here. And since there isn't anyone left in the Marlow family, no one will be opening it for future burials, so if we don't do something, no one will ever find me."

"I'm not too thrilled about opening a grave at nightfall. Maybe I should just call in a tip to the police."

"No, that won't work," Isabella insisted. "Think about it. They'll assume it's a prank call, and no one is going to just open the crypt on the basis of an anonymous call. Especially if you say it's me. Everyone thinks I'm alive. In a coma, but alive."

"You have a point," Danielle begrudgingly admitted. "Who put you in there?"

"I'm not really sure. I just remember waking up—although I wasn't really asleep. I was dead. But I didn't realize it at the time. So I went looking for my car. I can explain all that later."

"Okay, so we get it open, then what?" Danielle asked.

"Then you make your anonymous call—tell them you saw someone opening the crypt. When they come to check, they'll find me."

"I don't want to sound gross, but aren't you a little concerned about animals at night? I'd hate for some stray dogs to...umm... drag you off before the cops arrive."

"Let me worry about that. I'll keep the animals away. It seems I'm very good with animals since I died. I'm the one who led the dog to your friend at the rest stop."

"You did? Are you saying you were already dead when they dumped her there?"

"Yes. I told you I never left, at least not my body. I'd been dead for days—driving around with the people who had my car. That's who hurt your friend. I was afraid if I left her there, she'd die. I tried to warn her."

"Warn her?" Danielle asked.

"When she pulled into the rest stop, she was all alone. They wanted her car. I knew what they were going to do. I tried to warn her. She was using the bathroom, and I pounded on the door, told her to call 911—that she was in danger. But she couldn't hear me."

"Because you were already dead."

"Yes. After they attacked her and left her in the desert, I stuck around, waiting for someone to pull into the rest stop. But when people did, no one could hear me. That is, until someone came with a dog."

"The dog could see you, couldn't he?"

"Yes! And he seemed to understand me—and I could understand him! Like with your dog, Sadie. It's different when you're dead. I don't ever remember being able to—well, talk to dogs like I can now."

"So you led the dog to Lily?"

"Yes. And he led his people to her," Isabella said with a smile.

"Why did they have your car? You said you'd been dead for a while."

"We can go into that later. Please, let's get me out of here!"

Reluctantly, Danielle turned her attention back to the Marlow family crypt.

"I'm going to need a crowbar or something to help get this open," Danielle said as she surveyed the situation.

"I can help you. Together we should be able to open it."

Danielle turned to look at Isabella. "That's right. You picked up that rock and hit the man with it. You've obviously learned to harness your energy. I didn't consider that possibility."

"Harness my energy?" Isabella frowned.

"Some spirits—not all—learn to harness their energy—which enables them to move objects. I don't think Angela can do it. At least she said she couldn't."

"I couldn't do it before tonight. When I picked up the rock to hit the man, I forgot I hadn't been able to pick anything up since…well, since I died. But it worked. I can try opening the crypt by myself."

"Umm…you know…I could head on home and call the police with that tip while you open the crypt," Danielle suggested with a hopeful smile.

"Please don't leave me alone," Isabella pleaded. "I'm not sure I can do this myself. I know I picked up the rock, but it doesn't mean I can move anything again."

Danielle took a deep breath and gave Isabella a nod. "Okay, I'll stay and help you. If you hadn't helped me, I would have lost Sadie and possibly my life. It's the least I can do."

Danielle walked Sadie a short distance from the crypt and told her to sit. Obediently, Sadie sat. "I want you to stay right there, Sadie," Danielle told the golden retriever. Sadie let out a whimper and lay down. She rested her chin on her front paws as she watched Danielle.

Isabella's first attempt at opening the crypt wasn't as successful as her rock hurling. The stone door opened several inches before Isabella went flying into the crypt, landing inside. To Danielle it looked as if Isabella had just disappeared.

"Isabella, where did you go?" Danielle asked, looking around the crypt.

"It's so creepy in there!" Isabella said with a shudder as she stepped out from inside the stone structure.

"You moved it a little bit," Danielle observed. "Here, let me give it a try."

Using her shoulder, Danielle gave the stone door a firm push as she planted her feet against one of the stone pillars. It refused to budge. After a few more unsuccessful attempts, she took a rest, trying to catch her breath.

"Here, let me try again by myself," Isabella suggested.

Danielle stood back and watched as Isabella laid her palms flat against the stone door and deliberately pushed it to one side. *You really don't need to push it with your hands; your hands are only an illusion,* Danielle thought. *But if it helps you move it...*

Miraculously, the door began to open, revealing the crypt's interior. When the opening was about three feet wide, Isabella stopped pushing and stepped back by Danielle.

The sun was beginning to set, sending a shaft of late afternoon sunlight cutting through the trees and into the crypt, illuminating its interior. Danielle watched as Isabella entered the stone mausoleum. Silently, Isabella harnessed her energy, using it to move her body, which had been pushed into a far corner. She moved it closer to the now open doorway and, with it, the scent of decaying flesh.

The silence of the cemetery was deafening. In the distance, Danielle could hear the faint sound of breakers crashing on the beach. A wave of déjà vu washed over her—bringing back the memory of finding Cheryl's body at the beach shack. Since she was a child, Danielle had become accustomed to encountering wayward spirits, those ghostly creatures who'd reached out to her as they stumbled through the darkness, searching for the light. She'd accepted the spirits that only she could see—it was natural to her now. What was not natural or easy for her was encountering the evidence of their death—decaying bodies and rotting flesh.

A second wave hit Danielle, this one of nausea. She stepped back from the crypt, closing her eyes for a moment. The silence was broken when Sadie let out a bark. Danielle looked to Sadie, who was now standing at attention, barking at something behind Danielle.

"Danielle, what are you...what the hell?" It was Joe Morelli. He stood at the now open crypt, a flashlight in his hand. The beam of his flashlight hit the bare foot of Isabella Strickland's lifeless body.

"Joe..." Danielle groaned. *Just how am I going to explain this?*

"Who are you here with?" Joe demanded.

"Just Sadie..."

"Sit down," he ordered.

"Excuse me?"

"I want you to sit down by Sadie and don't move!"

Silently, Danielle sat next to Sadie and watched as Joe investigated the body at the crypt's doorway. Getting on the phone, he called for reinforcements while shining the flashlight into the now opened tomb.

When he got off the phone, he turned to Danielle. "I was worried about you. I drove by Marlow House on my way home and noticed your car wasn't there yet. I was afraid you might have had car trouble, so I swung back over here and found your car parked where we left you. I tried calling your phone. But it seems you left it in your car. I heard it ringing."

"So you found me." Danielle smiled weakly.

"Do you know who it is?" Joe asked, pointing his flashlight toward the body.

Before answering, Danielle glanced around. Isabella was nowhere to be seen.

"No," Danielle lied. She couldn't tell Joe the truth. As far as Joe knew, she had never met Isabella Strickland, which had been the truth until today.

"How did this get opened?" Joe asked.

"I think the more important question is who put the body in there?" Danielle said.

"I went through this way earlier this evening. I would have noticed had it been open."

"I opened it." Danielle remembered her hands had been all over the door while trying to push it open.

"You opened it? Why?"

"It was partially open," Danielle lied. "I was curious."

DANIELLE WONDERED if she was ever going to make it home. This had to be the longest Saturday in her life. She sat with Sadie and watched as several officers from the coroner's office moved the body from the crypt. Once again, she felt the wave of déjà vu. Many of the same responders here tonight were on the scene when she had found Cheryl's body.

"It's Isabella Strickland," Danielle heard one of them say.

"That's impossible," Joe said. "I just saw her today."

"Does this necklace look familiar?" one of them said.

Danielle heard Joe say, "That's Isabella's necklace. I recognize it from the picture Susan Mitchell showed us. Isabella had it custom made before she disappeared. Does she have a bracelet on?"

"No," someone said.

"It had a matching bracelet," Joe said.

"This is Isabella. I'd know that tattoo anywhere," someone said.

"I don't understand," Joe mumbled.

Silently, Danielle listened to the scene unfold. Sitting next to Sadie, she rested her chin on denim-clad knees as she wrapped her arms around her bent limbs and closed her eyes. It was the sound of boots crushing gravel that alerted her to someone approaching. She opened her eyes and found Joe staring down at her.

"If this is Isabella Strickland, then who was that I saw this afternoon?" Joe asked.

"Lily. Are you going to get her now?" Danielle asked in a weary voice.

"Do you know whose crypt this is?" Joe asked.

"According to the inscription, Walt Marlow's grandparents and parents."

"You knew Isabella was in there, didn't you?"

"How in the world would I know that, Joe?" Danielle asked.

"I don't know. But you knew. Who put her there, Danielle?"

"I have no idea. I've never met Isabella Strickland in my life." *Okay, so that is not entirely accurate*, Danielle told herself.

Danielle heard another set of footsteps approach. She looked up to see the chief.

"Joe, we're going over to the Gusarov Estate," the chief announced. "I want you to go with us."

"I want to go too," Danielle said, jumping to her feet.

The chief turned to Danielle, his expression unfriendly. "You go home, Ms. Boatman. You've caused enough trouble today. Just make sure you get to the station in the morning by nine a.m."

"No. That's my best friend they have up there. You can't expect me to just go home!"

"What makes you so certain it's Lily?" the chief asked. "Just because we've found Isabella Strickland's body doesn't mean that young woman up at the Gusarovs' is your friend."

"I saw her."

"Yeah, well, Joe thought he saw Isabella too," the chief grumbled.

"Let her go, Chief," Joe said.

TWENTY-FOUR

Danielle sat alone in her car outside the Gusarov Estate. The chief had agreed to let her come, yet insisted she wait outside in her car. Anxiously, she watched as the chief made his way up the front walk to the Gusarovs' front door, Joe and two uniformed officers by his side. Several squad cars pulled up behind her parked vehicle. In the distance, she could hear the sound of an ambulance siren. The chief had called ahead for medical assistance to meet them at the estate.

Humming with nervous energy, Danielle's right hand brushed over her braid. No longer tidy and neat, stray tendrils escaped their restraints. Her head was beginning to throb, which wasn't surprising considering she'd had very little to eat all day. She'd like to visit the bathroom but told herself she could wait. It was more important to see what was going to happen with Lily.

The front of the house was dark. After the chief and his entourage reached the front door, the porch light flickered on a few minutes later. Danielle watched as the door opened. She could see Stoddard Gusarov standing in the doorway, talking to the chief. Stoddard was animated, his hands waving erratically as if he were desperately trying to make some point. Finally, he moved to one side and the officers filed into the house, leaving the door open.

A few minutes later, she noticed the light in Lily's room go on.

Through the closed window coverings, she could see the silhouettes of the officers moving around in the room.

"THAT'S NOT ISABELLA," one of the officers announced when he looked at the woman sleeping in the bed.

"I don't understand. We already went through all this this morning," Stoddard insisted. "Joe identified Isabella, didn't you, Joe?"

"I knew Isabella," the officer said, staring down at the woman. "We went to school together. This isn't her. It looks a little like Isabella, but it isn't."

"You're wrong!" Stoddard insisted. "You just don't recognize her because she's been so sick. She's lost weight. Surely you recognize her arm—her tattoo!"

"That's Isabella! Don't be ridiculous. Don't you think we know our own niece?" Darlene Gusarov insisted.

Speechless, Joe stared at the woman in the hospital bed. He hadn't really looked at her face before, not closely. At the time he'd been so certain Danielle was delusionary, all he needed to do was look at the tattoo. He'd done exactly what Stoddard hoped he would.

"I'm calling my attorney!" Stoddard announced. "This is outrageous, you barging in like this, demanding to see my niece and then making all these ridiculous accusations. You forget who you are dealing with!"

"Stoddard, maybe you should call your attorney," the chief said calmly. "We found Isabella's body tonight. She's dead."

Stoddard's face went ashen. "What are you talking about?"

"Your niece, she's dead."

"You're wrong. There's been some mistake," Stoddard said.

"We recognized her. But before we came over here, we took her fingerprints. We had Isabella's on file. The body we found was definitely your niece. But the question now, who is the woman in that bed?"

"It's Lily Miller," Joe said at last.

"I didn't know!" Stoddard insisted. "I thought it was my niece. I haven't seen Isabella for months, and even Joe thought it was Isabella this afternoon! They have the same tattoo! What was I supposed to think? I didn't hurt her! I made sure she had the best medical care! You should be thanking me!"

"I don't believe any of this!" Darlene said. "Isabella's still alive!"

"We found Isabella's body tonight. Someone had put it in the Marlow family crypt at the cemetery," the chief explained.

"Are you insinuating someone murdered my niece?" Stoddard asked.

"The autopsy will give us a better idea. But someone locked her body in the crypt."

"None of this makes sense." Darlene shook her head. "If you say someone put her in the Marlow crypt, how did you find her?"

"Someone obviously opened the crypt," the chief said.

"Then I suggest you find out who opened it and you'll have the person who murdered our niece! They were probably going to move her body!" Darlene insisted.

DANIELLE CONTINUED to sit in her car. The ambulance had arrived, and she watched as the medical team rushed into the house, carrying a gurney. Someone was coming down the walkway toward the street. Because of the dim lighting, she wasn't sure who it was. It wasn't until he was a few feet from her car did she know it was Joe.

"You were right. It was Lily," Joe said when she rolled down the car window. He stood on the sidewalk by her car.

"Where are they taking her?" Danielle asked.

"The local hospital."

"How does Stoddard Gusarov explain it all?"

"He's insisting he thought it was Isabella. Claims the tattoo misled him, like it did me."

"He claims the tattoo was there when they found her?" Danielle asked incredulously.

"Apparently."

"That's bull," Danielle scoffed.

"I honestly thought it was Isabella this afternoon."

"We often see what we want to see."

"I still don't understand how you knew Lily was here. Or how you found Isabella's body."

"Maybe you need to stop wondering how I happen to know

things and start focusing on the real criminals—like whoever put Isabella in that crypt or Stoddard Gusarov, who knew that wasn't his niece he had locked up in his house."

A flurry of commotion behind Joe caught their attention. Turning toward the house, Joe and Danielle watched as the medical team returned with the gurney—now carrying Lily's unconscious body—and made their way to the ambulance.

"The chief wants to know if you have her family's phone number," Joe asked.

"I suppose it might be better if he calls them instead of me." Danielle grabbed her phone and searched for the Millers' phone number. After finding it, she jotted the number down on a piece of paper and handed it to Joe.

"I suppose you're going to the hospital?" Joe said.

"I'll have to go home first and drop Sadie off." *And tell Lily to get herself to the hospital and reconnect with her body, if possible.*

"We'll talk later."

Danielle responded with a nod and rolled the window back up. As she pulled away from the sidewalk, she picked the cellphone back up and pressed the speed dial for Ian.

"Hello, Danielle," came Ian's voice two rings later.

"Thank god you have your phone back on!" Danielle clutched the cellphone with her left hand as her right hand steered the car.

"I woke up about five minutes ago. I was getting ready to call you."

"We found Lily!"

"What do you mean?"

"She's alive, Ian. She's in a coma, but she's alive."

"Where is she?"

Danielle quickly gave Ian the abbreviated version of the day's events. Ian was so relieved to learn Lily was alive he focused more on questions regarding Lily's health. Danielle was able to skim over the harder to explain details—yet she knew those questions would eventually be forthcoming.

"Before you come back, I was wondering if you could find out something," Danielle asked.

"What's that?"

"Stoddard Gusarov insists Lily had the tattoo when they found her at the rest stop. I don't believe that. It doesn't make sense. Can you track down the cops that found her, talk to the medical team that worked on her. See if anyone remembers her having a tattoo. If we can prove he lied, then maybe we can figure out what he was up to."

"I sure as hell know Lily didn't get herself tattooed over Labor Day. But yes, I'll look into it."

When Danielle got off the phone with Ian, she called the private investigator she'd hired.

"I wanted you to know they found my friend and she's alive. As it turns out, she was the woman they found at the rest stop on Labor Day."

"So someone made a false identification?" the investigator asked.

"It looks that way. The authorities intended to identify Lily's body through her dental records, which they were hoping they'd have this week. But all that's moot considering they've found Lily alive."

"So what do you need me to do?"

"I'd like to find out who died in Lily's car. I suspect she might be one of the people who attacked her at the rest stop and took her car."

"I'll see what they're doing about it and get back to you."

"Thanks."

When Danielle got off the phone, she briefly considered stopping by the cemetery and talking to Isabella again. She pushed that thought aside. Danielle was anxious to get back to Marlow House and update Walt and Lily on the evening's events. She could talk to Isabella tomorrow—in the daylight. Hopefully, Isabella would still be around.

Marlow House was pitch-dark when she pulled up into the drive. There didn't appear to be a single light on. Parking the car by the side of the house, Danielle entered through the kitchen doorway with Sadie.

When she turned on the light, she found Walt and Lily sitting at the kitchen table, waiting for her.

"I thought you'd never get home!" Walt said as he stood up. He shifted his attention to Sadie. "I was so worried about you, girl!"

Sitting by Danielle's side, Sadie turned her head from Walt and closed her eyes. A low growl rattled from her throat. Walt stopped in his tracks.

"It's okay, girl, you're home," Walt said gently.

Danielle glanced down at Sadie and frowned. "Umm...I think she's pissed at you." Danielle reached down and stroked Sadie's neck.

Standing up, Sadie opened her eyes and lifted her head. She walked toward Walt and then strolled through his body as if he were not there, making her way to the other side of the kitchen, where she lay down and closed her eyes—her back to Walt.

"Aww, girl, don't be mad at me," Walt begged. "I was so worried about you."

Sadie lifted her head briefly, opened her eyes, and glared at Walt. She made what sounded like a grunting noise before turning her head from him again. Ignoring Walt, she rested her chin on her front paws and closed her eyes.

"I'm so sorry." Walt sounded heartbroken.

"She'll get over it, Walt. Give her time. Where are the Stewarts?" Danielle asked.

"They went back in their room," Lily explained. "Spent most of the evening poking through the library, looking for their imaginary diamonds. By the disgusting sounds coming from their room a little while ago, they're back to playing the honeymooners."

"You've been found, Lily!" Danielle blurted out.

"What?"

"After the police left the cemetery, I went to talk to Isabella. Her body was at the cemetery all along. According to what she said, she never let Frederickport."

"So how does this mean I've been found?"

"When Joe was on his way home, he drove by here and didn't see my car, so he wondered if I'd had car trouble at the cemetery. He found me there—with Isabella's body."

"Oh my god, how did you explain everything?"

"I didn't. Not really. He called the chief, and all these people showed up—it was Cheryl and the beach hut all over again. One of the officers knew Isabella personally and insisted it was her. After running her fingerprints, they knew the dead body was Isabella Strickland, which, of course, meant..."

"That Isabella Strickland wasn't the woman at the Gusarov Estate."

"Exactly. I followed the police over there. When I left, they were just taking your body to the local hospital. I gave Joe your parents' phone number. They've probably already called them."

"What about Ian?" Lily asked.

"I called him on the way over here."

Danielle's phone began to ring. She pulled it from her back pocket and looked at it.

"Lily, it's your mom," Danielle announced before taking the call.

TWENTY-FIVE

D anielle's head rested on a crown of curls, reminding Walt of a sleeping princess. Hovering protectively over her bed, he watched as she and Sadie slept.

Danielle woke to the sound of Sadie's snoring. Pushed to the far right side of the bed, Danielle opened her sleep-laden eyes and looked over at her bed partner. The golden retriever sprawled across the length of the bed, stretched out on her back, taking up more than three-fourths of the mattress's width. Her sleeping head hovered just inches from Danielle's face, making grunting snore sounds.

"Bed hog," Danielle grumbled, giving Sadie a gentle nudge. Feigning sleep, the dog refused to budge.

"Let the poor girl sleep," Walt scolded. "She's had a rough night."

Danielle sat up in the bed and looked over toward the fireplace where Walt stood.

"She's not the only one. How long have you been standing there?"

"Does it matter?" Walt asked.

"I don't like it when you watch me sleep."

"If it makes you feel any better, I was watching Sadie. Not you."

"Are our houseguests still asleep?"

"Yes."

"What time is it?" Danielle picked up her cellphone off the nightstand and looked at the time. "I'm supposed to be at the police station at nine."

"What about the Stewarts' breakfast?"

"I need to tell them they have to leave. There's too much going on. I'll make them a reservation down at the Seahorse Motel. That's right on the water."

"They aren't going to leave willingly."

"They tried to dognap Sadie! I can't have them here."

"And you can't prove it."

"Plus Lily's parents are arriving this afternoon. I told them they could stay here."

"You have plenty of room. I'm telling you the Stewarts are not going to go willingly."

"What am I supposed to do, let them stay indefinitely?"

"No. But I don't imagine you'll be able to get them to leave sooner than they originally planned. Weren't they staying for a week?"

"Yes." Danielle groaned.

"Maybe you need to find out who they really are. Like I told you, I don't think their name is Stewart."

"I'll see what I can do. I wonder..."

"What?" Walt asked after Danielle didn't finish her sentence and was silent for a few moments.

"You said they mentioned something about an Isabella saying diamonds were hidden here. If it was Isabella Strickland, then it must mean she knows them. I should go ask her. See what she can tell me."

"I thought she was down at the cemetery last night when you found Sadie."

"She was. I told you she was the one who nailed that creep with a rock."

"Didn't she see the Stewarts when they brought Sadie down there?"

"No. According to Isabella, she didn't see them. Oh..." Danielle looked up to Walt. "I don't think I mentioned it, but I saw your wife last night."

"I believe you mentioned something about it." Walt took a seat on the sofa.

"And you didn't even ask me how she was doing? Not one single question. Aren't you curious?"

"The woman tried to kill me."

"Yes, for which she's being punished."

"Oh, horse feathers! I wouldn't call being confined to a cemetery a fitting punishment for ending a man's life!"

"True. But she did try to stop her brother. You need to give her credit for that."

"I suppose…" Walt shrugged.

"Umm, I did promise her I'd ask you something. I forgot all about it."

"What in the world would she have to ask me?"

"Apparently, she's rather lonely down at the cemetery. Bored. She's been rethinking your marriage—her mistakes—and she wondered…" Danielle began to giggle.

"What's so funny?"

"She wants you to move down to the cemetery with her!"

"Surely you aren't serious?"

"She seemed serious enough. The only reason I agreed to ask you is it was the only way she'd show me where they'd taken Sadie."

"Sounds like Angela. Even in death she's selfish."

"If I happen to run into her when I go see Isabella, what would you like me to tell her—you know, about her request?"

"Tell her when hell freezes over. And then I'll gladly take her ice skating."

"I'm sure she'll appreciate that." Danielle grinned.

Sadie began to stir. Danielle reached over and ruffled her fur. The dog rolled over, stood up and gave a quick shake as if she were getting out of a bath. She looked over at Walt, let out a short bark, and then began wagging her tail.

"It looks like she's not mad at you anymore," Danielle said with a smile.

Sadie leapt off the bed and jumped onto the couch, sitting on Walt. Her body moved effortlessly through his transparent form.

"Still creeps me out," Danielle muttered under her breath.

"I'm just relieved she's safe," Walt said as he smiled down at Sadie.

"Oh, I had another question for you."

"More about Angela?"

"No. This one's about your family crypt. I told you last night that we found Isabella in there."

"If you think about it, an excellent place to stash a body. Since the Marlows are all gone—at least this branch of the family—no reason for the crypt ever to be reopened. If Isabella's spirit hadn't intervened, they would have gotten away with murder."

"They still may. The police don't know who put Isabella in there."

"Do they think she was alive when she was locked in the crypt?" Walt asked, sounding horrified.

"No. It didn't look that way, and from how the cops were talking, they didn't seem to think so. And when I talked to Isabella, she said she woke up there—as in woke up in death. I'm pretty sure she was already dead when her body was entombed. But my question to you: why weren't you buried there?"

"Me?" Walt frowned.

"It's a huge mausoleum. Your grandparents are there, your parents. You and Angela could have easily been entombed there too. Why weren't you?"

"What a chilling thought." Walt cringed. "After my grandfather died, one of the first changes I made to my will was where I'd be buried. I never wanted to end up in that grim place."

"The idea of a family crypt bothered you?"

"Horrified me." Walt shuddered. "I find those buildings of death morbidly grim. I knew it's what my grandfather wanted. I suppose he's furious I'm not there, which is just one of the many reasons I'm not anxious to move on to the next level."

"I suppose I can understand. Some people have an aversion to cremation, others to burial. I have one friend who insists when she dies she just wants them to prop her in the corner and let her dry out naturally."

"Lovely." Walt smirked. "I imagine that's one last request that won't be honored."

"I suppose you're right." Danielle chuckled. "Have you seen Lily this morning?"

"She told me to tell you she went to the hospital."

"Good. I hope she gets back in her body soon. I have a feeling the longer she stays disconnected, the more difficult it will be for her to jump back in."

"By the way, the Stewarts didn't stay in their bedroom all night."

"Really? What did they do?"

"They went downstairs to the parlor to watch television. Mrs. Stewart—or whatever her name is—was complaining because there isn't a television in her room."

"Oh goodie. I'll be sure to point out that the Seahorse Motel has a TV in every room!"

"I have a question about what they were watching—they called it a marathon. They kept playing one episode after another of the same show. Mrs. Stewart loved it—she seems to be a bit of a dumb Dora. I found the show quite unbelievable."

"What was the show?" Danielle asked.

"*Gilligan's Island*. Silly. Unrealistic."

Danielle began to giggle. "Well, it is *Gilligan's Island*. So tell me, what about it did you find so…umm…unrealistic?"

"The coconut pies."

"Coconut pies?" Danielle frowned.

"If they're stranded on a deserted island, how is it they're able to make coconut pies? I once helped the cook make piecrust when I was a child, and it took both flour and lard. I don't believe either of those ingredients are a commodity one might find on an uninhabited island."

"Really? The pie? That's where you draw the line at unrealistic? You didn't find anything unusual about Ginger's wardrobe?"

"What are you talking about?"

"Ginger's wardrobe. She had an endless supply of evening gowns. That didn't bother you, just the pies?"

"I assumed she was like most women and traveled with an extensive wardrobe. You should see what Angela packed for our honeymoon!"

Danielle stared at Walt a moment and then just shook her head. "Actually, the pies are the one realistic thing about the show."

"How do you see that?"

"Easy. The island has an abundance of coconut trees. From a coconut you can make coconut milk—and from the leftover pulp you can make coconut flour. You can also get oil from the coconut, which can be used for lard or shortening in the piecrust, and coconut sugar, so basically all the ingredients for the pie are found in the coconut."

Walt considered Danielle's explanation for a moment then

asked, "True, but wouldn't that take some sort of machinery to extract the coconut oil and flour?"

"That's why they have the professor, to make whatever they need." Danielle smiled.

"Humm…perhaps. But it still seems a little farfetched."

"Like I said, it is *Gilligan's Island*!" Danielle laughed.

She stopped laughing when she heard a door slam.

"It must be the Stewarts. They're awake," Danielle whispered.

"I'll keep an eye on them while you get dressed."

"Okay." Danielle jumped out of bed as Walt vanished. Sadie let out a bark.

"DID YOU JUST HEAR A DOG BARK?" Claire asked as she and Hunter started to walk down the stairs.

Hunter paused and looked back down the hall. "Sounded like it came from Boatman's room."

"You don't think she found the dog, do you?"

"There's no way she could have. I tied him up real good. He couldn't have gotten loose."

"She, you mean," Claire corrected.

"What are you talking about?" Hunter asked.

"You said he couldn't have gotten loose. The dog was a girl."

"It was a bitch, you mean, and what do I care?"

"But what if she found the dog?"

"There is no way she would have thought to go down to the cemetery to look for that mutt. Let's get out of here. I want to get down there and get our money before someone else finds it. Then we can get back here and have some breakfast."

Claire and Hunter were halfway down the staircase when Danielle opened her bedroom door. Sadie rushed out of the room, heading to the stairs. She stopped at the top of the staircase and looked down at Hunter and Claire. She began to bark. The pair froze and looked up at Sadie, who continued to bark and snarl angrily.

"It's the dog," Claire said under her breath as she clutched the handrail.

"I can see that," Hunter snapped.

"Good morning," Danielle said cheerfully when she reached

Sadie. She looked down at the Stewarts and gave Sadie a gentle pat, telling her to stop barking.

"I see you found your dog," Hunter said, his eyes fixed on Sadie.

"Yes. Some awful man tried to steal her. He's been arrested."

"How do you know he was trying to steal her? Maybe he just found her?" Hunter asked.

"I don't know about that. The police have him. I imagine they'll sort the whole thing out. Where are you two off to?"

"We were going out for breakfast," Claire blurted out.

"Really? Then I guess that means you won't be having breakfast here. It's probably for the best; a few things have come up." Danielle started walking down the stairs, Sadie by her side.

"Why did you say that?" Hunter grumbled under his breath.

"I don't know. I thought I had to say something," Claire whispered as she walked with him to the first-floor landing. Once downstairs, they waited for Danielle to join them.

"I suppose we could have breakfast here now," Hunter said. "We just thought you were still sleeping," he lied.

"Something came up last night—a family emergency, you might say. I'm expecting some more guests this afternoon, and I'm afraid you'll have to move. I can get you a nice room at the Seahorse Motel."

"Don't be ridiculous," Hunter said. "It's our honeymoon. We don't want to stay anywhere else."

TWENTY-SIX

"I told you they weren't going to be easy to get rid of," Walt said after Hunter and Claire drove away in the Cadillac. Walt stood with Danielle and Sadie at the front door of Marlow House.

"At least I don't have to make them breakfast this morning," Danielle said as she slammed the front door shut.

"You can thank Mrs. Stewart for that. Or whatever her real name is."

"What do you mean?"

"According to their conversation this morning, they were on their way down to the cemetery to pick up their ill-gotten money, and then he planned to come back here to let you cook for him."

"So why did the wife say they were going out for breakfast?"

"I think it threw her off balance when she saw Sadie and you asked them where they were going."

"I should have cooked for them. Put arsenic in their eggs," Danielle grumbled.

"What are you going to do about them?" Walt and Sadie followed Danielle to the kitchen.

"I'll deal with them later. I'm kinda overwhelmed at the moment. I have to be at the police station at nine. But first I want to grab something to eat, and then I have to swing by the cemetery."

"The cemetery?"

"I need to talk to Isabella. There are still a lot of unanswered questions. I hope she hasn't moved on yet."

"You know, it's a good chance she has. You helped her do what she came here for. Her body has been found, her friends know she's dead, and now she can have a proper burial. There's no reason for her to stay." Walt watched as Danielle fixed herself a bowl of cereal.

"I hope you're wrong." Danielle sat at the kitchen table. "There are too many unanswered questions."

"When do Lily's parents arrive?" Walt asked.

"They're supposed to get here this morning, but they're planning to go directly to the hospital. I don't expect them to show up here until this evening. I'll probably see them at the hospital first. Which reminds me, I won't be able to take Sadie with me."

"I didn't think you would."

"I'm a little nervous about leaving her here at the house, knowing the Stewarts are still around."

"I promise I won't let anything happen to Sadie," Walt vowed.

"I'll just feel better when they're gone."

"I promise, Danielle. I'll keep her safe."

After Danielle finished breakfast, she ran back upstairs to get ready for the day. By the time she headed out of the house, it was almost 8:00 a.m.

SADIE RODE IN THE BACKSEAT. Danielle knew Walt was annoyed at her for not trusting him to watch the dog, but at the last minute, she just couldn't bring herself to leave Sadie alone at Marlow House, knowing the Stewarts would be returning.

Walt's feelings were hurt, yet Danielle kept remembering Walt was also supposed to keep an eye on the Missing Thorndike when she wore it to the open house. That turned out disastrously, considering her cousin Cheryl managed to steal the necklace and ended up murdered for the prank.

Even if Walt focused all of his attention on keeping the dog safe, he couldn't protect Sadie when she was outside, and it didn't seem like a terrific idea to keep the dog locked up inside Marlow House all day long. Danielle wasn't sure what she was going to do when she got to the hospital, but she'd figure out something.

DANIELLE NOTICED the police cars first, parked along the street adjacent to the cemetery. There were no officers in sight, but by the yellow tape roping off the path leading to the Marlow Crypt, Danielle had a good idea where they might be. She hadn't considered that the area where she had found Isabella would now be a crime scene.

It would be awkward to have a conversation with Isabella with the police on site. As far as she knew, Joe, Brian, or the chief could be somewhere at the cemetery, and the last thing she wanted was for one of them to sneak up on her while she was in the middle of a serious conversation with someone they couldn't see.

Reluctantly, she parked her car. Debating if she should get out, she spied Angela sitting on a headstone.

"Well, girl"—Danielle reached into the backseat and patted Sadie's head—"I'll just be a minute. Be a good girl." Danielle got out of the car and started walking toward Angela.

"You didn't bring Walt?" Angela asked when Danielle reached her.

"I'm sorry. I gave Walt your message. But, well, he can't leave the house."

"He's still mad at me, isn't he?" Angela asked in a pout.

"He's still a little annoyed over that murder thing," Danielle said, keeping her voice low. "I was wondering, have you seen Isabella around?"

"You mean the one they put in the Marlow Crypt?"

"Yes. Is she still here?"

"I haven't seen her since last night after you found her body."

"Did she happen to say anything? Do you know if she's left for good?" Danielle sat down on a stone bench next to Angela.

"I don't have any idea." Angela then added with longing, "But I wish she'd stay around for a while. I'd love to know how she did that trick with the rock and the way she moved the stone door to the crypt! That could really come in handy around here!"

"You didn't happen to see who put Isabella in the crypt, did you?"

"Why certainly. I see everything that happens around here."

"Who was it?" Danielle asked.

"I don't know." Angela shrugged. "I don't know anyone alive. Except for you, of course."

"But you did see who it was, who put Isabella's body in the crypt?"

"Didn't I just say that?" Angela tossed her golden curls dramatically.

"How many were there?"

"Two." Angela sounded bored.

"Were they men? Women? A man and a woman?"

"Two men. About Walt's age. Not bad looking. They didn't speak English."

"Do you know what language they spoke?"

"I know it wasn't Spanish or French. I know a little of both."

"Could it have been Russian?"

"Russian?" Angela considered the question. "Yes, perhaps. Yes, they might have been speaking Russian."

"Do you remember anything about that night?" Danielle asked.

"I remember it was late. The sun had set hours earlier. I heard voices and saw two men carrying a woman's body. At first, I thought they were bringing her into the cemetery to have their way with her. But then I realized she was dead. As dead as me."

"And they went directly to the Marlow Crypt? Like they knew exactly where they planned to take her?"

"It seemed that way." Angela shrugged. "You know Walt and I were supposed to be buried in that horrid crypt. Can you imagine me having to spend eternity sharing that small space with my in-laws?" Angela cringed. "I'll have to thank Walt for changing his will so they didn't bury us there. That is, if he ever forgives me and sees me again."

"Angela, just like you're confined here, Walt really can't leave Marlow House."

"That's not what I heard."

"What I mean is, when he does leave, he'll have to move to the next level. He doesn't have the option of coming down here to see you or going anywhere for that matter."

"I don't understand. It's not like he tried to kill anyone. Why is he being punished?"

"I don't think he's being punished. I just think you each have your own separate destinies. And because of that, you don't neces-sarily have the same rules."

"Perhaps. But I don't believe Walt is really confined to Marlow House. He's simply holding a grudge. And frankly, I'm surprised he's being so petty."

"Danielle Boatman?" a male voice called out. Danielle turned around to see Officer Brian Henderson walking from the path leading from the Marlow Crypt.

"Officer Henderson," Danielle said, standing up.

"He's rather nice looking for an older gentleman," Angela noted.

"What are you doing here? It's a crime scene."

"He doesn't seem very friendly," Angela observed.

"I didn't cross over the yellow ribbon," Danielle said. "I stayed on this side."

"Why are you here?"

"I don't think he likes you."

Danielle tried to ignore Angela. She wanted to tell Brian *It's none of your business*, but instead she said, "I was on the way to the police station and decided to stop a moment and collect my thoughts. Yesterday was a bit overwhelming."

"Yes." Brian glanced down at his wristwatch. "The chief mentioned you were coming in this morning."

"Have you figured out who put Isabella Strickland in the crypt?"

"I don't know. You tell me, Boatman."

"What are you saying? You think I know who did it?"

"You seem to know everything else. You knew Lily was the one at the Gusarov Estate. You knew Isabella was in the crypt. You even knew your cousin Cheryl was at the beach hut."

"I had nothing to do with my cousin's death."

"I didn't say you did. But I'm not so sure about Isabella Strickland's."

"I didn't even know the woman."

"Maybe he's not that attractive after all," Angela decided. "In fact, he's rather unpleasant."

"It's funny how she went missing right about the time you took off for California."

"You mean when I went to Cheryl's funeral?" Danielle said angrily.

"Why was that again you waited so long to have her funeral? What was it, a month and a half after she was killed?"

"What are you getting at, Officer Henderson?"

"Just trying to get to the bottom of this. Seems whenever Danielle Boatman is around, unpleasant things happen."

"I don't know what it is I did to make you dislike me so much."

"He really doesn't like you," Angela agreed. "He almost acts like you plotted to kill him. You didn't, did you?"

"Trust me; it's not all about you. Although, you seem to think it is," Brian sneered.

"What does that even mean?" Danielle asked.

"Spoiled little drama queen, nothing but a magnet for trouble."

"How is any of this my fault?" Danielle asked angrily.

"To begin with, did you have to wear that ridiculous necklace to your open house? Nothing but trouble."

"Okay, you're right. If I had it to do over, I would never have worn it. It wouldn't have been stolen and my cousin would still be alive."

"I don't believe that for a moment." Brian laughed.

"What do you mean?"

"You wouldn't do anything different. If your cousin hadn't been killed, then you wouldn't have inherited all her money."

"That's a horrible thing to say!"

"I call them as I see them."

"Well, maybe I was foolish in the extreme to wear the necklace as a publicity stunt, but none of this with Lily or Isabella is the result of anything I've done."

"You say that, yet you are the only one who knew where both women were."

"I imagine Isabella's uncle also knew."

"We'll see. I have to go back to work. Just make sure you stay out of the roped-off area."

"Why certainly, Officer Henderson," Danielle snapped.

"He really doesn't like you," Angela said when Brian returned to the crime scene.

"The feeling is mutual."

TWENTY-SEVEN

Danielle sat with Sadie in the interrogation room, waiting to be questioned. She was five minutes late because she'd stopped by Starbucks to grab a cup of coffee to take with her. She glanced up at the clock. It was now 9:15 a.m. She had been waiting in the room for ten minutes.

When the door finally opened five minutes later, Joe Morelli walked in.

"Good morning, Danielle," Joe said as he shut the door behind him. "I thought you agreed to be here by nine?" He dropped the manila folder he was carrying on the table and sat down.

"I was five minutes late. Is that why you kept me waiting fifteen minutes?"

"It's rather hectic around here. A lot has been going on. When you weren't here at nine, there were other things vying for my attention that I had to jump on."

"A little crazy for me too right now." Danielle sipped her coffee.

"I see you brought Sadie." Joe looked down at Sadie, who lay next to Danielle's feet. At the mention of her name, the dog lifted her head and looked at Joe, then set it back down on her front paws again and closed her eyes.

"Is there a problem?" Danielle asked.

"No. I like dogs. Just surprised you didn't leave her at home."

"After yesterday, I'm not comfortable leaving Sadie alone at the house when there are guests coming and going."

"It seems your dognapper has quite a record. They found enough at his house to put him away for a long time."

"I hope they throw the book at him. I've no sympathy for anyone who'd do what he does to animals."

"It is a little strange. He keeps insisting you're lying. Swears he never said anything to you about dog fighting. He admits he was going to tie you up, but he swears he never said he was going to kill you."

"Does it really matter what he said to me? Didn't you just say they found enough at his house to lock him up?"

"But did we obtain it under false pretenses?"

"Seriously, Joe? The man had Sadie. He held a gun on me, and you're now wondering if he's being treated unfairly? What side of the law are you on anyway?"

"I'm just trying to understand, Danielle. What you told me just doesn't add up. A lot of what you told us doesn't add up. Why don't we forget the dognapper for right now and talk about Lily and how you knew it was her and not Isabella at the Gusarov Estate."

Danielle didn't answer immediately. Instead, she looked over at the two-way mirror. Finally, she said, "Before I say anything, I want to know who is in there watching us."

"Don't worry about that now. If you focus, we can get through this quickly and you can get out of here."

"Joe, unless you want me to invoke my right to an attorney and stop talking, I suggest you tell me what I want to know."

"Don't be ridiculous, Danielle, you aren't under arrest."

"Then I'm free to go?" Danielle stood up.

The door to the room opened and the chief walked in. "What is this about?" he asked.

"Morning, Chief. I take it you were in the next room? Who else?" Danielle asked, still standing.

"What is this about, Ms. Boatman?" the chief asked. "Joe's correct, you aren't under arrest. But considering all that went down yesterday, you can certainly understand why we need some more information from you. I would think you'd want to help since Ms. Miller is such a close friend."

"This morning I ran into Officer Henderson at the cemetery."

"Why were you there?" Joe asked.

"Why does everyone keep asking that?" Danielle was clearly annoyed. "If I want to stop by the flipping cemetery, why is that anyone's business?"

"Considering what we found you doing there last night, I don't think the question is unreasonable," the chief said.

"Perhaps, but I didn't appreciate all the other stuff Officer Henderson said to me. I don't know what I did to that man, but he hates me."

"I don't think he hates you," the chief argued.

"You're probably right, Chief. He doesn't care enough to hate me. But he made it clear he believes I'm nothing but trouble. According to him, everything bad that's happened in Frederickport since I arrived is my fault. Even Isabella Strickland's death."

"I'm sure he didn't say that," the chief said.

"Oh, I'm sure he did. My point in all this, the only way I will ever again speak to Officer Henderson is if my attorney is present. That includes discussing anything with anyone in this room if I even suspect that man is in the next room listening."

"I know Brian can be a little abrasive," Joe said.

"The man is an ass."

"Would you feel more comfortable if Joe took you into his office? You could talk there?"

"That would be fine, Chief," Danielle agreed.

"I CAN'T BELIEVE you let her manipulate you like that!" Brian fumed when the chief walked into the office next to the interrogation room.

"We kept her waiting until you returned from the cemetery because you were so determined to listen to the interrogation. What in the world did you say to that woman this morning?"

"Just the truth. You know how I feel about her."

"There's an old cliché about catching more with honey. I'd suggest you familiarize yourself with it."

"I'm too old and have been at this too long to tolerate bull. You should know that better than anyone," Brian said.

"The fact is, Danielle Boatman hasn't broken any laws. She's also a very wealthy woman, and if she wants to make our lives miserable, she has enough money to do it. I don't know what it is about her that irritates you so much, but back off."

"Are you serious? She hasn't broken any laws? Breaking and entering, to start with."

"That one would be a little hard to stick, considering Stoddard was holding her friend," the chief reminded him.

"Maybe we can't charge her with anything, but it's pretty obvious she's involved in something," Brian said.

"It's not that I disagree. But we're not going to learn anything if she lawyers up and refuses to talk to us. Let Joe handle Boatman. I think she trusts him. She definitely doesn't trust you."

"CAN I GET YOU MORE COFFEE?" Joe asked after Danielle and Sadie settled into his office.

"No, I'm fine." Danielle tossed her empty coffee cup in the trash can.

"Have you been to the hospital yet?" Joe asked.

"No. I called over there, but they won't really talk to me. I'm not family. But her parents are coming in this morning. They'll be staying with me. I hope to see Lily this afternoon."

"When will Ian be back in town?"

"In a day or so. He got the flu while he was down there, so I imagine he'll want to be better before he flies back. Lily doesn't need the germs, not to mention the other passengers on the plane."

"I'm sure he's anxious to see Lily."

"We all are. But she's still in a coma, so we'll have to take one day at a time."

"You're right."

"I know you didn't bring me down here to chat, Joe. What is it you need from me?"

"Can you explain how it is you knew Lily was at the Gusarov Estate? Did someone tip you off? Is that why you broke in?"

"Tip me off?" Danielle frowned.

"Maybe someone who worked for the Gusarovs knew that wasn't Isabella. Was that what happened?"

Not unless you consider Lily a tip. But you'd never believe that, Danielle thought.

After a few moments of silence Danielle said, "As you already know, I had a gut feeling Lily wasn't the one killed in the accident. Things didn't add up. For one thing, she would never race down the freeway that fast. I know Lily. Plus, she was supposed to be home on Labor Day. She was going to leave early to beat the holiday traffic. Instead of being back in Sacramento on Monday night so she could go to work on Tuesday, her car was involved in the accident not far from Palm Springs."

"But what does that have to do with Isabella Strickland?" Joe asked.

"There was an article in the newspaper about Isabella, with a photograph of the rest stop where they found her and her car. At least they thought it was Isabella. I started thinking of Lily and how if she had started for home when she was supposed to, she might have stopped there on Labor Day—the same day they found Isabella. What if she did stop there? Maybe they took her car because Isabella's was broken down. According to the article, there was something wrong with the car."

"So you jumped to the conclusion it was Lily they found at the rest stop and not Isabella?"

"I don't know what I was really thinking at that point. I just thought maybe Isabella knew something."

"But she was in a coma. Or at least, who everyone thought was Isabella was in a coma. How did you think Isabella was going to help you?"

"Joe, I'm trying to give you a general idea of my thought process. I'm not saying I expected Isabella to wake up and talk to me or that I thought it would be Lily. I had this gut feeling—an intuition—I just knew I needed to go to the Gusarov Estate and try to see Isabella. I didn't think they'd just let me in, so I broke in. I wasn't really thinking straight."

"So it was all just some wild hunch?" Joe asked incredulously.

"I don't expect you to understand, Joe. Most people don't. But sometimes I have these—intuitions. It's like when I found Cheryl's body. I just knew—instinctively—that I had to check out the beach hut. Just like I knew I needed to walk down the beach and try to retrace Cheryl's steps, assuming she tried to walk back to Marlow House that night. I know it doesn't make sense. When I was down at the cemetery, after finding Sadie, I was drawn to the crypt. I just knew I needed to try to open it the rest of the way."

"Are you telling me you have some sort of ESP thing?"

"I wouldn't call it ESP exactly." Danielle shifted in the chair uncomfortably. "I can't explain it. I know it makes some people suspicious—like your partner Brian."

"So this is your explanation for everything that happened yesterday—you had a hunch?"

"It wasn't just a blind hunch. I explained about the article, the coincidence with Lily, and the rest stop."

"I'm sorry, Danielle, it all sounds pretty farfetched."

"But it was Lily at the Gusarov Estate, and there was a body in the crypt."

"Yes, I know. But there is something about your explanation…" Joe leaned back in his desk chair and studied Danielle. "You see, I get gut feelings too. I've learned to trust my gut, and mine is telling me there's something more. Something you're not telling me."

"What is it you think I'm hiding, Joe?"

"I don't know. You tell me, Danielle."

"I honestly don't know what you want from me."

"Okay…" Joe leaned forward, resting his elbows on his desk. "Then let's go back to Jimmy Borge."

"Jimmy Borge?" Danielle frowned.

"Our dognapper. That's his name," Joe explained.

"I didn't know."

"Do you have any idea how he got Sadie?"

"I told you, when I got home yesterday—after leaving here—she was gone. I have a honeymoon couple staying at Marlow House; you met them. I suspect they accidentally let her out."

"What made you go to the cemetery to look for her?"

"I told you, a—"

"A hunch, right." Joe sighed.

After a few moments of silence, Danielle said, "Can I ask you something?"

"I suppose." Joe leaned back in his chair again.

"What is Isabella's uncle saying about Lily?"

"He insists he thought she was Isabella. I'm afraid he's intending to use me in his defense."

"You?"

"I went into the hospital room at his house, swore to you the woman was Isabella and not Lily. I was familiar with both women. He's saying if I could make that mistake, so could he."

"That's absurd. Lily didn't have a tattoo. Someone gave it to her so she'd look like Isabella."

"I understand that. But Stoddard's insisting whoever was driving Isabella's car and left it at the rest stop are the same people who killed her and put her in the crypt. He's saying Lily got the tattoo before she was dumped outside the rest stop."

They were both silent for a few moments, each playing over the conversation in their heads. Finally, Danielle spoke up. "What about her hair?"

"What about her hair?" Joe frowned.

"Was her hair short when they found her?"

"I assume so." Joe shrugged. "We didn't discuss her hair. But even if it wasn't, that doesn't prove anything. According to Stoddard, he hadn't seen her for months, and women do grow their hair out."

"But it's short now," Danielle reminded him.

"I know that. If it was long when they found her, I can understand why they'd cut it short, considering her head injury."

"Do you honestly believe Stoddard thought Lily was his niece?"

"I just know it's possible, considering I thought it was Isabella in that bed. And what motive would Stoddard have to pull such an elaborate hoax?"

"I can think of one reason," Danielle said as she stood up. "With Isabella Strickland dead, her half of the family business goes to Earthbound Spirits. I don't think Stoddard Gusarov wanted that to happen. It was in his best interest to keep his niece alive—at least until he figured out some way to change her will."

TWENTY-EIGHT

B efore going home, Danielle swung by the bank and withdrew some money from the ATM. While she hated giving the Stewarts a refund—not because she didn't want to spend the money, but because she believed they were evil crooks—she felt it would be money well spent to have them out of Marlow House.

Knowing the Stewarts were responsible for dognapping Sadie, she couldn't stay another night with them in the house, even with Walt standing guard. She wanted to go to the hospital and see how Lily was doing, but it was impossible until she had the situation with the Stewarts resolved and she knew Sadie was safe.

The Cadillac was parked in front of the B and B when she returned home. Danielle wondered if her guests were inside—treasure hunting—or down at the beach. She had her answer when she went into the library and found the Stewarts pulling books off the shelves as Walt stood nearby watching.

"Do you like to read?" Danielle asked when she walked into the library. Hunter looked up from a stack of books piled on the desk.

"You're back," Hunter said with a smile. "Yes, I love to read. You have a wonderful collection. I was just putting them back."

"Liars," Walt grumbled. "They've been searching through the books, looking for a secret compartment. Idiots."

"We wondered where you were. Since we didn't have breakfast here, we thought you might fix us lunch," Claire said as she stood up, walking toward Danielle. Standing by Danielle's side was Sadie, who began to growl. Claire froze; her eyes wide, she looked at Sadie. "Your dog is growling at me!"

"I'm afraid she's been a little jittery since Jimmy tried to dognap her."

"Jimmy?" Claire feigned ignorance.

"Yes. The man they arrested."

Claire and Hunter exchanged glances when Danielle looked down to Sadie.

"Don't bother putting those books away, I need to talk to you both," Danielle said cheerfully.

"Over lunch, perhaps?" Claire suggested.

"No. I'm afraid not. I don't do lunch." Danielle smiled.

"What is it you want to talk to us about?" Hunter asked.

"I mentioned earlier that there's been a bit of a family emergency. I have a friend who's been hospitalized, and her family is going to have to stay here. I'm afraid you'll have to leave." Danielle dug into her front pocket and pulled out the cash she'd withdrawn from the bank. She set it on the desk in front of Hunter.

"What's this?" Claire asked.

"We have a reservation. We've already paid for the week," Hunter argued.

"I'm giving you a full refund. I'm not even charging for the nights you've already stayed. But you'll have to leave now."

"This is our honeymoon!" Hunter said. "We don't want our money back. We want to stay for the week."

"Fortunately, there are a lot of vacancies in town since it's the off-season. You won't have a problem finding another place to stay."

"Do you want me to go pack for them?" Walt asked as he summoned a cigar.

"Ms. Boatman, you really don't want me to leave yet. You need me."

"I do?"

"Can't you smell that? It's the ghost of Marvin Marlow. I can help exorcise his ghost."

"Oh, I don't want you to exorcise old Marvin. I rather like him. He keeps me company."

"Don't call me Marvin," Walt grumbled.

"You can't just kick us out like this," Claire said as she snatched up the money from the desk. She began to count and straighten the stack of bills.

"I just assumed you'd want to leave now and avoid talking to the police," Danielle said with a shrug.

"Police, Danielle? What are you up to?" Walt asked as he took a drag off his cigar and lounged against the back of the sofa.

"You can't call the police on us." Claire panicked. "We haven't done anything wrong!"

"Mrs. Stewart, I never meant to imply I was calling the police on you. It's just that when I was down there this morning, being interviewed, they mentioned they would probably be stopping over here this afternoon to talk to both of you. I just assumed you'd want to avoid that, since it is your honeymoon. Nothing like a police interrogation to throw a bucket of ice water on the romance."

"Why would they want to talk to us?" Hunter asked.

"They have a man named Jimmy Borge in custody for trying to steal Sadie. I guess he has quite a record for dog fighting. They're trying to figure out how he got Sadie. Since you're the last ones to see the dog, they naturally want to talk to you both."

"I told you we didn't have anything to do with your missing dog!" Claire insisted.

"Yes, I understand that. But apparently, the police feel it's important to check everyone out. I guess this is more serious than just a dognapping, considering the man's record."

"This is ridiculous." Hunter snatched the money from Claire and shoved it in his pocket. "This is our honeymoon. First, you tell us we have to leave early; then you say we need to talk to the police because your stupid dog got out! Come on, Claire, let's go pack."

"The police aren't coming over to interview them, are they?" Walt asked as Hunter and Claire stormed out of the room.

"No." Danielle grinned.

"You're quite a good liar."

"I've had a lot of practice recently."

"I suppose I better go keep an eye on them."

"Yes, please do."

"IT'S ALL YOUR FAULT!" Hunter told Claire as he threw the suitcase on the bed.

"Why is it my fault?" Claire gathered up her cosmetics off the dresser.

"Your stupid idea to get a few bucks for that dog. Now we have to leave."

"I don't know why we have to go. They can't prove anything."

"Would you think a moment?" Hunter stopped packing the suitcase and looked at Claire. "All they have to do is run the plates on our car and they'll realize the name on the registration isn't the name we gave Boatman. Hell, the plates don't even match the car!"

"I don't think they'll run the plates. Why would they do that? You said yourself we look completely respectable with these lame clothes and that car. We can make up some story, say I went out to put something in the car before we left the house, and I accidently left the door open. The dog must have gotten out then. I never noticed. We're so sorry. Blah, blah, blah."

"You don't think your friend Jimmy won't give us up? According to Boatman, he's facing some serious jail time. He'll toss us to the cops in a heartbeat if he thinks that'll shave some time off."

"Jimmy wouldn't do that!"

"You don't think Jimmy's kind of pissed at us right now? Don't you think he's wondering how Boatman tracked him down to the cemetery and got the dog back? Hell, I'm wondering that myself!"

"But what about the diamonds?" Claire whined.

"I'm beginning to think Isabella was delusional. But even if she wasn't, we can't risk hanging around here if the cops are going to be asking questions."

"Where are we going to stay? Someplace on the beach?"

"Don't be stupid, Claire; we're not staying in Frederickport. Get your stuff together. We're heading back to Portland."

"What about Justina? I thought she was going to meet up with us here."

"She hasn't called. Probably drunk somewhere. We'll meet up with her in Portland. This trip was a bust."

"What about Marvin Marlow? I thought he was going to be our guide."

"Shut up, Claire, and pack!"

Fifteen minutes later, Walt followed Hunter and Claire down the stairs as the couple scrambled to get away from Marlow House before the police showed up. Danielle met them in the foyer. She stood by the parlor door, Sadie by her side.

Claire set her suitcase down a moment so she could adjust her purse's strap on her shoulder. Hunter was just reaching for the door-knob as Claire warily kept an eye on Sadie, who looked prepared to lunge at any moment. Her gaze moved from Sadie to the parlor door—and then she remembered. Her bracelet was still in the antique teapot.

"We can't go yet!" Claire blurted out.

"Come on, Claire, let's go." Hunter opened the door and stepped outside.

Swallowing nervously, Claire considered her options. If she went into the parlor, Danielle was sure to follow her into the room. Hunter would be furious if he found out she'd not only worn the bracelet but had left it in the teapot. Looking from Danielle to Hunter, Claire decided her only option was to leave the bracelet where it was—for now. She followed Hunter outside.

Danielle stood by the open doorway and watched the Stewarts scurry down the walkway toward the street, where they'd parked their car.

"You didn't get your keys back," Walt noted.

"I called the locksmith when you were upstairs. He's on his way over to change the lock before I take off to the hospital. Fortunately, their key only fits the front doorknob and not the dead bolt or any of the other doors, so it won't be too expensive to change."

"Are you planning to do this with all your guests?"

"I may do it once a month, just to be safe."

"If you get any more guests like the Stewarts, you might want to rethink this B and B business altogether. By the way, I have a feeling their car is stolen."

"How do you know that?" Danielle asked as she watched the Cadillac drive away. She shut the door and turned to face Walt.

"One reason Hank—who, by the way, also goes by the name Hunter—wanted to get out of here, he was afraid the cops were going to run his plates. Not only will the names not match, but also it seems the plates don't belong to that car."

"I wish I knew that before they left. I would have written their license plate down. I hate letting them get away with what they almost did to Sadie, but I really didn't have anything to tell Joe—aside from what you overheard. As it is, he thinks I'm nuts."

"Maybe you really should have had Joe come over to interview them."

Together Walt and Danielle walked into the parlor to wait for the locksmith.

"Perhaps. I suppose I could have said something to get Joe to interview them. But the truth was, I just wanted them to get out of here so I could have some sense of privacy and safety—and so I could leave Sadie here without worrying." Danielle dropped down on the sofa as if exhausted.

"I told you I would have watched Sadie."

"I just didn't want to sleep under the same roof with them. I wish you'd understand."

"I suppose I do," Walt said with a sigh, taking a seat across from Danielle.

"I got a text message that Lily's parents arrived okay. But I haven't heard anything else. I wish the locksmith would hurry up so I can get out of here."

"Sorry, I can't help you there."

"Do you think they'll be back, looking for the imaginary diamonds?" Danielle asked.

"I doubt it. I got the feeling this Hunter Hank character tends to lose interest quickly."

TWENTY-NINE

A t the hospital, Danielle found Lily's spirit form sitting on the bed, looking down at her unconscious body, which was hooked up to an assortment of monitors and medical gadgets. Lily's parents hovered nearby, speaking in soft whispers, discussing the next plan of action. When they spied Danielle entering the room, Mrs. Miller rushed to her with open arms, greeting her with a hug before breaking into a fresh round of tears.

"She's been crying nonstop since she got here," Lily called out from the bed.

"Can you believe it? My baby is really alive!" Mrs. Miller blubbered. "We just need to get her better. She needs to wake up."

Still embraced in the motherly hug, Danielle looked over Mrs. Miller's shoulder at Lily. "Yes, she does need to wake up."

"Ask them about my leg," Lily said.

Mrs. Miller released Danielle and returned to her husband's side. She used a tissue to dab tears from her eyes. Mr. Miller reached out and gave Danielle's hand a quick squeeze in greeting.

Danielle gave his shoulder a gentle pat as she walked around him to the hospital bed and looked down at Lily's body. The bedsheet was pulled to Lily's chest, exposing the top of her hospital gown. It looked as if one of her legs was bandaged under the sheet.

"Is something wrong with Lily's leg?" Danielle asked.

"Late last night they had to do emergency surgery. She got a bad infection and it settled on her knee," Mrs. Miller explained.

"No one told me." Danielle touched Lily's lifeless hand. "Is she going to be all right?"

"She's going to need six weeks of IV treatments—antibiotics," Mrs. Miller said. "It could have killed her. Thank god you found her."

"Apparently Isabella's dear uncle didn't have such a great private medical team after all," Lily said in disgust. "I could have lost my leg! Hell, I could have lost my life with that infection!"

"The doctors don't seem to know why she's still in a coma," Mr. Miller said.

"I've read about these things," Lily's mother explained. "Lily just needs to be surrounded by people who love her. We need to keep talking to her, letting her know we're here so she'll come back to us!"

"I've finally figured out why I talk so much." Lily looked from her mother to Danielle. "I've heard you guys making cracks about how Lily sure can talk. But you guys ain't heard nothing yet! My mother has been talking to me nonstop since she got here. I think I have a headache. How is that possible? I don't even have a physical head attached to me at the moment. Please, Danielle, you must make her stop!"

"Have you had anything to eat since you got here?" Danielle asked Lily's parents.

"No, we came directly from the airport. We didn't want to leave Lily alone," Mrs. Miller explained.

"Why don't you go get something to eat. You're going to need your strength. If there is any change in Lily, I promise I'll call you. You have your cellphone with you, don't you?"

"I could sure use something to eat," Mr. Miller grumbled.

"Then you go, dear. I'll stay here with Danielle."

"No, Mrs. Miller. We don't want you to get sick too. Go get something to eat," Danielle urged.

"Well..." Mrs. Miller walked over to her daughter and brushed her fingertips over the sleeping girl's forehead. "I suppose I should get something to eat." She leaned over the bed and kissed Lily's brow.

"I'll be here when you come back," Danielle said as the Millers left the room, shutting the door behind them. Danielle reached up and grabbed the privacy curtain, pulling it across the room. Should someone walk by the door and look through the window, she didn't want them to see her talking to herself.

"I love my mother, but I swear, I'm going to go insane stuck with her for six weeks," Lily groaned when her parents left the room.

With the privacy curtain drawn, Lily and Danielle failed to see the door to the hospital room open. Stepping into the room, Joe Morelli gently shut the door behind him and looked at the curtain. He assumed the nurse was tending to Lily, so he decided to wait quietly for her to finish before he went in to see Lily.

"Why haven't you taken your body back?"

"I was going to try last night, but then they wheeled me in for surgery and I wanted to watch. Oh, it was gross. I wish I hadn't watched."

"That doesn't explain why you're still here, like this."

Joe started to say something, to let whoever was behind the curtain with Lily know he was there, when he recognized the voice —it was Danielle. Instead of announcing his presence, he silently listened.

"Before I tried jumping back in, I wanted to hear my prognosis. I'm going to be hooked up to an IV three times a day for six weeks to get rid of this infection. That means I won't be going back to work."

"You have to stay in the hospital that long even if you come to?"

"No. They said if I keep progressing at this rate, once I wake up I can go home after about a week or so. I guess they want me under observation for a little bit after I come to. But after that I can go home, which means back to my parents'—god forbid—so I can finish my IV treatment for my leg. Mom thinks she's going to be the one to hook me up to the IV three times a day. You have met my mother, right? If her talking doesn't kill me, her nursing will."

"What about your apartment?"

"I suppose it's a good thing Mom is such a Chatty Cathy. In her attempt to reach me this morning, she told me—in detail—everything she and Dad have been doing since they got news of my death. This includes cleaning out my apartment. Do you realize they went through—All. My. Stuff. I'm just grateful I didn't have any sex toys!"

Danielle began to giggle.

"Fortunately, she wasn't quite ready to throw my things away—

thank god—so everything is boxed up and in their garage. That must thrill my father, who's always bitching about what Mom puts in there."

"I'm kinda surprised they moved you out of your apartment so soon."

"I can understand," Lily said with a shrug. "I forgot to drop my rent off before I left for Palm Springs. It wasn't that big of a deal at the time, because I intended to be back by the first. But when my landlord—and parents—thought I'd been killed in the car crash, and my rent hadn't been paid for the month, the landlord pressured my folks to get my apartment cleaned out. I don't think my parents minded paying for September, but Mom was a little nervous about the landlord going in there and getting rid of my stuff."

"I'm sorry, Lily."

"I can't really blame the landlord. But I don't want to go live with my folks. Not even for six weeks. But what am I going to do? I don't have a home. I don't even have a job."

"Come stay with me."

"With you? I can't do that."

"Yes, you can. You can stay in the downstairs bedroom. I'll even hire a private nurse to take care of you."

"I can't afford that."

"But I can. And Walt can help. Not to mention Ian. He was only planning on moving out of the rental because he wanted to be closer to you. This way he can stay where he is. It will be the perfect solution!"

"I can't live off you. It wouldn't be right."

"What are friends for, Lily, if we can't help each other? We're practically family."

"It would be better than staying with my folks; that's for sure."

"But you have to go back into your body."

Lily looked down at the sleeping woman. "I'm afraid. What if it hurts? It looked really painful when they opened my leg up last night."

"Don't be such a baby, Lily. Get in your body now!" Danielle shouted.

To Danielle's surprise, the privacy curtain flew open and she found herself standing face-to-face with Joe Morelli.

"How long have you been standing there?" Danielle squeaked, a blush covering her face.

"Long enough to hear you talking to yourself."

"I wasn't talking to myself; I was talking to Lily. And that's pretty rude to lurk behind the curtain like that and eavesdrop." Danielle turned abruptly from Joe and faced the bed. The only Lily in sight was the one sleeping under the sheets. Danielle glanced around warily, looking for her out-of-body friend.

"How is she doing?" Joe asked, stepping up to the bed.

"They had to operate last night."

"I heard."

"And you didn't tell me?" Danielle swung around angrily, facing Joe.

"I found out after you left this morning. The chief told me."

"That idiot Stoddard could have killed her with his incompetent staff."

"I got a call from Ian right before I left the office," Joe said.

"Ian? I'm surprised he hasn't called me." Danielle frowned, looking back down at Lily.

"He wanted me to know he spoke to the paramedics that worked on Lily at the rest stop."

"He did?" Danielle looked back at Joe.

"Lily didn't have a tattoo. In fact, Stoddard never mentioned any tattoo when they called him to identify the body. These days it's pretty common for young women to have tattoos, so it's something they tend to look for when making an identification. According to the paramedic, she didn't have one."

"Stoddard had her tattooed."

"That's what it looks like. The chief is having him brought in now. I'm not a doctor, but I have a cousin who has an artificial knee, and it got an infection just like the one Lily has. He was told the artificial knee didn't cause the infection, it's just where it landed. My cousin wanted to know the cause. The doctors said it could be anything, like dental work or a cut that got infected."

"Or a recent tattoo, one done under questionable conditions?" Danielle suggested.

"That's a possibility."

"Stoddard Gusarov has a lot to answer for," Danielle said angrily.

"He'll answer for it," Joe said under his breath.

Danielle stood by the side of Lily's bed, facing the door, Joe by her side. She leaned over and whispered into Lily's ear, "You must wake up, my dear friend."

To Joe's surprise, Lily, who had been catatonic and still since he found her at the Gusarov Estate, began to moan, restlessly tossing her head from side to side. One of the monitors began to buzz. As the medical staff rushed into the room, Joe looked up at Danielle, who calmly stepped aside, making room for the medical team. Her expression showed no signs of shock or awe at Lily's abrupt recovery.

Fluttering her eyes open, Lily licked her lips and looked around the room. When she spied Danielle, she smiled. "I'm back," her hoarse voice whispered.

"So you are!" Danielle laughed, rushing forward to take one of Lily's hands. She gave it a reassuring squeeze.

As the medical team chattered away amongst themselves, efficiently checking Lily's vital signs and reviewing the monitors, Lily told Danielle in a raspy whisper, "I'm holding you to your promise. You're stuck with me, you know. I'll be one of those houseguests who never leaves."

"I'm looking forward to it!" Danielle released Lily's hand and moved away from the bed, out of the way of the nurses, who continued to flutter around their patient. Joe followed her into the hall.

"She heard you," Joe said in awe.

"Of course she did." Danielle smiled and took her phone out of her pocket.

"She knows you invited her to stay at Marlow House while she recovers."

"What, did you think I was talking to myself in there?" Danielle felt giddy. Turning from Joe, she dialed Mrs. Miller.

"Is anything wrong?" Mrs. Miller asked when she answered her cellphone.

"When you're done eating, there is someone who would like to say hello. Lily woke up."

Joe could hear Mrs. Miller's shout of glee coming from Danielle's cellphone. Danielle quickly moved the phone away from her ear, trying to spare her eardrum. She laughed when she realized Mrs. Miller had hung up and was probably already on her way back to Lily's hospital room.

THIRTY

"Chocolate cake for breakfast, really, Danielle?" Walt chided good-naturedly.

Shamelessly, Danielle took another bite, savoring the treat. Wearing red plaid pajama bottoms and a pink T-shirt, she sat up on her bed, leaning against a pile of pillows. She'd forgotten to take out her braid the night before, yet most of her hair had already managed to escape while she slept. Wayward curls and tendrils gently framed her face.

"And this is why"—Danielle waved her chocolate-smudged fork and held up her now empty plate—"I will never lose that last fifteen pounds."

"Thank god for chocolate cake," Walt muttered to himself as he eyed Danielle appreciatively. He'd given up the notion that she might start wearing silk negligees to bed or trade her jeans for feminine dresses. While the flannel pajamas weren't sexy in the traditional fashion, he could imagine himself—if he were a flesh and blood man—snuggling under the covers with a flannel-clad Danielle as a fire roared in the nearby fireplace. Perhaps they might even share a piece of chocolate cake. It had been years—no, decades, practically a century—since he had enjoyed chocolate cake or the warmth of a woman.

"You know, I could have chocolate cake every day for breakfast if I just met a man who liked to dance." Danielle licked her fork. "Well, maybe not every day. But a couple times a week."

"Why is that?"

"I'd be dancing off all that cake." Danielle chuckled.

"Did Lucas like to dance?"

"Lucas? Hardly. No, Lucas would barely dance at our wedding —that should have been a red flag, I suppose."

"Does Joe like to dance?"

"I don't know." Danielle shrugged and tossed her fork on the plate. "Wouldn't want to dance with him anyway. At least not now."

"I enjoyed dancing. Back when I could still hold a woman in my arms."

"What kind of dancing?" Danielle asked curiously. "Ballroom… or something like the Charleston?"

"I like both." Walt smiled. "What about you?"

"I suppose if I want to burn off chocolate cake, something that gets me moving. I think it would be fun to learn the Charleston, especially dressed in one of those cute flapper outfits with the fringed skirts!"

Walt laughed. "I'd love to see you dressed as a flapper."

"I imagine that won't be happening." Danielle sighed. She set her plate on the nightstand. "Well, the cake was yummy."

"Do you intend to feed Lily's parents cake for breakfast?"

"They already left." Danielle leaned back on the pillows and tossed the blanket over her feet. "They told me last night they planned to get up early and go out for breakfast before heading to the hospital. They were leaving when I was getting my cake."

"Does Lily plan to tell them today that she intends to stay here?"

"She says she's going to."

"I can understand why she didn't mention anything yesterday."

"Yeah, it would have seemed strange if she just popped out of the coma and announced she was going to stay at Marlow House. But then, she practically did that with Joe standing there."

Walt smiled. "You told me."

"It was embarrassing. But I thought about it later and figured it was probably the least crazy thing he's seen me do. It's not like I'm the only person who's ever held a seemingly one-sided conversation with a comatose patient. If he'd shown up an hour earlier, he would have caught Mrs. Miller in the act."

"True. But how many of those comatose patients suddenly wake up and remember what was being said to them?"

"Yeah, that kind of freaked him out." Danielle grinned. She grabbed a pillow and tossed it at Walt. It flew through his body. "Out, I need to get dressed." Danielle jumped out of the bed. Walt vanished.

Thirty minutes later when Danielle came down the stairs, the doorbell rang. Walt appeared in the foyer, standing by the parlor door. "Someone's here," he announced.

"I heard," Danielle said, walking past Walt to the front door. Before opening it, she peeked out the window. "It's Joe. Please don't talk to me while he's here, it's distracting!"

"A social call?" Walt smirked.

"I seriously doubt it. He's in his uniform."

"Morning, Danielle," Joe greeted her when Danielle answered the door.

"Morning, Joe, what can I do for you?"

"Can I come in for a moment? I need to talk to you about Jimmy Borge."

"Sure, we can go in the parlor." Danielle opened the door wider and stepped aside for Joe to enter. Once in the parlor Danielle took a seat on the sofa while Joe sat across from her in a chair.

"Borge is cutting a deal with the DA, so you're not going to have to testify."

"Are you saying he's going to get off?"

"No. It looks like he'll be going away for a while."

"Good."

"So how's Lily doing?" Joe asked.

"I haven't talked to her this morning. Her parents left about an hour ago. They were going to stop for some breakfast, but they should be at the hospital about now." Danielle stood up suddenly and touched her back pocket. "Would you mind if I run upstairs real quick and get my phone? I left it up there, and Mrs. Miller just has my cell number."

"Sure, no problem."

Danielle flashed Joe a smile and dashed from the room.

"You and Joe seem rather friendly," Walt said as he followed Danielle up the stairs.

"He has his moments." Danielle shrugged.

"He's still interested in you. I can tell."

"He thinks I'm crazy, and I'm not interested."

———————

ALONE IN THE PARLOR, Joe stood up and stretched. Resting his hands on his hips, he looked around the room, surveying the walls. Walking toward the window, he noticed several new framed photographs sitting on a curio shelf. He picked up one of the pictures and looked closer. It was of Lily and Ian at the beach with Sadie.

While setting the picture down, an antique teapot on a higher shelf caught his eye. It reminded him of a teapot his grandmother owned. Reaching up, he picked it up off the shelf. When he did, something inside the pot rattled around. Curious, Joe looked inside. He couldn't see what it was, so he reached his hand inside the small opening and pulled out a gold and sapphire bracelet. Holding it in his hand, it took him a moment to realize what he was looking at. If he wasn't mistaken, it was Isabella Strickland's missing bracelet. If it wasn't hers, then it was one just like it. But how could that be possible? The bracelet was supposedly one of a kind.

Joe heard Danielle coming down the stairs. He quickly shoved the bracelet back inside the teapot and returned the pot to its shelf. He was still standing by the shelf when Danielle walked back into the room.

"This is a great picture of Lily and Ian," Joe said, turning to Danielle.

"Yeah, I love that picture." Danielle walked to Joe and looked at the framed photograph.

"I noticed that teapot up there." Joe pointed to the top shelf. "My grandmother had one just like it."

"Lily picked that up at a yard sale," Danielle explained.

"Can I look at it?" Joe asked.

"Sure." Danielle shrugged.

Joe reached up to the shelf and brought the teapot back down. As he did, the bracelet slid from one side of the pot to the other.

"Seems to be something inside," Joe said.

"There shouldn't be," Danielle said. In reply, Joe handed Danielle the pot. Curious, she tucked her hand inside and pulled out the bracelet. "What the heck?" Danielle stared at the gold and sapphire bracelet in her hand.

"I thought women kept their bracelets in a jewelry box."

"This isn't mine." Danielle shook her head. "I've never seen it before."

Joe studied Danielle's face. She continued to stare at the gold and sapphire bracelet. Finally, Joe said, "I have."

"What do you mean?" Danielle looked up at Joe.

He reached over and took the bracelet from her, holding it in his open palm. "Susan Mitchell showed me a photograph of a bracelet and necklace set Isabella Strickland commissioned. Supposedly, she designed it herself, see the little dragon clasp?"

Danielle picked up the bracelet and looked closer. "It looks sorta like the dragon in the tattoo."

"We found the necklace on her body. We didn't know what happened to the bracelet."

"How did it get here?" Danielle asked.

"That's what I was wondering."

Something about Joe's tone gave Danielle pause. She looked up into his face and noticed the intense way he studied her.

"Did you put the bracelet in the teapot?" Danielle asked, dumping it back in his hand.

Her question shocked Joe. "Of course not!"

Danielle stared at Joe. "You knew it was there, didn't you? You looked when I was upstairs."

"Do you have any idea how it got in the teapot?"

"No. I told you I've never seen it before," Danielle said angrily. "What, were you looking at the teapot, found the bracelet and put it back because you knew you needed permission from me to search my property?"

"Danielle, I believe you. I can tell you didn't know it was there."

"But you were testing me, weren't you?"

"You have to understand how this looked."

"Joe, just go. And take the bracelet. I have no idea how it got there. I'm not in the habit of stealing jewelry. I have a million-dollar necklace sitting in my safety deposit box at the bank that I'd love to sell. Not because I need the money, because it's just too much of a pain in the butt."

"We need to figure out how this bracelet got into the teapot. Who's had access to this room?"

"People come and go all the time. Can you give me a time frame?"

"When did you put the teapot on the shelf?"

"I don't know, before Lily went back to California, I guess."

"Is it possible the bracelet was in the teapot when Lily bought it at the yard sale?"

"No. It was empty."

"How can you be so sure?"

"Because I washed it before I put it up. You don't think I'd stick it up there without washing it?"

"Can I take the teapot with me?"

"Why?"

"There might be some fingerprints on it."

"Yeah, like yours and mine," Danielle grumbled. "Go ahead."

Joe looked at the teapot, trying to decide how best to pick it up without compromising the evidence any more than he already had. Danielle let out a sigh and told him she'd be right back. She returned in a few minutes and handed him a large plastic bag.

Walt was in the library when he heard voices from the foyer. Going to the doorway, he looked down the hall and saw Danielle opening the front door for Joe, who was carrying something in a plastic bag.

"Was that your teapot Joe was taking?" Walt asked after Joe left.

"You're never going to believe this," Danielle said. "Joe found a bracelet belonging to Isabella Strickland in my teapot."

"How would something like that get there?"

"I have no idea. You're here all the time, any suggestions?" Danielle asked.

"I've never seen anyone so much as look at that teapot. Do you think Joe planted it?"

Danielle laughed. "That's what I asked him. But no, I can't see him doing that. Although, I'm a little annoyed about how he handled it."

"What do you mean?"

"When I went upstairs to get my phone, he must have picked up the teapot to look at it and found the bracelet. Apparently, he recognized it. But he couldn't just tell me he found it. I assume the bracelet would be inadmissible in court had he found it while snooping around on his own. Improper search."

"But you let him take it?"

"I didn't really have a choice. And I certainly didn't want to make a scene. It's strange enough the bracelet was in this house. I'm surprised our treasure hunters didn't find it."

"They were more interested in loose floorboards and old books with secret compartments," Walt said.

"The only thing I can think of, someone planted it here to make it look like I'm someway involved with Isabella's murder. I am the one who found her body, and if she was wearing its matching necklace when she was killed, it's possible the killers took the bracelet."

"Danielle, if someone broke into this house, I'm sure I would have seen them."

"Then we need to remember who's been in this parlor over the last few weeks."

"The only ones I can think of recently are our treasure hunters."

"No, it has to be someone else. I can't believe they'd leave the bracelet."

"But they did mention an Isabella. Perhaps it was Isabella Strickland they were talking about all along."

THIRTY-ONE

D anielle called Sadie to the kitchen. She wanted to let her out one more time before putting her back in the house with Walt. Then she planned to go to the hospital and see Lily. Sadie raced through the house into the kitchen and out the back door. Danielle followed her outside. She had locked the back gate, which was why she was surprised to find a woman walking toward her, down her back drive. How the woman got through the gate, Danielle had no idea, because from where she stood, she could see the padlock hanging in the latch, still locked.

Sadie had run off to the trees by the back fence and was now busy investigating possible new smells.

"Can I help you?" Danielle asked as she walked toward the thirtysomething woman. The stranger wore faded baggie denim overalls and a tie-dyed tank top.

"I'm looking for Hunter and Claire. They're supposed to be here," the woman said.

Danielle stopped in her tracks and eyed the woman suspiciously. "Are you talking about the Stewarts?"

"Is that what they're calling themselves now?"

"They're not here," Danielle said. "They left last night."

"I was supposed to meet them here." The woman sounded disappointed. "Do you know where they went?"

"You were meeting them? I understood they were on their

honeymoon."

"Is that what they told you?" The woman began to laugh.

Just as she started to laugh, Sadie raced over from the back fence, charging headlong in the woman's direction. By the way she was running, Danielle was sure the dog was going to plow the woman down.

"Sadie, stay!" Danielle blurted out. Instead of stopping, Sadie flew through the woman's body—in the same way she had done with Walt countless times—and then in the next second the woman disappeared. Danielle's eyes widened as she stared at the spot where the woman in overalls had been standing just moments before. Sadie quickly circled back and began sniffing the ground.

"Walt!" Danielle shouted as she ran back into the house, Sadie on her heels.

Walt appeared in the kitchen. "What's with all the shouting?"

"I saw another spirit in the backyard."

"Spirit as in ghost?"

"I thought you hated that word."

"Only when applied to me. So who was it? Isabella Strickland? Whatever you say, don't tell me Angela figured out how to get here."

"Not Isabella or Angela. I've never seen this one before. But she asked for Hunter and Claire."

"Claire called Hank Hunter sometimes," Walt said.

"I remember you telling me. When the woman first started talking to me, I thought she was alive. It wasn't until Sadie decided to charge through her that I figured it out. But then she disappeared."

"Did she say what she wanted?"

"Only that she was looking for Hunter and Claire, that she was supposed to meet them here. And if I can believe her, I think you were right. Their name wasn't Stewart and they weren't newlyweds."

"I suppose if she comes back, you can ask her about them."

"I'd rather she not come back. I didn't get a good vibe." Danielle glanced at the clock on the wall. "I better get going. I told Lily I'd be there before lunch."

Five minutes later, after Danielle had opened the back gate and was preparing to back down the drive, her cellphone began to ring. She picked it up off the console and looked at the caller ID. It was coming from the Frederickport Police Station.

"What now?" Danielle grumbled as she put her car in park and answered the call.

"Ms. Boatman, this is Chief MacDonald. I was hoping you could stop in at the station. It's important."

"Now? I was on the way to the hospital to see Lily."

"I'd really appreciate it if you'd stop here first. But if you want me to come there, I suppose I can do that."

"No," Danielle said with a sigh. "I'll be there in five minutes."

After disconnecting the call, Danielle immediately called the hospital and asked for Lily's room.

"Hello?" came Lily's voice.

"Hi. This is Dani."

"You on your way over?"

"I was. But I just got a call from Chief MacDonald. He needs me to stop by the station first."

"Now?"

"Apparently it's important, because he told me if I didn't go there, he'd come to me. And if I'm at the hospital, I don't really feel like talking to him with your parents there."

"What do you think he wants?"

"I have a hunch, but I'll explain later. It's too involved."

"Okay. Hey, Ian called this morning. He's so sweet."

"When is he coming back?"

"Not right away. He's still getting over whatever crud he has, and he doesn't want to get me sick, especially with my current condition. But he said it Dani. He told me."

"Told you what?"

"He loves me!" Lily burst out.

Danielle smiled. "Yeah, I know. Did you tell your parents yet about you staying here?"

"Yes. Funny thing, they took it a lot better than I thought they would."

"Are they there now?"

"No. They went down to get some coffee."

"So they're okay with it?"

"I think Mom was a little relieved. That whole IV thing sorta freaked her out. But Dad insisted he wants to pay for the nurse."

"No. Please, he doesn't need to. I want to do this, honest, Lily."

"We can work out the details later. When do you think you'll be able to come to the hospital?"

"As soon as I'm done at the police station."

"See you later."

"Love you, Lily."

"Love you too, Dani."

Danielle drove directly to the police station. Upon arrival, the receptionist showed her to an office where the chief waited. Sitting behind the desk, the chief stood up and motioned for Danielle to take one of the two empty chairs facing his desk. He then told the receptionist she could leave and asked her to close the door on her way out.

"I appreciate you coming in," the chief said as he sat back down behind his desk.

"What is this all about?" Danielle asked nervously, glancing at the clock on the wall.

"Stoddard Gusarov insists you are in some way involved in his niece's death."

"He what?" Danielle sat up straighter in the chair. This wasn't what she expected to hear. "I didn't even know the woman."

"He didn't come up with a motive, aside from implying there might be something between Isabella's old boyfriend and you."

"Are you talking about Adam Nichols?" Danielle couldn't help but laugh.

"You did call Adam to pick you up after we brought you in the other day."

"I'm good friends with his grandmother. Hell, Gusarov's the one who was holding Lily prisoner!"

"He claims he sincerely thought Lily was his niece and insists that even Joe made the same mistake."

"Stoddard had Lily tattooed so people would think she was Isabella. Ian talked to the authorities in Southern California—she didn't have a tattoo when they found her on Labor Day."

"Yes, I know about that. But Stoddard insists they simply don't remember the tattoo. As far as he's concerned, all it means is that they failed to notice it. No one wrote down in the reports that she didn't have one."

"He's just trying to throw suspicion off himself."

"Stoddard says you put Isabella's body in the crypt—insisting that not only were you caught with the body, you also had Isabella's missing bracelet in your possession. According to her friend at the bank, Isabella told her she intended to never take it off. She was wearing the necklace when she was found, but the bracelet was at your house."

"Why would I..." Danielle paused a moment. "How did he know Joe found the bracelet at my house this morning?"

"Stoddard was here this morning. I showed him the bracelet."

"You did?" Danielle frowned. "But why would I keep the bracelet? I certainly can afford to buy my own jewelry."

"Stoddard believes you kept it as a souvenir."

"So now I am some thrill killer?"

"He believes after you killed Isabella and put her in the crypt, you took her car with you to California. For some reason Lily was driving it when she got attacked at the rest stop."

"So now Lily is involved?" Danielle snapped.

"Apparently, since she went out of her way to get a tattoo to match Isabella's."

"This is ridiculous!" Danielle fumed. "Do I need to get a lawyer?"

"I wouldn't get one quite yet." The chief smiled and leaned back in his seat.

"What is it you find so amusing?"

"I agree with you. Stoddard's version is a bit—farfetched. And yet, I am left to wonder how it is you happened to stumble across both Lily and Isabella, and how that bracelet came to be at Marlow House."

"But you don't think I killed Isabella?"

"No."

"So you believe me?"

"Not necessarily."

"Then why don't you think I killed her?"

"Because I know something Stoddard hasn't been told yet."

"What's that?" Danielle asked warily.

"Isabella's autopsy is back. She died of natural causes. She wasn't murdered. Plus we found fingerprints inside the crypt—they belong to two employees of Stoddard's."

"What are you going to do?"

"They're bringing in Stoddard right now. As soon as he gets here, I'm going to see what he has to say. I suspect they may have planted that bracelet at Marlow House, but we weren't able to get any usable prints off the teapot."

"I don't see how they could have planted the bracelet," Danielle blurted out without thinking.

"Are you saying you know how it got there?"

"No. I just mean there hasn't been any sign of a break-in at Marlow House. And Sadie's usually there when I'm gone." Not to mention Walt.

"But maybe that's how the dog happened to get out—perhaps whoever broke in to put the bracelet in your house inadvertently let Sadie out. If someone knows what they're doing, they can open a lock without you ever knowing."

"Perhaps," Danielle murmured, feeling foolish for arguing with the chief over a point that could cast doubt on her. "I suppose I can understand why he did it."

"Why is that?" He leaned forward, resting his elbows on his desk.

"According to Marie and Adam, Isabella left everything to Earthbound Spirits. That included half of the family business she owned with her uncle. It really was not in his best interest, financially, for her to die. So if he happened to find her dead, he might have decided to keep her alive by hiding the body somewhere no one would look. She had a history of just taking off. Maybe he was trying to buy some time to figure out how to have her will changed. And in the meantime, he could continue to run the business as he saw fit. According to Adam, they had a written agreement giving Stoddard full control of the business, and she pretty much stayed out of it. But she had the power to rescind that agreement at any time."

"And if he instructed his people to hide the body, then he knew your friend Lily was not his niece."

"Exactly."

"There are still a lot of unanswered questions. Hopefully, I'll get some of them answered after Stoddard arrives. In the meantime, I'd appreciate it if you'd keep this conversation between us."

Danielle stood up. "Can you tell me one thing, Chief?"

"I'll try." He stood up.

"Why are you telling me any of this?"

"Honestly?" the chief asked.

"Please," Danielle said.

"I have my own gut feeling about you, Danielle Boatman."

"I don't understand." Danielle frowned.

"Let's just leave it at that," he said with a smile.

THIRTY-TWO

B rian Henderson was bringing Stoddard Gusarov into the police station when Danielle exited the chief's office.

"Are you arresting her?" Stoddard called out when he saw Danielle walking down the hall in his direction. Danielle froze in her tracks, staring at the man who'd implicated her in a murder. The police chief, who'd been walking beside Danielle, stepped in front of her, blocking Stoddard from coming closer. In his hand, he carried a manila folder.

"Not today, Stoddard," the chief said, redirecting Isabella's uncle down another corridor and into the interrogation room, leaving both Danielle and Brian standing alone in the hall.

"Afternoon, Ms. Boatman," Brian said, sounding less hostile than normal.

"Officer Henderson," Danielle greeted him with a nod. Just as she was about to turn toward the exit door, a woman appeared next to Brian. It was Isabella Strickland. Danielle's eyes widened in surprise.

"Are you all right?" Brian asked when he noticed Danielle's sudden change in expression.

"Hello again," Isabella cheerfully greeted. "I'd stay and talk, but I really would like to see what Uncle Stoddard has to say."

"Umm...just a little exhausted with all that's been going on,"

Danielle mumbled as she watched Isabella disappear down the hall and go into the interrogation room.

———

"I DON'T KNOW why you dragged me down here again. Twice in one day and it isn't even noon yet," Stoddard grumbled as he sat down at the table.

"I thought you'd like to know how your niece died. We got the autopsy report back." The chief took a seat at the table, facing Stoddard. He set the folder on the table.

"How did she die?"

"Isabella died of natural causes. She had a brain aneurysm."

"So that's what happened," Isabella murmured from her place in the corner of the room.

Stoddard sat quietly for a few moments. Finally, he said, "Then Boatman must have put her in that crypt for the necklace."

"Stoddard, do you realize how outrageous that sounds?"

"Truth is stranger than fiction. I'm always hearing that."

"The problem is we didn't find Boatman's fingerprints in the crypt. But we did find some prints that had no business being there, considering that the last time that crypt was opened—before Isabella's body was put there—was almost a century ago."

"Whose fingerprints?" Stoddard looked up warily.

"I believe you know the owners. They both work for you."

"Even if they do, I didn't have anything to do with it."

"And there is the little matter of Isabella's dragon tattoo."

"I told you that woman had the same tattoo. They were trying to pull something, Boatman and her friend. They put Isabella in the vault and stole her car. Miller was trying to assume Isabella's identity, and it almost worked."

The chief let out a sigh and opened the manila folder. From it he removed a photograph of a man and slid it across the table to Stoddard. "Do you recognize this man?"

Stoddard briefly looked at the picture and pushed it away. "No. I've never seen him before."

"Interesting. He seems to know you. He's the tattoo artist responsible for Isabella's tattoo. And he admitted he's the one who tattooed Lily."

"So. What does that have to do with me?" Stoddard moved restlessly in his seat.

"Considering he's from Washington, you probably didn't expect we'd be able to track him down. But as it turns out, Adam Nichols remembered the name of Isabella's tattoo artist. And when we checked into the man's bank account, we noticed a substantial deposit made just a couple days ago. I'd say it was for a little more than just a tattoo. I'm surprised you'd use a business check. You didn't do a very good job at covering your tracks."

"He put my tattoo on that poor woman?" Isabella gasped. "I knew he could be a little hinky, but that is totally unethical!"

Stoddard started shaking his head in denial, yet before the chief could give him the men's names, he cried out, "I didn't want anyone to get hurt!" Folding his arms on the table, he laid down his head and began to weep. After a few moments, he lifted his head and looked at the chief.

"Stoddard Gusarov, you have the right to remain silent. Anything you say can and will be used against you in a court of law. You have a right to an attorney. If you cannot afford an attorney, one will be appointed for you. Do you understand the rights I have just read to you?"

"Yes. But I don't need to call my attorney. It's not like I had anything to do with Isabella's death."

"What happened, Stoddard?"

After Stoddard regained his composure, he began to talk. "I went to Isabella's house. I needed to talk to her about the company taxes, and she kept brushing me off, like she always did. So I had to go to her. When she didn't answer the door, I just went in. It wasn't locked. I found her on the couch; the TV was on. At first, I thought she was asleep. But she was dead."

"Why didn't you just call us?"

"She was never involved with the business—never wanted any responsibility. She just wanted her dividend checks and was perfectly happy with me doing everything, keeping the business running. But she was going to leave her half to that cult. She wasn't even apologetic about it. Kept saying she had the right to leave her money to whoever she wanted."

"It was my money, Uncle Stoddard. Don't act like you didn't get financially compensated. And admit it; you never wanted me involved in the business. I tried at first, but you made it so unpleasant I just gave up."

"Did you really think no one would ever wonder where she was?"

"She was already dead. It wasn't like I could help her. I just needed time to figure out what to do. I tried to think of the one place I could put her where no one would ever find her body. I figured no one was ever going to open that crypt again."

"What happened to her car?"

"I left it at the beach, with the door unlocked and the keys in the ignition. I left her purse in the car. I figured someone would steal it and take it out of town. And if they started using her credit cards, even better. If any of her friends started to wonder where she was and they came to you, you'd see activity on her cards and assume she was doing what she always did—taking off without thinking of anyone else."

"So that's how my car got to the beach!" Isabella said as she walked closer to Stoddard. "I was so confused. I found myself at the cemetery. I didn't know how I got there. I started looking for my car and somehow ended up at the beach."

"What if we found the car first? Or if someone started looking for her before it was taken?"

"I figured it would look like foul play, but without a body she really couldn't be ruled dead, at least not right away."

"Why did you identify Lily Miller as Isabella?"

"At the time, it just seemed like the answer. When the police in California called me, telling me they found a car registered to our company, I knew they were talking about Isabella's car. Her purse was still in it, with her driver's license. By the photo, they were pretty sure Miller was Isabella, but they wanted to see if I could identify her. They told me her condition; she was in a coma. And when they showed me her picture—I just said yes, it was her. I didn't even think it through at the time. In some way I felt it was fate."

"It wasn't fate," Isabella said angrily. "Those fools who took my car—the one you left for them—almost killed that poor woman!"

"When did you decide to have her tattooed?"

"At the hospital, I realized if anyone visited, they would know immediately it wasn't Isabella just by the arm. That's when I decided to move her home and have private medical care. I contacted Isabella's tattoo artist, and he seemed more than willing to provide his service, no questions asked, for the right amount of money."

"Once we started questioning him, he folded fairly quickly."

"That doesn't surprise me," Isabella scoffed.

"In my defense I made sure she had the best medical care."

"She wouldn't have needed medical care if you hadn't left my car at the beach with the keys in it! Then those people would never have stolen it, and they wouldn't have broken down at that rest stop! If it wasn't for your actions, that woman would never have been attacked!"

"What did you intend to do if she suddenly woke up?"

"I had already made arrangements to move her to a private hospital in Canada. If she eventually woke up, I would have dealt with it." Stoddard stared at his hands, his fingers fidgeting.

"Dealt with it?"

"I wouldn't have hurt her. I figured I could pay her off. She could go home, and no one would have to know where she'd been. After all, I paid for her medical care and it's not like I'm the one who hurt her."

"You tattooed her arm."

"I intended to compensate her for any…well….any perceived pain and suffering."

"You think money will take care of everything, don't you, Uncle Stoddard."

"Did you put Isabella's bracelet in Marlow House?"

"No!" Stoddard said emphatically, looking up into the chief's eyes. "I never saw Isabella's bracelet. She wasn't wearing it. I had nothing to do with putting it in Boatman's house." Stoddard took a deep breath then said, "I think I should probably call my attorney."

"I don't know how much that attorney is going to help you now, Uncle Stoddard." Isabella moved toward the door. "And to think it was all for nothing. If you had just looked in the files at your house, you'd see I changed my will. I put a copy in your filing cabinet six months ago. But obviously, you haven't found it yet. I assumed you'd find it before I died, but I never expected to die so young and suddenly. Perhaps part of this is my fault, since I led you to believe I was still leaving my money to Earthbound Spirits."

THIRTY-THREE

D anielle didn't see the woman when she pulled into the parking lot at the hospital. She let out a scream and slammed on her brakes, but she wasn't quick enough. Her car plowed into the pedestrian before screeching to a stop. There was no thud—no sound or bump from impact. The woman wasn't sprawled unconscious or dead in the parking lot; she stood before Danielle, her body disappearing through the hood of the car. She continued to stand on the pavement where the front part of the car had stopped. It was the woman in overalls—the one who had been looking for Claire and Hunter at Marlow House.

Danielle's heart raced as she stared at the ghost. In the next instant, the woman disappeared. Danielle heard a honk. Glancing up in the rearview mirror, she saw a car behind her, waiting for her to move. Taking a deep breath, she finished parking her car.

When Danielle got to Lily's hospital room, the Millers were just preparing to leave.

"You girls have a nice visit," Mrs. Miller said as she patted Danielle's arm on her way out of the room.

"Where are you going?" Danielle asked.

"To get something to eat," Mr. Miller explained before giving his daughter a quick kiss on the cheek.

"How did it go at the police station?" Lily asked after her parents left. "You look a little rattled."

"In the parking lot, I thought I hit someone. But then I realized..." Danielle stopped talking, her attention drawn to a shadow in the corner of the room. In the next instant, the shadow transformed. It was the woman from the parking lot—the one wearing overalls. The ghost walked toward the bed, her attention focused on Lily.

"What's wrong?" Lily asked. "You look like you just saw a ghost."

"I think I'm seeing one," Danielle muttered, her gaze still locked on the mystery woman.

"Where?" Lily sat up in her bed, looking around frantically.

"She's alive," the woman said in awe, now standing over Lily. "I thought I killed her. I hit her hard. I could hear her skull crack," the woman said with no emotion.

Danielle swallowed nervously.

"Where is it?" Lily asked again.

"Who are you?" Danielle asked.

Lily's eyes widened, noting whoever Danielle was talking to was obviously standing close to the bed. Grabbing the top of her blanket, she pulled the covering up past her chin as she slid down in the bed. Anxiously, she looked from Danielle to the space where she imagined the ghost stood.

"You can see me. No one else can except for that woman at the gas station." She glanced down at Lily. "Your friend can't see me, can she?"

"What do you want?" Danielle asked.

"I want to go home," the woman said sadly. "But I can't. They tell me I must move on, but that place scares me."

"Follow the light," Danielle suggested. She was tempted to ask the woman what she meant when she had said she thought she killed Lily, yet Danielle kept quiet, worried it would frighten her bedridden friend.

"No one knows I'm dead," the woman said, looking from Lily to Danielle. "But I am dead, aren't I?"

"Yes, you are," Danielle said quietly.

"Everyone thought it was your friend in that car, but it wasn't, it was me. If I had switched the license plates like I was supposed to, maybe they would have realized it wasn't her."

"You need to follow the light," Danielle said again.

"But there is no light for me…just darkness. I don't like the sound."

"The sound?" Danielle asked.

"Screams. The painful screams. They're waiting for me, but I don't want to go." The woman vanished.

"She's gone," Danielle said.

"I never considered it, but this being a hospital, I imagine there are all sorts of spirits wandering around—patients that didn't make it."

"I suppose," Danielle murmured, glancing around the room, looking for any signs of the woman. After she was confident it was just herself and Lily in the room, she sat down on a chair.

"What did the ghost say?" Lily sat up in the bed.

"She was confused. Asked me if she was dead. Mentioned I was the only one who could see her. She seems to be gone now." Danielle forced a smile. "So how are you feeling?"

"I'm okay. The physical therapist was here for a few minutes this morning. Tell me what happened at the police station."

"The chief wanted to see me. Apparently, Isabella's uncle is trying to convince the chief I killed Isabella and put her in that crypt. And that you were trying to impersonate her."

"What?" Lily sat up even straighter. "That jerk! Do the police actually buy that bull?"

"No. The autopsy came in on Isabella; she died of natural causes. So I obviously didn't murder her. Plus my fingerprints weren't anywhere inside the crypt, but they found fingerprints belonging to a couple of Gusarov's employees. But the chief doesn't want me to say anything about it right now. I suppose I shouldn't be telling you, but I think you have a right to know. Don't mention anything to your folks yet. I'd rather stay in the chief's good graces."

"That Gusarov guy is a real piece of work." Lily shook her head in disgust.

"There is something else."

"What?"

"Joe stopped by this morning to tell me the guy who tried to steal Sadie was making a plea deal, so I probably wouldn't be called to testify. While he was there, he found a gold and sapphire bracelet hidden in that teapot you picked up at the swap meet."

"First of all, why was he looking in your teapot? And whose bracelet was it?"

"It belonged to Isabella Strickland. She had it custom made. It matched the necklace she had on when we found her. Has a dragon clasp that matches her tattoo."

"Oh please, don't get me started on dragon tattoos!" Lily looked down at her tattooed arm and frowned. "How did it get in the teapot?"

"The chief seems to think Isabella's uncle had someone plant it in Marlow House to implicate me."

"Is that possible?"

"I don't see how. Walt swears no one's been in the parlor recently—aside from the Stewarts."

"Is there some connection between the Stewarts and Isabella?" Lily asked.

"I'm beginning to wonder." Danielle leaned back in her chair, folding her arms over her chest.

"How so?"

"If you'll remember, they mentioned an Isabella when talking about the diamonds supposedly hidden at Marlow House." *And the woman in the overalls asked about them and then claimed to have killed you—or at least she thought she had until she saw you were still alive.*

"That creep makes me so angry," Lily fumed.

"You talking about Isabella's uncle?"

"Yes. It's like I've been violated. It's not just that tattoo—which makes me furious—but everything about it. He cut my hair. Arrogantly made decisions regarding my body. I could have lost my leg due to the neglect of his so-called private medical staff. I swear, I'm angrier today than I was yesterday."

"Maybe you need to talk to someone about it," Danielle suggested.

"You mean a lawyer?"

"No, although I imagine it would be a good idea to get an attorney."

"So like what, a shrink?"

"You've been through a lot, Lily. I think it might help if you talk to someone."

"Yeah, my mother sort of suggested that too." Lily slumped back on her pillows and let out a weary sigh.

"Knock, knock," a man called out from the doorway.

Danielle turned around in her seat to face the man attached to the voice.

"Hello, Joe," Lily greeted him before Danielle could comment.

Joe Morelli, dressed in his police uniform, stood in the open doorway, holding a vase of flowers. "Can I come in?"

"Sure. Are those for me?" Lily beamed.

Joe stepped into the room. "Yes. Wow, you look great." He turned to Danielle and smiled. "Hello, Danielle."

"Hi, Joe, those look pretty," Danielle greeted him, looking at the flowers.

"Where would you like me to put them?"

"Can I smell them first? Then you can set them on the dresser."

Joe grinned at Lily's request. He walked to the bed and handed her the flowers. Closing her eyes, she took a deep breath. Smiling, she opened her eyes and handed the flowers back to Joe.

"They're beautiful, thanks."

"Glad to see you're looking so good," Joe said as he set the vase on the dresser.

"Now I feel guilty. I didn't bring flowers." Danielle was only half teasing.

"You did something better," Joe said. "You rescued your friend."

"Yes, she did." Lily grinned.

"I wanted to come over here to give you a heads-up," Joe began. "Don't be surprised if the Gusarovs' attorney shows up and offers you a settlement."

"What's going on?" Lily asked. "I understood he was trying to implicate Danielle and me—he's the innocent victim." She glanced at her tattooed arm and frowned.

"Stoddard has been arrested. But I imagine he'll be out on bail by tomorrow, if not sooner."

"On what charges?" Danielle asked.

"Kidnapping, assault, to name a few."

"I'm glad to hear it," Lily said.

"Which is why I wouldn't be surprised if he tries to pay you off, hoping you'll be willing to persuade the court to drop some of the charges. He's probably anticipating a lawsuit, and if he settles now, he might be thinking he can buy your silence at the same time."

"He'll be paying for what he did to me all right," Lily said angrily. "I intend to sue his butt for maiming my arm, cutting my hair, and kidnapping me. But I also want to see him go to jail."

"I suggest you speak to your lawyer before you agree to anything his attorney offers. And if you're serious about wanting him to see jail time, you don't want to do anything that might weaken our case against him."

"I don't want that either. I'm furious about what he did to me, but I'm also pissed about how he tried to implicate Dani."

"Has anyone made funeral arrangements for Isabella?" Danielle asked.

"Yes. The services will be at the local cemetery chapel, day after tomorrow. I believe it's at ten in the morning. But I could be wrong about the time," Joe said.

"I'd like to go to the service," Danielle said.

"Who's planning it? Surely not her uncle," Lily asked.

"From what I understand, someone from their company is handling the arrangements."

"I guess this means Earthbound Spirits will be taking over half of the company," Danielle said.

"From what I understand, they don't have a copy of her will yet," Joe explained.

"Well, that's convenient," Lily said.

"Wouldn't her attorney have a copy?" Danielle asked.

"Yes, but her attorney was Clarence Renton."

"Wonder if Clarence and Stoddard are going to be cell mates." Lily snickered.

"Surely Gloria Comings would have access to his files," Danielle said.

"Gloria left Frederickport not long after Renton was sentenced. I thought you knew," Joe said.

"I forgot about that. But someone must have access to his files."

"I suppose someone does. I just know they haven't located a copy of her will yet."

After Joe left twenty minutes later, Lily said, "You know, Joe can be a nice guy."

Danielle shrugged. "I never said he wasn't. It's his partner I can't stand."

"That was sweet of him to bring me flowers."

"It was." Danielle glanced up to the flowers and then back at Lily. "You haven't asked me how Walt's doing."

"I talked to him last night."

"Last night?" Danielle arched her brows.

"He visited me in my dream." Lily grinned.

THIRTY-FOUR

It was Wednesday morning, the day of Isabella Strickland's funeral. Lily had been at the hospital for four nights and was improving daily. According to the doctors, she was tentatively scheduled for release on Monday.

Danielle sat at the kitchen table at Marlow House, reading the morning paper and waiting for the pot of coffee to brew. Sadie lay on the floor, curled up by Danielle's feet.

Walt appeared by the table. "Good morning."

Danielle and Sadie looked up. "Morning, Walt. Interesting article in the paper about Stoddard Gusarov."

Walt looked down at Sadie, who wagged her tail at him. "I thought I heard Ian arrive. Figured he'd take Sadie with him." Walt sat down at the table. "Not that I'm unhappy to see she's still here."

"Ian just stopped by to let me know he got into town this morning. He's on his way to the hospital to see Lily. I told him he could just leave her here since I won't be taking off for a couple hours. I gave him a key to the house, so he'll be stopping by to pick her up after I leave for the funeral."

"Lily's parents are gone?"

"They left a few minutes before Ian arrived. Where were you? I'm surprised you didn't hear them. Mrs. Miller isn't exactly quiet." Danielle set the paper on the table.

"I returned about the time Ian was leaving. I heard his voice, but when I came downstairs he was gone."

Danielle arched her brows, looking at Walt curiously. "Returned? Returned from where? Since when have you been able to leave Marlow House?"

"A little dream hopping."

"Ah, visiting Lily?" Danielle grinned.

"Yes. Our visit was interrupted when a nurse woke her up. Which was a shame because we were just getting ready to go skydiving."

"Skydiving?"

"Lily's getting a little antsy. I thought an outing would be good for both of us."

"Wow, skydiving?" Danielle muttered. "Aside from being antsy, how is she?"

"Excited to see Ian. Anxious to get out of the hospital. Still furious over the tattoo."

"I don't know what she can do about that. I understand they can remove tattoos, but I've heard that can be more painful than getting one, and her arm still won't look like it did."

"Do women today really have as many tattoos as I see on television?" Walt asked.

"It's pretty common these days." Danielle shrugged.

"Why don't you have one?"

"How do you know I don't?" Danielle teased.

Walt replied with a knowing grin.

"Hey! You promised never to go into my bathroom!" *The only place I ever undress in this house.*

"That was before you set the ground rules. And you weren't in the bathroom."

"Yeah, well, that was obviously before I considered I might have an audience if I undressed in my own bedroom."

"You keep forgetting it is also my bedroom," Walt smirked.

"Used to be your room."

"You never answered my question. Why no tattoo?"

"I don't care for pain. Or putting anything that permanent on my body."

When Danielle started to get up to get a cup of coffee, Walt told her to sit back down and went to pour her a cup.

"What's so interesting?" Walt asked when he returned to the table with Danielle's coffee.

"It's the article about Isabella's uncle. Guess I don't have to keep mum about all the stuff the chief told me; it's all in here. Plus some stuff I didn't know."

"Like what?" Walt asked.

"They have the tattoo artist Stoddard hired. The guy totally gave it up, admitted to taking a hefty bribe from Isabella's uncle to tattoo an unconscious woman. In exchange for the money he had to duplicate Isabella's tat, no questions asked. Apparently he held up his side of the bargain right up until the cops knocked on his door."

"Do you think Gusarov's attorney will be able to discredit him?"

"Doesn't look like it. Gusarov paid with a check, even signed it himself."

"Gusarov doesn't sound like a criminal mastermind."

"I don't know about that." Danielle closed the paper and set it back on the table. She looked at Walt. "If it hadn't been for my—gift—then he could have gotten away with it. Even if I had someway stumbled into the estate and found Lily, without finding Isabella's body, Lily would now be out of the country, and Gusarov could have very well gotten away with it. After all, when Joe saw Lily the first time, he insisted it was Isabella."

DANIELLE LEFT for the cemetery at 9:30 a.m., hoping to see Isabella. Cheryl hadn't hung around for her funeral. She had moved on weeks before her service, which was one reason why Danielle knew spirits didn't necessarily stick around to witness their send-off. She hoped Isabella was still lingering. There were still a few questions she wanted to ask her.

While Danielle had always been uncomfortable at cemeteries, the few times she had visited the Frederickport Cemetery, she hadn't been overwhelmed with spirits. The only two she had encountered there were Angela and Isabella. She was hoping today to see just one—Isabella's.

Danielle parked near the chapel. It was on the opposite end of the cemetery from Angela's grave. One perk of parking on this side of the cemetery, she might avoid being drawn into a conversation with Angela. She simply did not want to deal with Walt's wife today.

Before leaving that morning, she had talked to Adam on the phone, who told her where in the cemetery Isabella's family plot was located. It wasn't far from the chapel. Since the services weren't to start for another thirty minutes, she had a little time to visit Isabella's gravesite—and hopefully talk to her.

If anyone had arrived early for the service, they were already in the chapel, because Danielle didn't see anyone meandering in the area. She began walking toward the gravesite.

It was another sunny day in Frederickport. The temperatures had been hovering in the seventies. Danielle wore a lavender dress, which garnered compliments from Walt before she had left Marlow House that morning. She had decided to wear her hair—still holding a curl from the recent braid—free flowing.

Danielle walked by a dozen or more grave markers when she came upon an elderly woman kneeling by a headstone. The sound of Danielle's shoes crunching the gravel along the walkway caught the woman's attention. She turned from the headstone and looked up at Danielle, a friendly smile on her wrinkled face.

"Good morning. Lovely day, isn't it?" the woman said as she stood up and brushed her hands off on the skirt of her pink and white gingham sundress. On her head she wore a floppy white hat, its wide brim shielding her eyes from the sun.

"Yes, it is." Danielle stopped by the woman and glanced down at the headstone.

"My husband..." The woman nodded to the grave. "I like to come down here and tidy up his grave." She then lowered her voice and said, "I'm afraid they just don't keep the place up like they used to."

"I imagine he appreciates that."

"Oh, he does," the woman said with a smile.

Danielle silently read the dates on the headstone. The woman had lost her husband ten years earlier. Danielle wondered how often the elderly woman visited her husband. Since Lucas's funeral, Danielle had not been back to his grave—not even when the marker was set.

"It's what we do for someone we love," the woman said.

Danielle looked back at the marker. This time she noticed the surname: MacDonald.

"That's the police chief's last name. Are you related?" Danielle asked.

The woman broke into a broad smile. "Why yes, dear, he's my grandson. Are you one of his friends?"

"Umm, I don't really know him well, but we've met."

"Are you married, dear?"

"No." Danielle couldn't bring herself to say, *No, I'm a widow.*

"What is wrong with my grandson? A pretty, single girl like you, and he hasn't tried to snatch you up?"

"Isn't your grandson married?" Danielle couldn't help but grin.

"Oh no, dear, he lost his wife a few years ago. Cancer. Such a shame, their two boys and all. They need a mother. Do you like children?"

"Umm…" Danielle blushed. "I don't think I'm your grandson's type."

"Well, he's a foolish boy, then. You're absolutely lovely! And I think you'd make a wonderful mother for those boys."

Danielle started to respond, but something caught her eye. It was Isabella. She was walking in her direction, and then suddenly she flew by—moving in the direction of the chapel.

Crap, I missed her! Danielle silently cursed. "It was nice meeting you, but I should head to the chapel."

"We didn't really meet," the woman reminded her. "You never told me your name."

"I'm Danielle Boatman, ma'am." Danielle wondered what Chief MacDonald might have said about her—the infamous innkeeper who'd recently come into not just one but two sizable inheritances. The news of her arrest for her cousin's murder—even though it had been brief—had made it into the local newspaper.

If the chief's grandmother recognized the name, she made no indication of the fact. Instead, she said, "My name's Katherine MacDonald. You can call me Kathy. Although, when my grandson was little, he'd call me Gamma Kat."

"It was nice to meet you, Kathy." Danielle smiled.

"And I enjoyed meeting you. When you see that grandson of mine, tell him to start paying attention to what's in front of him."

WHEN DANIELLE REACHED THE CHAPEL, people were starting to arrive. She recognized a number of them, including Susan

Mitchell from the bank. She was surprised to see Stoddard and his wife, but figured he must be out on bail.

Standing at the door to the chapel, waiting for the people in front of her to go in, she heard someone behind her say, "Good morning, Ms. Boatman." Danielle turned around. It was the police chief.

"Morning, Chief," Danielle greeted him.

"I'm a little surprised to see you here, considering you'd never met Isabella Strickland."

"I figured with all that's happened, I should at least come and pay my respects."

"I suppose I understand that."

"By the way, I just met your grandmother Katherine, although she tells me you used to call her Gamma Kat," Danielle teased.

"Excuse me?" The chief frowned.

Danielle pointed in the direction of the cemetery. "She was over at your grandfather's grave. Said she was tidying it up; she's not really happy with how they're maintaining the cemetery. I thought it was sweet. Do you know if she visits your grandfather's grave often?"

"Did she say anything else?" the chief asked in a flat voice.

Danielle eyed his odd expression. He seemed uncomfortable. Then it hit her. She suspected his grandmother Katherine had a habit of playing matchmaker, perhaps in the same way Marie did with Adam, often with embarrassing consequences.

"Hey, it's okay," Danielle said, trying to soothe his discomfort.

"What do you mean?" he asked.

"Yeah, she did do the matchmaker thing—if that's why you look so appalled. Don't worry; I understand how grandmas can be sometime. I just love Marie, but she's constantly trying to hook up her grandson. While I don't care if she does it with other women, when she tries to get Adam and me together, it's awkward."

"My grandmother Katherine passed away last year," he said, his expression blank.

"Oh crap," Danielle groaned under her breath.

THIRTY-FIVE

D anielle took a seat on the end of the back row. Sitting alone, she inwardly groaned over her brief conversation outside the chapel with the police chief. After announcing his grandmother had passed away last year, he walked away from Danielle without looking back. She could only imagine what he might be thinking now.

She watched as more people poured into the chapel, filling the seats. Looking across the room, she spied the chief sitting with the receptionist from the police station. He stared at her, his expression unreadable. Embarrassed, Danielle quickly looked away.

Two rows up, she noticed Marie sitting with Adam. The elderly woman gave her a cheery wave and started motioning for her to come up and sit with them. Before Danielle could respond, an elderly man took the empty seat being offered. Marie frowned and gave Danielle a shrug before turning back around to face the front of the chapel. Adam looked to see who his grandmother was waving to and saw Danielle. He smiled and gave her a brief salute before turning back around.

Glancing over the room, Danielle didn't see Joe or Brian and wondered if either of them planned to attend the service. The back row began filling up, yet the two seats closest to Danielle remained empty.

"It looks like a good turnout," came an unexpected voice next to

Danielle. It was Isabella, sitting in the seat next to her. Isabella anxiously looked around the chapel, curious to see who was attending her service.

Placing her hand over her mouth to conceal the movements of her lips, Danielle whispered, "I've been wanting to talk to you."

"Here I am," Isabella said cheerfully. "I see Uncle Stoddard is here with his wretched wife. He wasn't always so bad. He was actually very good to me when I was growing up. But then he kept getting married, and each wife was worse than the previous one."

"Can you meet me after the service somewhere so we can talk?" Danielle whispered, her hand still covering her lips.

"I suppose," Isabella said reluctantly. "I almost didn't come today, but then thought it will probably be the last time I see many of my friends—well, until they join me. I assume they will eventually join me, won't they?" Isabella turned to Danielle as if she might have the answer.

"I think so," Danielle muttered as she faked a cough, her hand now fisted over her mouth.

"I suppose it would look funny if we got into a discussion around all these people." Isabella giggled. "Makes me wonder about a homeless man I used to see wandering the streets in Portland. He'd talk to himself. But maybe he really was talking to someone." Isabella looked over at Danielle. "Perhaps he was like you and could see people like me."

Danielle smiled weakly as she glanced around, looking to see if anyone was watching her. She was too embarrassed to look over the chief's way. Considering what she had told him about his deceased grandmother, the last thing she wanted was for him to witness her talking to herself. She lowered her hands to her lap, sitting up straight in her seat.

"After the service, I'll meet you by the trees over at my gravesite. But I can only stay a few minutes. It's time for me to move on."

Danielle looked at Isabella, meeting her gaze. She smiled and gave her a little nod, then turned her attention to the front of the chapel.

"They're burying me by my mother. She and I weren't close. Truth be told, I barely knew her. I wonder if I'll see her when I move on."

Suddenly Isabella noticed Adam sitting up with his grandmother. "Oh, there's Adam!" Isabella sat up straighter and began to wave, calling, "Adam, hey, it's—" Realizing her blunder, Isabella let out a sigh and sat back in her seat. "Well, that was stupid. I keep forgetting they can't see or hear me."

Isabella continued to watch Adam. "I dated Adam for about a year. My uncle loathed him. I believe the feeling was mutual. Uncle Stoddard was convinced Adam was only with me for my money. What he didn't know, if Adam wanted me for my money, he certainly wasn't prepared to marry for it. That's why we broke up. I swear, if that boy so much as heard wedding bells, he broke out into hives." Isabella let out a long sigh and added, "But he could sure be a lot of fun."

The chapel grew quiet as the minister approached the pulpit and faced the mourners. After welcoming the group to celebrate the life of Isabella Gusarov Strickland, he started to tell her story. Overhead a slide show presentation began to play, showing still shots of Isabella, beginning when she was just a small child.

"I don't know why they're having him do my eulogy," Isabella said as the minister continued to talk. "I think he's Uncle Stoddard's minister, but I never went to that church. I wonder what the minister thinks about what Uncle Stoddard did. I would assume the entire town knows. Things like that get around fast in Frederickport. I was there when they arrested him."

Danielle glanced over to Isabella, curious to hear what she had to say.

"Poor Uncle Stoddard did it all for nothing. I changed my will months ago. If I would have just told him instead of putting the new will in his file cabinet at his house, then none of this would have happened."

Danielle's eyes widened at the news. *Could this mean Earthbound Spirits is not the beneficiary of Isabella's will?*

"I don't see anyone here from Earthbound Spirits. Back then, when I originally changed my will, I told them I'd be leaving my estate to them. It was just sort of what was expected for members to do. I never gave them a copy of the will—although they repeatedly asked for one. I think that's what disenchanted me with the group. I suspect they already know I changed my will back, which is why they aren't here making a show—pretending they care I'm dead. But poor stupid Uncle Stoddard, he doesn't have a clue."

Something the minister said caught Isabella's attention. She stopped talking and started listening to her eulogy. Danielle only half listened, instead trying to remember all the questions she wanted to ask Isabella when she had her chance—because it appeared it would be her last opportunity.

Opening her purse, Danielle pulled out a pen and a small pad of notepaper. She began jotting down words—bracelet, diamonds, Lily…When Danielle was finished making her list, she looked up and found Isabella gone. Looking around the chapel, she didn't see her anywhere. Tucking her notebook and pen back in her purse, Danielle prayed Isabella would keep her word and meet with her one last time.

After the service, Marie—with Adam in tow—caught up with Danielle and insisted the three go together to the gravesite portion of the service. Marie took Danielle's left arm while Adam walked along Danielle's other side.

"You were sure right about Lily," Adam said as they walked toward the gravesite.

"I'm surprised Stoddard dares show his face today!" Marie snapped. "The man should be in jail!"

"From what I understand, he's out on bail," Danielle explained.

"How is poor Lily doing? I've wanted to stop by the hospital and see her, but Adam said I should wait."

"She's improving every day. I don't know if you heard, but they had to operate on her leg the night they found her—emergency surgery. She had an infection and it settled there."

"No! I didn't hear that. Is she going to be all right?" Marie tightened her hold on Danielle's arm.

"She's going to be fine, but she has to have six weeks of IV antibiotics, three times a day. Fortunately, she doesn't have to stay in the hospital for the treatments. We're hoping she'll be released on Monday. She'll be staying at Marlow House while she recuperates."

"Doesn't she have an apartment and job back in California?" Adam asked.

"Well, she did until everyone thought she was dead. Her parents cleaned out her apartment, and another teacher has taken over her class. Of course, she's in no shape to go back to teaching right now, anyway."

"Stoddard needs to pay for what he did to that poor girl!" Marie fumed.

"I never cared for Stoddard, but even I'm surprised he pulled something like this," Adam said.

When they reached the gravesite with the other mourners, Danielle looked to the right and saw Isabella waiting some distance away under a grove of trees. The minister said a few more words over the casket before ending the service.

Mourners milled around, chatting with one another. Marie and Adam knew most of those attending the service. Handshakes, hugs, and introductions moved steadily through the crowd.

"If you'll excuse me," Danielle said after Marie introduced her to another couple. Adam had moved to the other side of the crowd, talking to people he knew. "I promised I'd give Lily a call right after the service," Danielle lied as she held up her cellphone and nodded toward the grouping of trees where she was heading.

By the time Danielle reached Isabella, Marie was already involved in a conversation with the couple she had introduced to Danielle.

Isabella watched the crowd mill around her gravesite. She glanced at Danielle, who held a phone by her ear. "I thought you wanted to talk. Who are you calling?"

"No one. But I figured I'd look less strange if people thought I was talking on the phone."

"Very clever. I just realized you're the one who inherited Marlow House. You're the one who found the Missing Thorndike."

"Yes, I am."

"I was going to come to your open house with a friend of mine from the bank, but then I heard Adam was going to be there with—well, I guess it was your cousin."

"You still cared for him?"

"I've always been in love with Adam." Isabella sighed. "Is there something going on between you two?"

"Me and Adam?" Danielle cringed at the thought.

"I noticed you walking with him."

"No. I'm good friends with his grandmother, that's all."

"Marie was always nice to me. I think she wanted Adam to marry me. But if you like him, it's okay. I mean, I want Adam to be happy."

"No, seriously. There's nothing between Adam and me."

"Whatever." Isabella shrugged. "So what do you want to ask me?"

"Your bracelet, the one you had custom made, do you know what happened to it?"

"Do you mean this one?" Isabella put out her wrist for Danielle to see. The bracelet she wore matched the one found in the teapot. Danielle knew it was only an illusion. No more real than Walt's cigars, despite the smell of smoke.

"Yes."

"Let's see." Isabella considered the question a moment. "The latch kept coming undone. I was afraid I was going to lose it, so I decided to take it to the jeweler to have it fixed. I stuck it in my car's glove compartment, but then I got that horrid headache, so I went home instead and took a nap. I think that's when…when I died."

"You never took it out of your glove compartment?"

"No." Isabella looked down at the bracelet. "But that really doesn't matter now. I have it again."

"Do you know anything about diamonds hidden in Marlow House?"

"Diamonds? You don't mean my story, do you?"

"Story?"

"I'm a writer," Isabella explained.

"Yes, I heard you liked to write. But what does that have to do with diamonds hidden in Marlow House?"

"After you found the Missing Thorndike I came up with a plot for a mystery about a jewel thief. In the story, he doesn't just steal the Missing Thorndike; he steals valuable diamonds and hides them in his house, which remain there for almost a hundred years, waiting to be discovered. The story is written in first person, from the perspective of a woman who finds his diary at a local thrift store, and she uncovers the clues about the missing diamonds. Why are you asking about my story?"

"In your story, you didn't happen to mention Marlow House by name, did you?"

"Yes, but I intended to change it. I just couldn't think of what to call it at the time, so I used its real name."

"Is it possible someone got a hold of your story and thought it was real?"

Isabella considered the question for a moment. As if a light bulb went off, she smiled and said, "I know exactly who did—Hunter."

"Hunter?" *Hank's other name, according to Walt.*

"He stole my car. Him and those two skanks. I didn't realize at the time that Uncle Stoddard was the one who left it at the beach parking lot—or that I was dead. I was confused and went with them."

"How did he read your story?" Danielle asked.

"He found my notebook. I'd left it in my car. They didn't find it until after they cleaned it out, taking what they wanted before abandoning it at that rest stop. After Hunter read it, he thought it was true. Stupid man."

"Who hurt my friend Lily?"

"That was Hunter and Justina. Justina is Hunter's cousin. Of course, Claire didn't try to stop them. She was just as guilty. Justina was the one that actually hit her with the rock when your friend stepped out of the women's bathroom. But don't worry about Justina; she can't hurt anyone anymore. She didn't want to fly to Oregon, so she talked Hunter into letting her drive your friend's car back while he and Claire flew."

"Was she the one killed in my friend's car?"

"Yes. After the accident, I found her at a nearby gas station. She was trying to get people to help her. Of course, no one could see or hear her. Except for me. I followed her back to the motel Hunter and Claire were staying at. I actually felt a little sorry for her. She was so confused."

Danielle tried to process all that Isabella was telling her. If she understood correctly, the Stewarts were actually the people who had tried to kill Lily. They had slept in her home. She had made them breakfast. Danielle felt ill.

"You know what's funny?" Isabella asked. Danielle couldn't imagine anything about this being funny. "I think sometimes Hunter could hear me—or at least sense my presence."

THIRTY-SIX

D anielle stared at the open page of her novel. Dressed for bed in plaid pajama bottoms and a T-shirt, she leaned against the pillows fitted between her and the headboard, blankets covering the lower half of her body.

"I swear, you've been staring at that same page for fifteen minutes. I can't believe you're that slow of a reader," Walt said as he appeared by her bedside.

Danielle closed the book and set it on her lap. Scooting to one side of the mattress, she made room for Walt to sit down. He accepted her silent invitation.

"Have you been watching me for that long?" she asked.

"What's wrong, Danielle? You've been out of sorts all evening."

"I keep thinking about what Isabella said today—about Hank, or Hunter or whatever his name is, and that horrid Claire. They almost killed Lily, and they're going to get away with it, and there is nothing I can do about it! Not to mention what they almost did to Sadie."

"If what Isabella told you is accurate, it looks like one of them put the bracelet in the teapot—since Isabella claims to have left it in the car they stole."

"I know, but why? That doesn't make sense," Danielle said.

"Maybe we can think of some way to make them pay for what they've done," Walt suggested.

"I don't know what. The car they were driving was probably stolen, and I don't even know what their real names are. I should have done more when I figured out what they tried to do with Sadie —while they were still here."

"Why don't you let it rest for now and get some sleep. You've had a big day."

"I suppose you're right. Nothing I can do about it right now anyway." Danielle tossed her book onto the nightstand.

"Where did Lily's parents go? I noticed they took a suitcase." Walt stood up.

"They went into Portland to do some shopping. They're going to spend the night. Apparently, Mrs. Miller got rid of all Lily's clothes when she thought she died."

"I thought you said Lily's mother put all her things into storage, that she didn't have the heart to get rid of her belongings so soon."

"It seems that didn't apply to Lily's clothes, cosmetics, underwear, and shoes. The girl has nothing to wear besides hospital gowns. Her mother is buying her a new wardrobe before she comes home from the hospital."

"You should have gone with her. An outing would be good for you."

"She asked me if I wanted to go with them, but I'm too exhausted. It'll be interesting to see how she decides to dress Lily."

"I hope she buys her lots of feminine dresses. Maybe she'll bring you a couple too."

"Oh hush." Danielle grabbed her pillow and gave it a punch, reshaping it. "Get out of here, and let me sleep."

***

THE OLD TRUCK and camper belonged to Claire's stepfather. He was the only person willing to loan her a vehicle for the night. She hated driving the truck, yet now realized it was probably the best vehicle for her mission.

Parked two doors down from Marlow House, in front of a residence that appeared to be vacant—if the stack of newspapers on the front porch were any indication—Claire lay on the cab-over bed in the camper and peeked through the curtains, looking up the street. She had been watching for several hours now.

When she had first arrived, a sedan was parked in front of

Marlow House. Five or ten minutes later, a man and woman got into the car and drove away. The man had been carrying a suitcase, so Claire assumed that whoever they were, they weren't spending the night at the bed and breakfast. The only car parked in the driveway belonged to Boatman.

Not long after the couple drove off, a man from across the street walked over to Marlow House. He returned home a few minutes later with the golden retriever. Claire remembered Boatman mentioning she was dog sitting and that Sadie belonged to her neighbor. Claire had been trying to figure out how she was going to deal with the dog, yet now she didn't have to worry about it. Smiling, she had a good feeling about her little reconnaissance mission.

There was just one light on in the house—coming from Boatman's bedroom. Claire waited and watched. Finally, the light went off; the house was dark. She decided to give it another twenty minutes; hopefully by that time Danielle would be asleep.

Claire closed the curtains and scooted off the bed, dropping down to the camper's floor. From her pocket, she pulled out a set of keys. She had found them when rummaging through the library at Marlow House. Danielle had labeled the keys, making Claire's task easier. One key was for the back gate and the other for the door to the kitchen. She wasn't even going to try the front door key she still had. Claire would bet money that Boatman had already changed that lock.

Claire knew Hunter would eventually ask her about the bracelet. Recently, he had been so distracted by Justina's disappearance that he seemed to have forgotten about it. But she knew he would eventually ask her. Before he did, she intended to have it back in her possession.

Slipping out of the camper, Claire hastily made her way up the street to Marlow House. It was practically a full moon, enabling Claire to see her way without turning on her flashlight. When she reached the back gate at Marlow House, she glanced around nervously and then quickly unlocked the gate. She opened it just far enough to slip through and then closed it again, hanging the lock back in the latch to make it appear locked.

With her adrenaline pumping, Claire raced to the kitchen door and nervously unlocked it. Slipping into the house, she gently closed the door behind her and turned on her flashlight. Making her way through the kitchen, she noticed the knife block sitting on the counter. Impulsively, she grabbed the butcher knife from the block and held it firmly in her right hand while holding the flashlight in her left. She felt safer knowing she could defend herself should Danielle Boatman surprise her.

From the kitchen, she moved into the hallway and made her way to the parlor. She was almost there. All she had to do was grab the bracelet and get back to the truck and camper. Hunter would never have to know how she'd foolishly left the bracelet behind.

Once in the parlor, she pointed the ray from her flashlight along the far wall, looking for the shelf with the teapot. She froze—the teapot was not sitting in its normal spot on the shelf. Frantically, she waved the flashlight around the room, searching for the teapot. She couldn't find it.

Against her better judgment, Claire flipped on the parlor light. She searched the room. The more she looked, the angrier she got.

Turning off the light, she clutched the knife and took a deep breath. *Danielle Boatman has my bracelet, and she better give it back!*

UPSTAIRS, Danielle tossed restlessly. She hadn't been able to get to sleep. Instead, she kept thinking of how she had let the Stewarts get away. Then she heard it—creaking coming from the staircase. Sitting up in the bed, she clutched the blankets to her and listened. Someone was coming up the stairs and it wasn't Walt—he never made the stairs creak.

Once, when first arriving at Marlow House, Lily and Danielle had discussed the noisy stairs and how they might be quieted by adding carpet. Lily had laughed and said the stairs would make a good alarm system. Danielle had countered that she would prefer a system that kept the burglars outside.

"Walt?" Danielle whispered as she scooted out of bed, looking for something to use as a weapon. The moonlight flooded the room, enabling her to see. "Walt!" she repeated, this time a little louder.

Dropping to her knees at the side of the bed, Danielle remembered the baseball bat Lily had tucked under her bed before she went back to California.

Nothing better than an all-American baseball bat to protect yourself from intruders, Lily had told her.

But I have Walt, Danielle had countered. *But where is Walt now?*

She reached under the bed, desperately searching for the bat. Just as she found it, the bedroom door flew open. Peeking over her mattress at the doorway, bat now in hand, Danielle watched as a woman entered the room. Danielle's eyes went immediately to the woman's right hand held high over her head, carrying a wicked knife.

"Where is it?" the woman screeched as she ran into the room, waving the knife. She stopped at the bed and looked down—it was empty.

At first, Danielle did not recognize the voice, yet now that the intruder was standing on the other side of the bed, she could see her face. It was Claire Stewart—at least that was what she called herself.

Danielle jumped up, bat in hand, prepared to take a swing. "Don't you come any closer!" she yelled.

Claire stumbled back, surprised by the outburst. The two women faced each other, one clutching a knife, the other a vintage wooden baseball bat.

"Just give me my bracelet and I'll leave!" Claire demanded.

"It's not here. The police have it. And I suggest you leave before they arrive."

"Why would they arrive? You don't have an alarm system; I've been through this entire house." Claire laughed.

"The bracelet's not here. Just leave."

"I don't believe you!" Claire held the knife up higher. "Give it to me. It's mine!"

"That cop who was here when you first arrived—Joe Morelli—he found it in the teapot and recognized it. It belonged to Isabella Strickland."

"What do you know about Isabella Strickland?" Claire snarled.

"Don't you read the paper? It's been in all the news. She was found dead at the Frederickport Cemetery—she'd been missing. Her funeral was today."

"I didn't have anything to do with her death," Claire shouted.

"I know you didn't." Danielle eyed Claire warily, prepared to bring the bat down hard should the woman lunge toward her with the knife. "She died from a brain aneurism."

Claire looked confused.

"She died of natural causes," Danielle explained.

Danielle heard it again—squeaking stairs. Claire didn't seem to notice—either that or she already knew who was on his way up to the second floor.

"Did you bring your husband with you?"

"My husband?" Claire began to laugh. "I don't need him for what I have to do. But he was right, you know…"

Danielle's eyes widened when she saw the source of the noise. It was Ian sneaking up behind Claire. When his gaze met Danielle's, he pressed his finger to his lips. Danielle's heart raced; she considered lunging forward and clobbering Claire over the head with the bat before she had a chance to stab Ian, but the bed was in the way.

Desperately looking for a way to keep Claire's attention away from Ian, she decided her only recourse was to keep her talking. "What do you mean he was right?"

"He told us Isabella was with us—that she had died and her spirit was still in her car. He could feel her. Just like he did with Marvin."

Yes, Marvin. I need to have a few words with him. Where are you, Walt, skydiving with Lily?

Before Danielle could think of another question, Ian grabbed Claire's right wrist from behind. Claire cried out in surprise, trying to pull from his grasp. Ian twisted her arm cruelly, forcing her to release the weapon. It fell to the floor. Danielle charged forward, scooping up the knife, putting it out of Claire's reach.

"I already called the police," Ian said as he pushed Claire down on the bed face-first.

THIRTY-SEVEN

W hen the call came in about a potential break-in at Marlow House, Joe and Brian were just leaving Pier Café. They arrived on the scene just minutes after Ian made the initial call. They found the front door open, the foyer dark, but they could hear shouting coming from upstairs. Removing their guns from their holsters, they raced down the hallway and up the stairs. Just as they reached the second-floor landing, the light in Danielle's bedroom turned on.

Bursting into the bedroom, the officers found Ian holding a young woman down on the bed while Danielle stood next to the doorway.

"Get him off me!" Claire shouted when she turned her head to the side and saw the police officers standing in the doorway. "He attacked me!"

Holstering his gun, Joe took Claire off Ian's hands, holding her by the forearm.

"Aren't you going to arrest him?" Claire demanded as she rubbed her now red wrists.

"Ian, what happened here?" Joe asked.

"I caught this woman breaking into Marlow House; she was holding that knife"—Ian nodded to the knife now sitting on the dresser—"over her head, like a weapon."

"That's a lie!" Claire looked up at Joe, who continued to hold her forearm. "Don't you recognize me? You were here when my husband and I checked in on Friday."

Joe took a closer look at the alleged burglar. At first, he didn't recognize her. The woman he met on Friday was well dressed, with her hair neatly styled in a somewhat severe but conservative hairdo. This woman wore tattered jeans, a dirty T-shirt, and her hair needed washing. Unlike the woman he had met on Friday, this one wore no makeup. Yet he was fairly certain she was the same woman.

"Are you saying you're a guest here?" Brian asked.

"Of course I am!" Claire tried to pull away from Joe, but he continued to hold her arm.

"No, she's not." Danielle spoke up. "She was a guest over the weekend, but they checked out on Sunday."

"That's not true!" Claire insisted. "And that isn't even my knife. If you check the kitchen here, I bet you find it's part of a set."

"If you're still staying here with your husband, where is he?" Joe asked.

"He went out to get something to eat," Claire lied.

"Which of the rooms are you staying in?" Brian asked.

"Why are you asking me all these questions?" Claire cried. "He attacked me; you even saw him!"

Joe pushed Claire down in a chair and told her to stay put. He knew Ian had been the one to call the police, so he asked him to explain what happened that led up to the call.

"I was standing at my window, looking across the street, when I noticed what looked like someone moving around the parlor of Marlow House with a flashlight. The rest of the house was dark. I knew Danielle was home alone. Lily's parents have been staying with her, but they went to Portland for the night to do some shopping."

"So as far as you know, this woman isn't a guest here?" Brian asked.

"I know she isn't," Ian said. "Lily's parents have been staying here all week. I know they're the only guests."

"That's when you called the police, when you saw the flash-light?" Brian asked.

"No. After I noticed a light moving around the parlor, the over-head light went on. I don't know why, but I just assumed it was Danielle. But then I saw the woman through the window, and it clearly wasn't Danielle. She had this massive knife in her hand, holding it over her head like she was getting ready to slash someone."

"That's not true! She threatened me with a baseball bat! See, it's over there!" Claire pointed to the wooden baseball bat sitting in the corner of the room. She started to stand up. Joe placed his hand on her shoulder and told her to sit back down. He told Ian to continue.

"Then the light went out again and I could tell she was moving through the house with the flashlight. I immediately called the police and headed over here. Danielle gave me a key this morning. She's been watching Sadie. I used it to get into the house. When I got upstairs, the woman was standing at the bedroom doorway, threatening Danielle with the knife. I grabbed her wrist, and the knife dropped to the floor. You arrived a few minutes later."

Joe looked at Danielle and said, "Tell me what happened before Ian arrived."

"I'd gone to bed but hadn't fallen asleep yet. I heard someone coming up the stairs. I started looking for something to protect myself with—then I remembered the bat Lily put under my bed. Just as I grabbed it, the door opened and Claire came into the room. I didn't know who it was at first; I couldn't see her face. But then she came closer and demanded I give her the bracelet back."

"Bracelet?" Joe frowned, looking from Danielle to Claire.

"She's the one who put the sapphire bracelet in the teapot," Danielle explained.

"That's not true!" Claire shouted. "I don't know what she's talking about."

"She calls herself Claire Stewart, but I don't think that's her name. And I also think she's the one who took Sadie and tried to sell her to that Borge jerk," Danielle said.

"She's lying! I had nothing to do with that stupid dog getting out."

"You say she's lying, let's have a look at your ID. That should help clear up the part about your name," Brian said.

"I don't have my purse with me. I left it in our car," Claire grumbled.

"In the car with your husband, the one who left you here to get something to eat?" Brian asked.

"Yes," Claire said, sounding like a petulant child.

THEY LEFT Danielle in the house to get dressed while they took Claire outside to take downtown. She didn't go silently, insisting all the way that she was the victim and she intended to sue them all. After they locked her in the backseat of the patrol car, Joe stood with Brian and Ian on the sidewalk.

"Danielle Boatman is a magnet for trouble," Brian said, shaking his head in disgust.

"This is hardly Danielle's fault," Ian argued. "That woman broke into her house."

"She wouldn't have gotten in had Boatman not been so careless with her keys," Brian countered. Just before taking Claire downstairs, they found the keys to Marlow House in Claire's pocket.

"I'd like to know how she got here," Joe said.

"Maybe her husband dropped her off and is driving around and intends to pick her up," Brian suggested.

"Or maybe she drove herself," Ian said, looking down the street. He pointed to the truck and camper two doors down. "That wasn't there earlier today, but it was parked there when I got home tonight. The people who live at that house are gone for the week. I've never seen that truck in this neighborhood before."

"I'll go check it out," Brian said.

"WHY ARE YOU DRESSED? Where are you going this late?" Walt asked when Danielle stepped into the hallway from her bedroom.

"Where have you been?" Danielle asked angrily. "Oh, never mind, I know, skydiving with Lily."

"Danielle, what's going on?"

"I'm on my way to the police station, if you must know. My favorite law duo is waiting outside—Joe and Brian."

"What are they accusing you of now?" Walt asked.

"It's not me this time, although if I know Brian, by the time we get to the police station, he'll turn this around to make it my fault."

"What happened?"

"Claire Stewart, or whatever her real name is, broke into the house tonight. I guess she's the one who put Isabella's bracelet in the teapot—and she wanted it back."

"I'm sorry, Danielle, I should have been here."

Danielle took a deep breath and shook her head. "No, I'm sorry,

Walt. You're not my watchdog. I shouldn't have snapped at you like that. None of this is your fault."

"I should have been here for you. I knew you'd be alone."

"No." Danielle shook her head again. "I'm just a little rattled. I'm glad you have a way to visit Lily."

"Tell me what happened tonight."

"I heard someone coming up the stairs. It was Claire wielding one of my larger kitchen knives, demanding I give back the bracelet. Fortunately, Ian noticed something from across the street; he called the cops and then came over here. Scared the crap outa me. He took the knife away from her, and all I could think of, if he gets hurt, Lily is going to kill me!"

"But Ian's okay?"

"Yes. He's waiting outside to take me to the police station. I swear if I never see the inside of that police station again, it will be too soon!" Danielle started to head downstairs when she heard the front door open and Ian call out her name.

She hurried down the stairs. "Coming!"

"Go put your jammies back on," Ian said when they met in the middle of the foyer.

"Why?" Danielle asked.

"You don't need to go down to the station tonight. They said you can come down in the morning. They found the car she was driving. Her purse was inside, with her ID. You were right; she isn't Claire Stewart. She's Claire Manning, and she has a record and an outstanding warrant."

"So what's her husband's real name, do they know?"

"She's not married. Looks like she came by herself. Claims the truck she drove over belongs to her stepfather."

"When I asked her if her husband was with her, she said she didn't need him here. Since she was holding the knife at the time, I figured she didn't have a reason to lie."

"I know you've had a scare tonight; if you want me to sleep over, I'll be happy to."

Danielle glanced over at Walt, who stood silently by Ian's side.

"I think I'm okay now." Danielle smiled. "But I appreciate the offer."

THIRTY-EIGHT

W hen Danielle arrived at the police station the following morning, Joe was standing near the front desk. He immediately walked to her, reached out and gently touched her elbow, guiding her to a private area of the office.

"You're putting in some long hours," Danielle greeted him as Joe led her to the corner.

"I've been worried about you," Joe began. "You had quite a scare last night. Were you able to sleep?"

"I slept fine."

"Do you still think the bed and breakfast is really such a terrific idea?" Joe asked.

"What's this about, last night's break-in?"

"I've mentioned this before. There's no reason for you to put yourself in these situations. You've had nothing but trouble since you decided to open a bed and breakfast. And now with your inheritance, there's really no reason for you to do it."

"Just because I had one bad experience with guests doesn't mean I should quit my dream."

"It's not safe. I hate to say this, but you don't seem capable of making good choices."

"What are you talking about?" Danielle frowned.

"Breaking and entering, defiling a grave…"

232

"And if I hadn't done those things, we wouldn't have found Lily."

"But you didn't really know that at the time," Joe argued.

"I didn't come here to discuss my business plans."

"Just think about what I'm saying. I'm not trying to be heavy handed, Danielle. But I worry about you, and I'm afraid one of these days you're going to do something that will land you in serious trouble, and I won't be able to help you."

"I think that would make your partner incredibly happy."

"Brian doesn't understand you."

"And you do?" Danielle asked.

"I don't believe you're manipulative or malicious."

"And Brian thinks I'm those things?"

"Like I said, he doesn't understand. If you would just let people help you…"

"What kind of help are you talking about?"

"It wouldn't hurt if you could talk to a counselor. Help you better understand how you allow yourself to get in these situations."

"Are you saying the break-in last night was really my fault?"

"Not exactly. But Brian has a point. Had you not made certain choices, you wouldn't have been in that situation."

"Excuse me, Joe," the receptionist interrupted their conversation. "The chief asked if Ms. Boatman was here yet. He wants her to go to his office."

"The chief? I thought this would be Joe and Brian's case since they made the arrest." Danielle dreaded the thought of facing the chief after yesterday's embarrassing encounter at the funeral. *I'm sure the entire Frederickport Police Department thinks I'm a psycho nutcase.*

When Danielle walked into the chief's private office a few minutes later, she found him sitting at his desk, reviewing some papers. He glanced up, motioned for her to shut the office door and sit down, and then gathered up the papers on his desk and set them aside.

"Good morning, Chief," Danielle said with a weak smile.

"Sounds like you had quite the night last night."

"Just a regular day in the life of Danielle Boatman," she quipped with forced humor.

"When I was little, I used to call my grandma Gamma Kat. I hadn't thought about that in years."

Surprised, Danielle's eyes widened. While she had expected him to say something about their encounter the day before, she hadn't expected that. She sat speechless, uncertain how to respond.

"After my grandfather died, Grandma would go several times a week to tidy his gravesite, as she called it. When I asked her why she felt she had to do it, she said the cemetery wasn't taking care of the place like they used to. One day, I told her I'd call the cemetery's maintenance department and shake things up a bit for her—so she wouldn't have to keep doing their job. But she begged me not to and finally told me the real reason she went down so often."

Silently, Danielle listened, her hands folded neatly on her lap.

"She told me she went to the cemetery to talk to my grandfather. At first, I thought she meant a one-way conversation, where she spoke to his gravesite. But that's not what she meant—she insisted it was a two-way conversation with grandfather's ghost."

Danielle shifted nervously in her chair, unsure where the chief was going with this conversation.

"I'll admit, at first I thought she was delusional. After all, she was getting up there in age. But the only problem was, aside from claiming to have regular conversations with her dead husband, she showed no other signs of dementia. My grandmother had always been very sharp. When she saw the concern on my face, she told me it was all right if I didn't believe her. That if it made me feel better, I could just think of it as an old woman indulging in a private fantasy—something that gave her comfort. She reminded me that as long as she behaved normally in other areas of her life, I shouldn't let it bother me."

"She admitted it was all a fantasy?" Danielle asked.

He laughed and said, "Not exactly. She went on to tell me that someday after she was gone, she would find a way to send me a message. To let me know that she really had been talking to my grandfather when she visited the cemetery."

"And you think I'm that message?" Danielle asked in a small voice.

"Did she say anything else to you? Anything she asked you to tell me?"

Danielle remained silent for a moment before answering. "Your grandmother said, 'Tell him to start paying attention to what's in front of him.'"

The chief began to laugh—uncontrollably. Tears slipped from his eyes. He wiped them away with his fingers, still laughing, shaking his head, until the laughter subsided, leaving him with a satisfied grin.

"I don't understand?" Danielle asked in a quiet voice.

"Everything makes sense now," he explained.

"It does?"

"Growing up, whenever I was trying to figure out a difficult problem, Grandmother would tell me all I had to do was stop looking so hard for the answer, that it was probably already right in front of me. And in this case, she was right."

"Right about what?"

"My problem."

"What was that?" Danielle frowned.

"You." He smiled confidently.

"Me?" Danielle moved restlessly in the chair.

"It all makes sense now. Your actions. Why you've behaved the way you have. Joe was wrong; you aren't some fragile creature, nor are you the manipulative woman Brian thinks you are."

"You believe I spoke with your grandmother?"

"Yes, I do."

Danielle wasn't sure how to process what the chief was telling her. She sat quietly, replaying his words in her head.

After a few moments of silence he said, "You told Joe you had ESP. But you don't, do you?"

"I didn't say ESP exactly," Danielle muttered. "But no, I don't have ESP."

"So the stories about you claiming to talk to ghosts when you were a child—those were true. Not just that you made those claims but that you actually did speak to spirits."

"Yes," Danielle whispered.

"How did you really find Isabella's body?"

"She told me."

"Isabella?"

"Yes." Danielle nodded.

"And Cheryl? How did you happen to find her?"

"I suppose Cheryl helped me find it, but she wasn't sure where it was exactly."

"Does anyone else know?"

"You mean how I see things?" Danielle asked.

"Yes."

"Just Lily. I told my husband, but I don't think he ever believed me."

"But you once told your parents…your cousin Cheryl?" he asked.

"Yes. When I told my parents, they sent me to a doctor. I suppose that's why Joe is convinced I have a history of mental instability. I know he looked into my background after hearing about Cheryl's stories."

"You could tell him the truth," he suggested.

"And you think he'd believe me?" Danielle scoffed.

"Probably not." He shrugged. "But I take it Lily did?"

"Yes. Of course, she's witnessed a few things that enables her to believe."

"Like with your encounter with my grandmother?"

"Do you honestly believe me?" Danielle asked.

"I think I do…it does answer a lot of questions."

"Then maybe you could help me put the people who hurt Lily behind bars?"

"How can I do that?"

"I know who they are, but considering my sources, I can't really go to Joe with my information."

"What do you have?"

"The woman who broke into my house last night—"

"Claire Manning?"

"Yes. After Isabelle's uncle left her car at the beach, Claire and a man by the name of Hunter or Hank—the man who claimed to be her husband when they checked into Marlow House—and his cousin, a woman named Justina, took Isabella's car and ended up in California. They are the ones who attacked Lily and took her car."

"How can we prove it?"

"From what I understand, they haven't been able to identify the woman who was killed in Lily's car. She was so badly burned, the only thing they can use is dental records, which is really no help since they have no idea who she is. If you can find out who this Hunter or Hank is that was with Claire and then see if he has a cousin named Justina, perhaps you can match her dental records to the body found in Lily's car."

"Your source?"

"Isabella," Danielle said with a sheepish grin.

"Is there anything else?"

"I know Claire and Hunter Hank were the ones who took Sadie —Ian's golden retriever—and left her down at the cemetery. That's how I knew where to find her in time."

"Isabella told you that too?"

"No. Walt Marlow."

"Walt Marlow?"

Danielle nodded.

"From what I understand, you told Joe and Brian last night that Claire was the one who put Isabella's bracelet in the teapot—and that's why she broke in, to retrieve it."

"According to Isabella, the clasp kept coming undone, so she was taking it to the jeweler to have it fixed. She put it in the glove compartment, and Claire found it after they took the car. I have no idea why she stuck it in the teapot. You'd have to ask her that question."

"Why do you think Claire and this Hunter guy posed as a married couple and stayed at Marlow House?"

Danielle told him about Isabella's notebook and the story about diamonds. The chief began to laugh. "That sounds like Isabella. She once told me she wanted to be a writer. I told her to go for it, and she said she would, as soon as she had some adventures to write about."

"So what do we do now?" Danielle asked.

"I assume you don't plan to say anything to Joe?"

"I don't see the point." Danielle shrugged.

"Joe is a good man, Danielle, and I know he genuinely cares about you."

"I know. But there's really not a future for us. And that's okay."

"I just have one favor to ask you," the chief said.

"What's that?"

"The next time a ghost wants to lead you to its corpse, would you please call me first?"

"Fair enough." Danielle grinned.

"By the way, if you see my grandmother again, tell her she doesn't have to keep playing matchmaker. I've been seeing a very nice lady, and the boys like her." He got up from his chair.

"Will do," Danielle said as she stood up. "So what are you going to do now?"

"Have a little talk with Claire Manning. See what I can find out about this Justina."

"Oh, there is one more thing, although I hate doing any favors for Stoddard Gusarov," Danielle said reluctantly.

"What's that?"

"Isabella had a new will made about six months ago. She left everything to her uncle. She put the will in a file cabinet at his house. It's been there all along."

THIRTY-NINE

C laire sat alone in the interrogation room. She had forfeited her right to an attorney, convinced she could ultimately talk her way out of the situation. It was her word against Boatman's, and she had overheard Officer Henderson discussing the innkeeper in not-so-flattering terms. She would just have to convince him she was the real victim, not Boatman. Of course, she had to spend the night in Frederickport's little jail, which actually had better accommodations than some places she had crashed during her recent California road trip.

One thing Claire wanted to avoid was Hunter discovering she had broken into Marlow House. As it was, she was still trying to figure out how she might explain the missing sapphire bracelet to him.

The door opened and an officer she had never seen before entered.

"Ms. Manning, I'm Chief MacDonald."

"What happened to Officer Henderson? I thought he was handling my case?"

"Officer Henderson has gone home. He had a long night." The chief sat at the table across from Claire.

"This is all a mistake, you know. I was a guest at Marlow House."

"You also registered as a married woman with a…Mr. Hank Stewart?"

"Yes," Claire muttered, looking down at her hands.

"But you aren't married, are you, Ms. Manning?"

"Is that really a crime?" Claire set her hands on the tabletop. "So we were playing house a little. People check into hotels as married couples all the time."

"But it is against the law to steal someone's dog."

"I told them I had nothing to do with that stupid dog getting out."

"That's not what Jimmy is saying. You sold him the dog."

"I don't know what you're talking about. No one gave us any money."

"Only because Jimmy got arrested before he had time to leave the money, which he had on him, by the way, when he was arrested. And he's not real happy with you right now. Thinks you set him up."

Claire swallowed nervously. "He thinks that?"

"Yeah, and he's pretty pissed. If we can't make the charges stick, I imagine one of the first things he'll do when he gets out is look you up."

"You got to protect me! Jimmy is crazy sometimes!"

"Maybe we could work out something. If we knew more about where those dogfights are held, I imagine then he'll be going away for a long time, and then you won't have to worry about him."

Claire sat silent for just a few moments before she started talking, telling the chief everything she knew about the dog fights—where they were held and who was involved." After she finished, she took a deep breath. "Can I go home now?"

"No, not yet. I have a few more questions for you."

"But I told you everything I know about the dog fights!"

"I'd like to hear about how you, Hunter, and Justina found Isabella Strickland's car at the beach parking lot."

Claire's eyes widened in surprise. "I don't know what you're talking about."

"Come on now, Claire. Your fingerprints were all over that car when they found it outside of Palm Springs."

"That's impossible!"

"Why, because you think you wiped the car clean?"

"But we did!" Claire blurted. Realizing her blunder, she looked back down at her hands.

"It doesn't matter. Justina's told us everything. I just wanted to give you a chance to tell your side of the story."

"You found her?" Claire looked up. "I don't know anything about the car she was driving. She took off. I can't be responsible for what she did."

"According to Justina, you were the one who hit that girl over the head with a rock at the rest stop. Left her for dead in the desert."

"She lies!" Claire shouted, standing up. "I didn't have anything to do with that! It was Hunter and Justina; I stayed back in the parking lot. They're the ones who killed her, not me!"

BRIAN AND JOE stood in the observation room, watching the chief interrogate Claire Manning.

"Who is Justina?" Brian asked.

"I have no idea, but did he just get Manning to confess to stealing Sadie and being an accomplice to Lily's attack in California?"

"It sure as hell looks that way." Brian frowned. "Where is the chief coming up with all this?"

"He didn't mention anything about it this morning when we talked."

"He must have talked to someone," Brian said.

"Only Danielle."

"Danielle?" Brian glanced from Joe to the window into the interrogation room.

ON FRIDAY AFTERNOON, Walt watched Danielle hang up Lily's new clothes. The Millers had returned to Frederickport late Thursday evening. After breakfast on Friday, they headed out to the hospital with Ian and hadn't yet returned. Sadie lay on Lily's bed at Marlow House, watching Walt watch Danielle.

"I don't think they're all going to fit in that closet," Walt noted.

"As long as they fit Lily—that's all that matters. Mrs. Miller actually picked out some nice stuff. I should send her shopping for me."

"Not enough dresses," Walt grumbled.

"Was that the doorbell?" Danielle paused, listening for a second chime.

Walt looked out the window. "Yes, there's a police car out front."

"You know, the neighbors are going to start talking—if they haven't already!" Danielle tossed the outfit she was preparing to hang up on the chair and headed for the door. Sadie leapt off the bed and followed her down the hall.

"Joe, to what do I owe the honor?" Danielle asked after opening the front door a few moments later.

He glanced down at Sadie. "Dog sitting?"

"Ian's at the hospital with Lily. Sadie and I are buds."

"Can I come in?"

Danielle peeked out the doorway and looked around. "Where's your partner?"

"The chief told Brian I could handle this. I get the feeling he's trying to keep you two apart."

"Handle what?" Danielle asked as she opened the door wider, silently inviting Joe to come in.

"They've identified the woman who was killed in Lily's car."

"Come into the parlor. We can talk there." Danielle led the way.

"So what happened?" Danielle asked after they were sitting down.

"Apparently the chief got a tip and followed up on it. The couple you knew as the Stewarts—Claire Manning and Hunter Hodges—along with Hodges's cousin, Justina Marker, were the ones who took Isabella's car. They went joyriding on an extended car trip through California, using Isabella's credit cards and what cash there was in her purse. But the car broke down at the rest stop, and unfortunately, Lily had the bad luck to pull in."

"I know Lily had over five thousand dollars in her car, from what she won at the casino. I imagine they found that."

"They used Lily's money to fund their trip back to Oregon. Hodges's cousin was driving Lily's car when it had the accident. Manning and Hodges didn't even know there'd been an accident. They thought Marker was still alive somewhere, driving around in Lily's car. The positive ID came in this morning from her dental records."

"Are they going to make the charges stick?"

"Manning broke down, completely rolled over on Hodges. Of

course, Hodges is blaming his cousin, who's not here to tell her side of the story."

"I hope those two don't manage to wiggle out by blaming everything on the dead woman."

"I'm sure Hodges'll try, but it doesn't look good for him. When they searched the place where Hodges was staying, they found Lily's credit cards, among some other things we're fairly certain belonged to her, including some brochures on Marlow House she'd written notes on. Of course, she needs to verify it's her property. We're turning all this over to authorities in California."

"What about the charges up here?"

"After California finishes with them."

"I'm glad the Millers are going to be able to know what happened before they go home."

"How much longer are they staying?"

"Lily's getting out of the hospital on Monday, and her parents plan to take off on Tuesday. Mrs. Miller wants to make sure her daughter is all settled in. We've hired a private nurse, and we want to have all that set up by then."

"So you're really going to have Lily stay here while she recuperates."

"Yes. She doesn't have an apartment anymore, and Ian is here. They've gotten pretty close."

"You're a good friend, Danielle."

"Lily is a good friend too."

"I was wondering," Joe began.

"Yes?"

"You said Lily won't be getting out of the hospital until Monday. How about letting me take you out to dinner this weekend?"

"Ah, Joe..." Danielle let out a weary sigh and smiled sadly. "I don't think so."

"It's just dinner, Danielle."

"I appreciate the offer, honest. But I have a lot to do before Lily gets home." Danielle stood up.

"Maybe another time?" Joe asked as he followed Danielle to the front door.

"You're a nice guy," Danielle said as she opened the front door for Joe. Slowly he walked through the doorway, waiting for Danielle's answer. "But I don't think so."

FORTY

"I feel guilty taking the only downstairs bedroom at Marlow House," Lily said as she hobbled into the room. Located adjacent to the parlor, the room's window faced the street, unlike the kitchen and library windows, which looked out to the side yard. "It's the only room you have for guests who can't use the stairs."

"You can't use the stairs," Danielle reminded her.

"True that." Exhausted from her short drive from the hospital to Marlow House, Lily plopped down on the side of the bed to catch her breath.

"You okay?" Danielle opened the curtains to let in more sunlight.

Lily glanced over at the IV stand already set up next to the bed. "Are you sure you want to do this, Dani? I have a feeling I'm going to be more trouble than you bargained for."

"Too late, friend. Your clothes are already in the closet," Danielle said cheerfully. "Anyway, Joanne comes back to work tomorrow, the nurse will be coming over in a couple hours for your next IV treatment, and then there's always Walt."

"Where is he anyway?" Lily glanced around.

"He's probably in the attic. Said he was going to stay out of the way until your parents go home. But I think he wanted to give us a chance to talk without him lurking."

"While I'm glad to be back—in my body—I have to admit I'm going to miss being able to see and hear Walt."

"There's still the dream hopping," Danielle muttered.

"Hey, what's wrong?"

"Nothing." Danielle shrugged.

"Come on, out with it!"

"You and Walt went skydiving," Danielle said with a pout.

"We didn't really go skydiving—it was a dream."

"But did it feel real?"

"Well…" Lily considered the question a moment. "They have a different quality from regular dreams. But yeah, it felt real without the fear of death factor."

"Do you always know it's not a regular dream?"

"I do now. The first two times he visited me, I didn't. Hasn't he ever hopped in your dream?"

"No." Danielle shrugged indifferently. "No reason to, since I can see and hear him."

"I'm surprised he hasn't." Lily scooted back on the bed, grimacing a bit from the pain.

"Can I get you anything?"

"No. I took a pain pill before I left the hospital. Are my folks still across the street with Ian?" Lily pulled the blanket and sheet up over her body.

Danielle looked out the window. Ian had taken the Millers across the street to show them his rental. "Looks like it. He's giving them the grand tour." Danielle turned from the window and took a seat on one of the two wingback chairs in the room.

"My folks seem to really like Ian. I think at first Mom thought he was just a summer fling, but after seeing how he stuck by me, even going to California to see if he could find out anything about the accident, I think that really won them over."

"He's definitely crazy about you."

"I'm pretty crazy about him." Lily yawned then asked, "Dani, do you mind if I take a nap?"

"No problem. You want me to shut the blinds?"

"No, that's okay. Just turn off the light, please."

Danielle walked to the doorway and looked back at the bed. Lily lay curled up on her side under the blankets, her eyes closed. Danielle smiled and turned off the light, then walked out of the room and shut the door behind her.

"I THOUGHT I'd find you up here," Danielle said when she walked into the attic and found Walt at the window, looking through the spotting scope across the street at Ian's house.

"Lily's folks have been over there for quite a while," Walt said, turning from the window to face Danielle.

"I called Ian. Told him Lily was taking a nap. Wanted to warn Lily's parents so they don't come barreling in and wake her up."

"I noticed the Millers aren't exactly a quiet family," he said with a chuckle, turning back to the window.

Danielle stood by his side, looking across the street. "It will seem a lot quieter around here when they leave tomorrow."

"You never mentioned, are you planning to take any reservations while Lily's laid up?"

"I was thinking about it. But after the fiasco with the fake Stewarts and all that's gone on, I think I'll wait until Lily gets back on her feet again. It'll be easier for her to rest if we don't have strangers coming and going. I figure I can open again by Halloween."

"That might work. After all, you are running a haunted B and B."

Danielle grinned. "I suppose I am."

"Have you told Lily yet about the police chief?"

"No, I haven't had the opportunity. Either her parents or Ian have been around when we've been together."

"Does she know anything about Justina?"

"Only what the police told her. She doesn't know Justina's spirit was wandering around here and the hospital. But I think she's moved on. After all, her family and friends now know she's dead. Although, I have a feeling she's not going to be thrilled with the next leg of her journey."

"I wonder if she'll be seeing Roger," Walt smirked.

Danielle chuckled at the thought then said, "Mrs. Miller asked Lily today if she was going home after she recuperates."

"What did she say?"

"Lily reminded her mother that she technically does not have a home anymore. Mrs. Miller got all apologetic about moving Lily out of her apartment. Lily told her mother it was probably for the best since she couldn't go back to work anyway. Basically, she just wants to take everything one day at a time."

"Do you think she'll eventually go back to California?"

"I don't know." Danielle shrugged. "I suppose part of that will depend on what happens between her and Ian."

"And what about you, Danielle?"

"What do you mean?"

"I heard Joe, he keeps asking you out."

"That will never work."

"You know, he just wants to save you—take care of you. I see it in his eyes."

"I know. And I find it very irritating."

"Most women would find it flattering."

"Maybe women from your era, not mine. At least not me."

"What about the chief?"

"What about him?" Danielle frowned.

"He accepts your abilities. He's single. And apparently his grandmother thinks you'd make a wonderful wife and mother."

"Sheesh…" Danielle looked over at Walt, a frown on her face. "What are you trying to do, get me married off?"

"No. I was just curious." Walt feigned indifference, yet silently studied her reaction.

"The chief is a nice enough guy and not bad to look at. But he's really not my type."

"What's your type?"

"I don't know. I just know he's not it."

"Joe's not your type either?"

"He could have been at one time. But not now."

"If you don't know what type you like—how do you know you have one?"

"I just know I'd like someone who accepts me as I am, has faith in me. And…" Danielle paused a moment.

"What?"

"My type likes to dance."

IT WAS after 11:00 p.m. when Danielle finally crawled into bed on Monday night. Exhausted, she hugged one of her pillows as she slipped off to sleep.

Someone was playing music. It was a happy beat. She wanted to move her feet. Danielle opened her eyes and looked into the mirror.

She let out a gasp, her right hand flying to her hair. It no longer fell down her back but was cropped into short curls. She had never considered cutting her hair so short, but she had to admit, it made her eyes look enormous.

"It's called a Castle Bob. Quite the rage, you know. It suits you," Walt said.

Danielle looked from the mirror to Walt, who stood by her side. He wore a pinstripe suit she had never seen him wear before. He looked rather dapper, she thought. Reaching out impulsively, she touched the cuff of his jacket.

"What fabric is that?" she asked.

He only smiled. Danielle looked down; she wore a short, fringed skirt. It felt silky against her nylon-clad thighs.

"I'm dressed like a flapper!" She laughed, looking back in the mirror.

"Of course, we're going dancing." Walt took Danielle's hand in his. Without question, she went with him.

They stood in the center of a huge dance floor, surrounded by other couples, all dressed in a similar fashion to Danielle and Walt.

The music began to play. Walt showed Danielle how to move her feet—her arms—until it was second nature, and together they moved with the music, dancing the Charleston on the crowded dance floor.

Danielle laughed; she moved her feet faster, leaned forward, her arms swinging back and forth in a steady rhythm with the music. Walt's dance steps matched hers, and at one point, he caught hold of her hands and twirled her around the floor. She threw her head back and laughed, never wanting the night to end.

"Lily was right," Danielle said breathlessly, her feet still moving at a rapid speed. She and Walt locked gazes as they danced.

"How so?" he asked.

"It doesn't feel like a regular dream."

"Are you upset?" Walt asked, still keeping up with Danielle's steady dance movements.

"How so?" she managed to say.

"This probably isn't going to burn up any chocolate cake," he said.

Danielle laughed and grabbed Walt's hands, urging him to twirl her again. "That's okay, sometimes the dance is enough."

THE GHOST WHO WANTED REVENGE

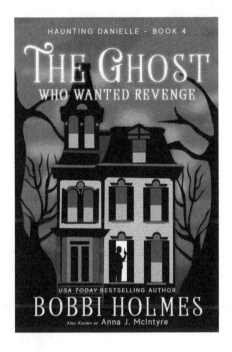

RETURN TO MARLOW HOUSE IN

THE GHOST WHO WANTED REVENGE

HAUNTING DANIELLE, BOOK 4

With his dying breath, Stoddard Gusarov names his killer: Danielle Boatman.

Danielle had a score to settle with Stoddard Gusarov, but murder him? Never.

Proving to the police she is innocent is the least of her problems. She has an angry spirit to contend with, the ghost of Stoddard Gusarov—and he's out for revenge.

NON-FICTION BY

BOBBI ANN JOHNSON HOLMES

HAVASU PALMS, A HOSTILE TAKEOVER
WHERE THE ROAD ENDS, RECIPES & REMEMBRANCES
MOTHERHOOD, A BOOK OF POETRY
THE STORY OF THE CHRISTMAS VILLAGE

BOOKS BY ANNA J. MCINTYRE

COULSON FAMILY SAGA

Coulson's Wife

Coulson's Crucible

Coulson's Lessons

Coulson's Secret

Coulson's Reckoning

UNLOCKED 🔒 HEARTS

Sundered Hearts

After Sundown

While Snowbound

Sugar Rush

CPSIA information can be obtained
at www.ICGtesting.com
Printed in the USA
LVHW031236260121
677404LV00002B/112